The Ghosts of War

The Ghosts of War

A novel by Michael Diaz

Writers Club Press
San Jose New York Lincoln Shanghai

The Ghosts of War

Writers Club Press
an imprint of iUniverse, Inc.

For information address:
iUniverse, Inc.
5220 S. 16th St., Suite 200
Lincoln, NE 68512
www.iuniverse.com

ISBN: 0-595-24173-5

Printed in the United States of America

This book is dedicated to all the veterans, past, present and future. To the Prisoners of War and Missing in Action of the Vietnam War, to the gallant men of Bravo Co.1/503rd, 173rd Airborne Brigade, 1967-1968 and to CWO Anderson L. Mann, Black Hawk pilot, who also answered the call of duty.

Author's Note

It has been over thirty years since I landed at Cam Ram Bay, Republic of South Vietnam, to start my year-long tour of duty as a member of the 173rd Airborne Brigade. The Vietnam War has been over for a long time, but it is obvious that the images of the war and the passions that arise in the American conscience, are very much still a part of us. I know well that the memories and images of that long ago war still have the power to move me like nothing else does. To this day, I can't get closer than forty feet to "The Wall" without breaking down. The memories of long ago, even when buried deep in my mind, are my constant companion and I am sure that it is the same for countless other Vietnam veterans. I cannot think of any other event in my life that helped to shape my life and my character as much as the Vietnam War did and I'm sure that it has been the same way for countless other Americans who served in that country.

I count myself lucky in the fact that I returned from that war, more or less in one piece. Many others did not and even now, their lives are torn apart by thoughts of what they went through in Vietnam and how they were received once they returned home.

Vietnam was a war different from any other we had fought and eventually the American people were not able to fully support it, losing their faith in the government, sick and tired of the quagmire that our country was sinking into. Many people believe that we lost the war. We did not. The U.S. Armed Forces never lost a battle in Vietnam and we, the soldiers who fought there, sure didn't lose the war. For my own experiences in Vietnam, I can say that we did our duty to the best of our ability. We fought, died, shed our blood, sweat and tears just like any other GI who was ever asked to serve his country. But instead of a word of thanks from our fellow Americans or from the Government we served, we came back home to the roar of crowds calling us names such as baby killers, along with many others, and the Government and the public were willing to forget about us.

I, for one, will never forget. Not the war, not the faces of friends who paid the ultimate price for freedom or the images of a war torn country. The memories are too deep, too painful to just brush them aside and forget. And so, my fellow soldiers, this one is for all of us and for the memories that bind us together.

"Let every nation know, weather it wishes us well or ill, that we shall pay any price, bear any burden, meet any hardship, support any friend, oppose any foe, to assure the survival and the success of liberty."

—Inaugural Speech by John Fitzgerald Kennedy
President of the United States

PROLOGUE

The White House
Washington, DC
The Oval Office
1962

The President of the United States, John F. Kennedy, gathered the papers in front of him and remained still in his chair for a long moment, his eyes glancing at the men gathered in the Oval Office. It was early in the morning and he had ordered the meeting as the first order of business for the day. He knew well that when it came to Viet Nam and the ongoing war in Indochina, the discussions could go all day and at the end nothing would really be decided. It baffled him at times that such a distinguished group of men, intellectuals all, could get so bogged down on the issue. But then he wasn't doing too well either, he thought grimly, knowing that the Vietnam War and the U.S. involvement in it, was a very complex issue. With a deep sigh, he stood up from his desk and came to stand by his brother, Robert Kennedy, Attorney General of the United States. The faces of the men gathered in the room were serious, intent and at the moment, the only noise heard was the clink of coffee cups being lowered onto saucers. Everyone in the room was digesting the previous words of the President, trying their best to look at the big picture.

It was quite a gathering, the President thought, letting his eyes rest on each one of the men in the Oval Office. The Secretary of Defense was there, Robert McNamara, as was the Secretary of State, Dean Rusk, the Ambassador to South Vietnam was also there as well as his primary military advisor, General Taylor, the National Security Advisor, and the Vice President of the United States, Lyndon B. Johnson.

"I want a consensus on this, gentlemen," the President said, shaking the sheaf of papers in his hand, glancing at the Vice President. "If there is any opposition, I want you to speak up now."

Several heads nodded in assent and finally his military advisor, General Taylor, stood up.

"Mr. President," he started, his eyes fixed on his Commander in Chief, "I believe that we need to keep all our options open in this conflict and one of them is the use of our conventional forces in the Republic of South Vietnam. Another is the use of nuclear weapons if the situation arises." He stopped then, clearing his throat. "Maybe we just need to go in there with all our power and put an end to this, once and for all."

"I agree with the facts about our options, Max," the President said, shaking his head, his Boston accent clipped and precise. "We will keep all our options open, but right now I'm not thinking of escalating the war in Indochina or sending our conventional troops over there." He paused now, his face showing clearly the conflicting emotions playing in his mind. "As far as any use of nuclear weapons in Indochina, Max, I'm deeply opposed to that." He stopped talking now, his eyes hard and uncompromising. He shook his head, glancing at the men in the room and then he continued.

"For God's sake gentlemen, I'm thinking that our involvement in South Vietnam is getting too deep already and that maybe we should be thinking about getting out altogether."

The Secretary of Defense nodded his head in assent at the words of the President. He had just returned from a tour of South Vietnam, together with General Maxwell Taylor and he was not overenthusiastic about that country's prospects for winning the war against the National Liberation Front (NLF). Also he had no doubts that by now the NLF was taking their marching orders from Ho Chi Minh in North Vietnam and with their involvement, things were about to really heat up in South Vietnam. And that meant that the U.S. was either going to get out or get increasingly involved in the conflict.

The Secretary of Defense thought fleetingly about his meeting with Diem a few days past and he shook his head grimly. Ngo Dinh Diem's government was full of corruption and mismanagement and altogether unable to come to grips with the guerrillas and the different factions vying for power, always in a struggle with each other instead of working together to make the lives of their people better. There were more than a handful of differences that kept coming up in South Vietnam, making the job of holding the Diem regime in place a nightmare.

The leader of South Vietnam was not a very amiable man and working with him was a difficult enterprise, something that the previous administration (President Eisenhower) had learned early in their dealings with him. He was Catholic and as far as McNamara was concerned, the man had a great deal of antipathy against the Buddhist of his country and was not willing to allow religious freedom or compromise with them in any form whatsoever. Sooner or later, the Secretary thought, that was going to be the catalyst that would ignite the fall of the government in South Vietnam. That and the stupid ideas Diem's regime had about the land and the farmers. Instead of making reforms and splitting the immense tracts of lands held by a few landholders, he had reaffirmed their ownership, creating mistrust and anger among the very people he needed for the support of his policies. The majority of the population in South Vietnam were Buddhist and peasants and Diem was on a collision course with both groups.

The President glanced at his men, waiting for their words, himself thinking about the country that was uppermost in their minds of late. The only reason South Vietnam was holding its own so far, the President thought, was because of the thousands of Special Forces advisors roaming the country with the CIDG forces, helping the government hold against the enemy encroaching against it. The political situation was grim and he had begun to think that they (the U.S.) had rushed to help South Vietnam too fast. Yes, he had made a commitment to South Vietnam, but he was beginning to get nervous about the possible consequences. The country was a mess and after almost two years of providing equipment and advisors, the war was at a stalemate and the country was in shambles. He thought back briefly at the meeting with President Eisenhower just before his inauguration. Viet Nam and the whole of Southeast Asia had been the topic of conversation, with Eisenhower forcibly stating his point of view that the United States must do all it could to help them and keep them out of communist hands. Eisenhower was a firm believer in the so-called "Domino" theory and was convinced that if the United States didn't support Indochina strongly, the countries would fall pray to communism one by one. At one point in time, he had agreed with Eisenhower's statement, but lately he had been anxious about the question of South Vietnam and the whole of Indochina. And Truman and Eisenhower probably had their reservations too, the President thought. Truman had helped the French during their war in Vietnam during the 1950's, sending material, money and technicians and after the French were defeated at Dienbienphu and the country divided in two, Eisenhower had done the same with South Vietnam, providing military aid and advisors to help them in their fight against North Vietnam and the Viet Cong. In the end, his administration had inherited the mess that was Viet Nam today.

"I believe we are all with you, Mr. President," the Secretary of Defense finally said, glancing at General Taylor. The General, after all, was a soldier and he saw Viet Nam as a place to hold the line on communism by the United States, using the conventional forces of the Army, Navy and Air Force to do just that. He had felt the same way, he thought, at the beginning, but now, like his President, he was beginning to have a bad taste in his mouth about the whole situation. They needed to be careful on this one and take it easy, one step at a time. There was no sense in rushing into a full-scale war with a foreign country just because communism was knocking on the door, especially a place so far away from the U.S. And in the final analysis, it was their war and they needed to do more than what they were doing so far, he thought, grimly shaking his head. He knew well that if the U.S. went in to fight conventionally, the body bags would really start to mount up and the American public would react to that.

"Our policy so far has been to supply the Republic of South Vietnam with equipment and advisors and I intend to keep doing just that," the President said, running fingers through his hair in what was a characteristic gesture for him when he was under pressure.

"We will continue to supply technicians and equipment and increase the number of Special Forces for now gentlemen and we will see what develops." He stopped for a second, his eyes settling on General Taylor again.

"Get the proper orders in place and advise Special Forces headquarters at Fort Bragg that we are increasing the number of advisors in Vietnam. The Secretary of Defense will see to the numbers for manpower requirements.

"Yes sir, Mr. President," General Taylor said, standing up. His face was etched in worry lines and it was obvious that he didn't like the idea of more Special Forces going in, but his commander in Chief had spoken and right now that's what they would do. With that, the meeting was over and the men filed out of the Oval Office one at a time, leaving the President and his brother alone.

"What do you think, Bobby?" the President asked, his faced etched with worry lines.

"I'm with you on this one, John. We don't need this mess to escalate any deeper than it is right now. The best thing we could do is to continue to try for a peaceful, political solution at all cost."

The President of the United States nodded his head slowly, his mind searching for answers to the thousands of questions running wild in his head. He had made a commitment to continue helping the government of South Vietnam just like Truman and Eisenhower had done and at the beginning it had looked like the right thing to do; helping a so called democratic country stay free and holding the line in Indochina against communism. He had never expected to go this far, getting in so deep. He had thought that his Special Forces and the Army of the Republic of Vietnam (ARVN) could deal with the guerrillas of the NLF in a short amount of time. But instead of a quick fix, the situation had become a tangled mess. The ARVN had proved to be incapable of sustaining an aggressive drive against the NLF due to the lack of training, lack of effective leadership and intervention from Diem's regime personally. The only inroads that were made had been made by his Special Forces and the CIDG they had trained. Everything else seemed to conspire to make things worse and the government in power was too weak to manage the situation any better. The political, economic and religious situation was bad and getting worse by the minute, with no end in sight as far as he could tell, and the body bags of American service men were beginning to come home, he thought, sighing deeply. He was the Commander in Chief and he felt bad about it, responsible for putting his men in harm's way for a country that in the end was not of any real significance to the U.S., neither politically nor militarily.

He had no intention of escalating the war or of using American troops and nuclear weapons to prop up the South Vietnamese government, but at the same time, he was concerned about the possibility that the country might be lost, falling into the hands of the Communists. His detractors would have a field day if South Vietnam was lost to communism during his tenure as President, and he had his own soldiers to worry about. Special Forces and other advisors and technicians numbered well over eighteen thousand now and he was not about to let them die for nothing. But he couldn't appear to be soft on Communism, Moscow and China would love that, he thought, frowning at the prospect.

The President sat down in one of the vacated chairs, his strong fingers massaging his temples, thinking about a country thousands of miles away from the United States and the morass that it had become for him. And he had just ordered more of his Special Forces into the quagmire. But he sure as hell didn't have much of a choice, did he? He shook his head slowly, his forehead creased in thought, feeling the tension eating at him. He couldn't appear to be weak concerning Vietnam, but every fiber of his body right now was telling him that the best thing America could do as of this moment, was to get out completely. Or at least just keep things the way they were until a peaceful solution could be found. If they couldn't achieve a military solution to the problem, perhaps they could achieve a political one.

But what if even with the Special Forces in place and the ARVN, the NLF and North Vietnam took over the country before steps had been taken to find another solution? he asked himself.

Then my administration is doomed, the President thought, a weary grin flickering across his face momentarily. His detractors in Congress and elsewhere will blame him for loosing the country and for his inability to act decisively and he would have to eat his words concerning the willingness of America to come to the help of the oppressed.

He stood up, exasperated with the whole situation and the doubts that kept creeping into his head. He walked back to his desk and stood behind his chair. He put his hands on the back of the chair and squeezed the leather with both hands, shaking his head.

"What's wrong, John?" his brother asked, seeing the doubts etched clearly on his brother's face.

"I have a feeling that this war is going to be a long and bloody one," the President of the United States said softly, his eyes fixed on his brother, "and in the end, the side that has the greatest resolve and staying power, is going to be the one that will be successful." He stopped talking; his brow creased in thought, and then he added, "And I don't think it's going to be us."

Bobby Kennedy didn't say anything, just shook his head pensively at his brother's words. As far as he was concerned, in order for the United States to get anywhere in South Vietnam, sooner or later the full power of the Army, Air Force and the Navy would have to be unleashed, and that in any bodies book was a conventional war. That, as far as he was concerned, was the last thing his brother's administration needed. It would tear the fabric of the country and he was sure it would enmesh the American people into a terrible debate. For a moment longer, he stood still and then with a deep sigh, he exited the Oval Office, leaving his brother alone with his thoughts.

CHAPTER I

Republic of South Vietnam
Chuong Thien Province
Special Forces Camp A-28
December 12, 1963

1st Lt. Paul William Gallagher stood still at the entrance to the heavily fortified command bunker, a lukewarm canteen cup of black coffee in his hand, looking intently at Sergeant First Class (E-7) Lee Ashworth and the 140-man company that comprised the Vietnamese Civilian Irregular Defense Guard (CIDG). Ashworth was checking equipment and distributing ammo to the men, making sure that everything was in order prior to their departure on a combat patrol. Gallagher glanced at the sky above, noticing that the sun was on its way down. Soon the evening shadows would descend upon the valley below the small hill and darkness would follow suit. Despite the fact that the sun was going down, it was still hot, the humidity incredibly high and he could fell the sweat running down his body in rivulets.

The camp was located atop a small hill, giving it a commanding view of the valley below and the dense mass of jungle that stretched in every direction. It was a small camp, surrounded by barbed wire, with M-60 machine guns protecting the most vulnerable positions. Like most Special Forces camps doting the landscape of South Vietnam at the time, it was a Spartan place to live and work.

The CIDG force was equipped with M-1 and M-14 rifles, and .30 cal. carbines, coupled with an assortment of French and Chinese made equipment. Several 81 mm mortars were scattered around the compound, under the care of a heavy weapons (18B), Special Forces A-team member. There were almost three hundred civilians, including family members of the CIDG, and usually five to twelve Special Forces in the compound. At the moment one of the members of the team was at a hospital in Saigon with a case of malaria. Sickness and a chronic shortage of qualified personnel were always interfering with the job of the advisors in the camp.

They were part of the 5th Special Forces Group, based at Ft. Bragg, N.C. and had come to Viet Nam as special advisors to the Republic of South Vietnam in an effort to train the civilian population in the government's fight against infiltrating communist guerrillas. The camp was fairly new and had been put in place right in the middle of a suspected VC (Victor Charlie or Viet Cong) stronghold. Combat patrols sent out on a daily basis engaged the enemy almost continuously, denying them the mobility and obscurity they once enjoyed. Recently Captain Pierce had begun to send out night patrols, scoring some hits and on several occasions mauling them pretty bad, making the Victor-Charlie in the vicinity weary of traveling at night in what used to be their uncontested territory. Special Forces soldiers didn't mind fighting at night, as a matter of fact, they relished the fact that they were able to take the fight right into Charlie's back door and keep the pressure on the enemy.

Apparently the VC commanders had not taken the threat of the Special Forces camp lightly and had made arrangements to get rid of it. The American top brass in Saigon had received intelligence that a Main Force VC battalion was going to take out the camp and A-28 had gotten the assignment of finding the battalion and ascertaining their movements. If they could do that, then the artillery and the choppers would come in, followed closely by the ARVN troops.

They were supposed to have twelve men with them, but replacements were hard to come by and it was a cause for celebration when another Green Beret showed his face in the camp. Being shorthanded, 1st Lt. Paul Gallagher was the acting XO (Operations Officer), while SFC (Sergeant First Class) Lee Ashworth was the medic, cross-trained in radio communications and languages. The man spoke some Vietnamese also and was proficient as an armorer too.

Gallagher sipped the strong, bitter liquid that passed for coffee in the command bunker, finally throwing the remaining liquid on the ground, turning around and walking back inside.

"It looks like we will be ready to go in a few minutes," he said softly, glancing at the man with railroad tracks on his collar, a Captain, pouring over a map of the Mekong Delta. This was War Zone D in South Vietnam and it was part of the area assigned to the group of Special Forces advisors helping the local province in their fight against the Viet Cong. Next to the captain, there was a radio, a "buck" sergeant (E-5), Steve Miller, operating it. Miller was twenty-one, a serious, competent young man who enjoyed his work and the fact that he was in Vietnam, doing what he did best. He glanced rapidly at Lt. Gallagher, a smile on his boyish face, continuing his transmission, his voice clearly overheard in the small hutch while talking to other units in the vicinity.

Captain Pierce, the detachment commander, lifted his eyes from the map, throwing a grease pencil down, glancing quickly at Gallagher.

"We better get going then," he said, reaching for his LBE (load bearing equipment), his M-14 rifle and a Swedish "K" sub-machine gun with a thirty-five round clip, 9mm caliber. Besides the rifle and sub-machinegun, a 1911A1 Colt .45 could be seen in a leather holster strapped to his waist. A green beret with the rank of captain sat on his head at a jaunty angle and a rucksack with the remaining ammo and food was quickly strapped on his back. He reached for the map, folded it carefully and unbuttoning two of his shirt buttons he put the map under his shirt.

"Its getting late," he said, checking the wrist watch, making his way to the entrance, exiting and walking toward Sgt. 1st Class Ashworth. Lt. Gallagher followed him closely, reaching for his gear and his rifle on the way out. Once outside he stood to the side of the bunker, waiting for Captain Pierce to finish. He glanced at Sgt. 1st Class Ashworth, noticing the man was ready, a Thompson sub-machine gun .45 caliber in his hands. A 1911A1 Colt .45 ACP could be seen also on his waist together with a long blade knife resembling a machete. He was a black man, originally from the Bronx in New York, tall, slight of build, with short-cropped black hair and piercing brown eyes. The oldest of the three men, he was thirty-one years old and had served in Korea, where he had received two Purple Hearts, a bronze star with V device denoting valor and a host of other medals. He was single, with no family anywhere and he was fond to say that his mistress was the Army as well as his family. His mother had died several years ago from a brain tumor and according to Ashworth, he had never met his father. He was a quiet, competent NCO (Non-Commissioned Officer) and Paul had found out that he really enjoyed the man's company and his biting, sarcastic humor. He was a fountain of information about Viet Nam and its people, having served two tours there, and Paul didn't wasted any time in picking his brain, much to the chagrin of Ashworth who had to contend with a 'cheery' lieutenant following him around and asking a million questions.

He remained still, waiting for his Captain to finish, his hand going to the right breast pocket, feeling the letter there. He smiled, a happy grin etched on his face, remembering the contents of the letter now. He was going to be a father by next April and he was still getting use to the idea. He had kept the news to himself, waiting for the right time to tell his friends, savoring the feelings bursting in his heart at the prospect of another Gallagher at the old family farm. A father, he thought happily, shaking his head. Figure that one out, he told himself, the grin back on his face. He was brought back to reality by Ashworth's voice.

"Atten…hut," Ashworth barked, his voice loud.

The men snapped to attention and Captain Pierce stepped in front of the assembled company, receiving a half way decent salute from Ashworth who stepped aside ready for inspection.

A smile flickered across Captain Pierce's face for a second as he returned the salute and then he was all business.

He was a stocky built man, twenty-seven years old, with sandy color hair and bright, intelligent hazel-green eyes. A 1960 graduate of West Point, he had been in the country almost two years and as far as Gallagher was concerned, he was one of the bravest and honor bound men he had ever known. He was a soldier, pure and simple, the epitome of what a Special Forces officer should be. He was also a religious and compassionate man who firmly believed they were doing the right thing in Viet Nam, following their motto, "To free the oppressed." They were not only training soldiers, but also helping them build for the future and the most important thing all of them subscribe to; freedom.

Paul Gallagher walked over next to Ashworth and stood still, watching Pierce going through the men's rucksacks, making sure that the ammo and rations were there. Captain Pierce knew that Ashworth had already check the equipment, but he was a man who double checked everything, making sure that things were as good as they appeared, never taking anything for granted. This was war and as far as Pierce was concerned, nothing should be left to chance. Paul kept his eyes on him, learning all he could, absorbing the lessons given and taking the advice of the man. He had been in the country only three months and realized that he was an amateur at this very dangerous game while Pierce was a first class warrior and very knowledgeable about the country and the enemy they fought. This was Gallagher's fourth patrol and he was looking forward to it, hoping to learn something from it. He had received his baptism of fire on the second one when a company of Viet Congs had ambushed his patrol. He had come out of it with a Purple Heart and a healthy respect for his enemies. He was not a gambling man, but he would bet his bottom dollar that the black, pajama clad farmers, the Viet Cong, could teach the boys at the Pentagon something about unconventional warfare and jungle fighting.

On this day they were about to depart to an area west of Chuong Thien, searching for proof that a battalion size Viet Cong unit, the 371st Main Force, was in the area some ten clicks away. The MAAG (Military Assistance and Advisory Group) commander in Saigon had requested the patrol and Captain Pierce's CIDG were given the task by their commander, Colonel Ashley Brown.

"Okay men," Pierce said in Vietnamese, "saddle up."

Pierce glance behind him, winked at Ashworth and Paul and with a nod of his head sent the Vietnamese scout forward, heading west, the rest of the company following suit. Captain Pierce glanced at the evening sky, noticing the shadows beginning to lengthen, the overhead sky clear, the dying sun painting the sky in a multitude of colors. At any other time he would have had several HU-1B choppers transporting the men to an undisclosed LZ (landing zone), but this time the brass had been adamant that the patrol should head for the designated area on foot. Apparently they didn't want any indication that a company size force was heading toward the suspected area of the VC battalion and by walking out of the encampment a veil of secrecy could be kept. The only people with any knowledge of the mission were Captain Pierce, Paul and Ashworth, minimizing the chance that a spy or some one pre-disposed warmly toward the Viet Cong would reveal their plans. Captain Pierce was sure that among the myriad of people in the compound, somebody was more than likely a Viet Cong sympathizer and if the opportunity arose, they would inform on them readily.

Captain Pierce walked toward SFC Ashworth who was serving as the RTO (Radio Operator) and tapped him on the shoulder. Ashworth glanced back, stopping in his tracks at the sight of his Captain.

"Let me do a radio check, Lee," Pierce said, reaching for the handset. Besides his equipment and personal load, Ashworth was also carrying a PRC-25 radio on his back and now he handed the hand set to his Captain.

"Charlie-Bravo Niner, this is Alpha 1, how you read, over," Pierce said into the handset.

"Alpha 1, this is Charlie-Bravo Niner, read you five by five, over," the response came back, loud and clear.

"We are on our way, over and out," Pierce said, handing the handset back to Ashworth and starting to walk before the final transmission had been acknowledged.

"Roger, Alpha 1, over and out."

In single file they cleared the perimeter, taking care about the position of the Claymore mines and the flares. Once in the jungle, they made their way in silence or as quiet as the passage of over a hundred men through the jungle could be, doing their best to keep the noise down, cursing softly when the noise of rifles banging against equipment was too loud. There was no conversation and when something had to be said it was passed forward in whispers, the unit conforming to the order of complete silence. They were walking into the enemy's lair and it would not do to underestimate them.

They walked until the evening shadows descended on the jungle, having covered almost two miles in the dense undergrowth. Pierce decided it was time to bed down and he halted the company in a small clearing. They would make a cold camp and start early the next morning. After seeing to the guards and the welfare of his men, the two officers and Sgt. Ashworth put a couple of ponchos together, making a tent where they could sleep half way comfortably. By then it was completely dark, night descending on the jungle within minutes after the patrol had stopped.

While Gallagher and Ashworth busied themselves preparing something to eat, Captain Pierce got under a poncho with his map and a flashlight, marking his coordinates. A few minutes later he came out, the red glow of the flashlight barely penetrating the shadows. He gave the map to Ashworth who in turn got on the radio, passing the coordinates to base camp.

After their meager supper, Paul Gallagher stood up, making his way to the perimeter, checking on the guards, leaving Ashworth and Pierce talking in a low voice. Sgt. Ashworth had been working on the radio and now he shook his head slowly. He had noticed some poor reception during the last transmission and was concerned about the radio.

"What's wrong with it?" Pierce asked, wondering about the damn thing. It would not do to be without a good working radio in the area where they were heading. In case they got in trouble, it was the only way for them to get artillery or support in a hurry.

"Don't know," Ashworth said, raising an eyebrow, a characteristic gesture for him when he was concerned about something. "Maybe the battery is going bad or something is corroded." Both of the men knew that the humidity in the jungle was overpowering and things didn't last long in that type of climate. Cloth would rot away within days and any wound or cut could easily get infected with what was called "jungle rot" if not properly taken care of.

"I'll change batteries and check it in the morning," he said, not at all sure that the damn thing was going to work come morning time.

He stood up, stretching his body, glancing at the sliver of sky seen above, sniffing the air like a hound dog. It was a clear night, with a full moon and a million stars shining brightly, not a cloud in sight. He wiped the sweat from his face with the ever-present olive drab towel that hung around his neck, marveling at the humidity in this place. Even after hours, the humidity hung around like a parasite, sucking every drop of moisture from their body, forcing then to be vigilant about drinking their water and taking their salt tablets through the long days.

"It's going to rain soon," he said softly, whirling around and crawling inside the small tent.

Pierce looked up at the sky and shook his head, a grin flickering across his face. "Sure it is," he said, whispering to the shadows around him. There wasn't a dark cloud in sight and no sign of rain anywhere. He sighed deeply, his ears catching the soft murmur of his men talking. Glancing around him one more time, he rummaged in his rucksack and came out with a pad of paper. Getting under the poncho he proceeded to write a letter home to his parents, something he did almost daily.

He was still immersed in his writing when he heard furtive steps approaching the poncho. Shortly after he heard Gallagher's voice.

"Pierce, what are you doing?" Gallagher asked in a barely audible whisper.

The poncho came off and Pierce stood up, turning the flashlight off. Even with a red cover, it would not be hard to spot the damn thing in the night, he thought, putting it away.

"I was writing a letter to my parents," he said softly, dropping his body unto the hard ground next to Gallagher.

"Did you tell the 'General' all about me?" he asked, a smile etched on his face.

The General was Robert W. Pierce, Major General (Retired), father of Captain Pierce and a man who had served in the Second World War and in Korea with the 15th Infantry Regiment, 3rd Infantry Division.

"I sure did," Pierce said, his thoughts going back to his parents who right now were enjoying the sunshine in the Florida Keys.

Ever since Gallagher had become a part of his team, Pierce had made it a point to talk about him in his letters to his parents and the old man had even started writing to him, something that Paul enjoyed tremendously.

There was no doubt in Lt. Gallagher's mind that Pierce and his father had a very close bond, both men being extremely patriotic with an incredible sense of respect and love for God and for country. Words like honor and duty were part of their lives, not just words to be said and then forgotten, but also words to live and die for.

Many times Paul Gallagher had thought that if the father was anything like the son, then they were the epitome of what America was all about. Men like them were the backbone of the country, doing their duty, fighting the wars in order that their people could remain free. He had wondered many times if he himself was anything like Pierce and finally had reached the conclusion that they both shared some of the same ideas and had similar points of view about life in general. He was as patriotic as the next man was and he would gladly give his life to uphold that which in his heart was most dear—freedom. He had learned the same words, had heard the same speeches from his father as Alton Pierce had heard from his, and he could bet that the 'General' and his father would hit it off if they ever came into contact with each other.

They remained silent for seconds, each man immersed in their own private thoughts, until the silence was broken by Pierce saying, "We better get some shut eye Paul. Tomorrow is going to be a long day." Paul Gallagher nodded his head and they crawled inside the small tent, listening to Ashworth gently snoring and within minutes both men were sleep.

Sometime in the early hours of the morning, Pierce crawled out of the small tent. His bladder was full and he walked a few paces away from the tent to empty it. He stood still enjoying the complete silence that permeated the jungle. He glanced at the sky above, watching the black clouds rolling by and he shook his head. Something soft and wet hit his face and Pierce chuckled softly to himself. Ashworth had been right, as usual, and it was beginning to rain. He glanced at the luminescent dial on his watch, noticing the time. It would be daylight in about an hour or so, time to get moving.

He made his way back to the small tent, whispering Gallagher's and Ashworth's names, at the same time kicking their legs.

The two men woke up instantly, their hands searching for their weapons, relaxing when they realized it was Pierce outside the tent. They made their way out, yawning and stretching, glancing around, noticing that it was still completely dark. Sgt. Ashworth looked up, feeling the wetness on his upturned face and then he smiled in the darkness.

"Well, what do you know," he said softly, "It's raining."

"Oh you smart ass," Pierce said, a grin flickering on his rugged face. "You guys go check on our boys while I pack the equipment. We are moving out in forty-five minutes."

While Ashworth and Gallagher went about the business of waking the company and getting the men ready to continued their trek, Captain Pierce packed their meager equipment, wishing he had a hot cup of that good, old Army coffee to start the morning. He was a typical Army man who ran on the dark brew, the stronger the better and he really missed his daily shot of it. The rain that had started in a gentle mist was coming down hard now, cutting visibility to a minimum, soaking them through and through, making them shiver in the early morning hours. Pierce glanced at the sky above again, hoping that the rain was a passing cloud. But it wasn't going to be as he had hoped. The sun was hidden behind dark clouds and the jungle surrounding them was almost as dark as night.

"It is going to be a lousy day," Pierce told himself, relegating the thoughts to the back of his mind. Pain and discomfort was nothing new to them. They couldn't do anything about the weather, therefore they would put up with it without complaining. He rummaged in his rucksack, his hand coming out with a poncho. He put it on and then squatted down to wait for his men, reaching for his rifle and inspecting it, checking on the ammo, making sure that everything was in working order.

Several minutes later Ashworth and Paul made it back, finding Pierce munching on a cracker, drinking tepid water from his canteen.

"Lee…get on the radio, check it out," he said.

Sgt. Ashworth sat down on the wet ground, covering the PRC-25 radio as best he could from the rain and for the next twenty minutes he fiddled with it, checking and rechecking everything. When he was finished he unfolded the eight-foot long antennae and started transmitting. For long minutes he worked the radio controls, but there was nothing coming back, just static. Unable to get anything, he unscrewed the eight-foot antenna and reached for his rucksack. The operating range of the FM, PRC-25 "line-of-sight" radio with the eight-foot antenna was between three to five miles, depending on terrain and obstructions and this time SFC Ashworth had taken a spare antenna that when rigged together, it would increased the range of the radio between twelve and fifteen miles. The antenna consisted of several aluminum sections that when joined together produced a twenty-foot mast. The minutes passed slowly as Pierce and Ashworth worked to get the antenna rigged and when it was finally ready, Ashworth tried again.

The results were the same and frustrated Ashworth stood up, pushing the damn thing away from him in disgust.

"It's no use. The damn "Prick"(nickname for the PRC-25) is busted captain." He stood up, his hands on his waist, his eyes taking the radio, glancing at the sky above. "And this damn weather is not helping any either".

Captain Pierce shook his head at the ominous event. Things had barely started and they were having problems already. "Damn…this sure isn't good," he told himself, thinking about his options. They needed a radio, no doubt about that. It was their only link to safety and help if they got in trouble. He could abort the mission, but he had a feeling that the brass back in Saigon would be pissed to no end at their delay, or he could send some men back to base camp for a new radio and batteries.

He thought about his options and decided that the best thing to do would be to send a couple of men back for a spare radio and new batteries and let them catch up with the company as soon as they could. They were only a couple of miles from camp and it would not be hard for a couple of men to go back and get a radio. His mind made up, he turned to Gallagher.

"Paul…get Tranh Kinh over here."

Gallagher nodded his head and walked toward the huddle of men waiting patiently after finishing their meager breakfast. The rain was coming down hard now and they were wet and miserable, waiting stoically for the word to move. He glanced at their upturned faces and finally spotted Tranh Kinh.

"Tranh Kinh," Gallagher said softly in his best Vietnamese, "we need you." Immediately a small, wiry figure detached himself from the men, approaching Gallagher. The man was small, barely over five feet tall, with brown eyes and a mouth full of rotten teeth. A perpetual smile was etched on his face and Paul Gallagher knew him to be a spirited fighter with a deep hate of the Viet Cong and everything they represented. He spoke a smattering of English and was the official interpreter for the company.

He walked up in front of Paul and snapped to attention, saluting.

Paul returned the salute, smiled and said, "Captain Pierce needs you."

Tranh Kinh and Lt. Gallagher made their way swiftly toward where Pierce and Ashworth were waiting. Morning light was getting stronger and they needed to move out soon. Pierce was bending over the map, calculating distances, running his figures in his mind. Seeing Tranh approaching, he stood up swiftly.

"Tranh...pick two men, good runners, and send them back to camp to pick up a new radio and some spare batteries," Pierce said, pausing for a moment. "They shouldn't have any problem catching up with us by noontime."

They talked briefly for a few more minutes and then Tranh whirled around, ready to go. Pierce turned too and then as an afterthought, turned back around, calling Tranh.

"Tranh...wait."

The wiry Vietnamese stopped and came back. His intelligent brown eyes rested on Pierce, waiting while the Captain searched for something under his shirt, his hand coming out with a crumpled envelope. He passed it to Tranh, speaking a few words in Vietnamese. Tranh folded the letter carefully, came to attention, saluted again and was gone. Shortly afterward, two men detached themselves from the group of Vietnamese soldiers and in seconds disappeared in the impenetrable jungle.

Pierce glanced at the sky, noticing the black clouds rolling by and the rain coming down. Morning had come, but with the rain and the clouds hiding the sun, darkness still had a hold of the jungle. It was going to be slow going, Pierce thought, hefting his pack, the straps cutting into his shoulders.

He glanced around one more time, looked at his point man and the flankers and nodded his head to move out. In silence, the long line of men uncoiled like a giant snake, making their way into the dark, forbidding forest.

And like Pierce had predicted, it had been slow moving, barely making two clicks by noontime. He rested his men every hour on the hour, sending flankers out, maintaining an eye on the rear, expecting Tranh's men to catch up with them soon. But by the end of the noon rest period there was no sign of them and reluctantly Pierce gave the word to move out again. He was beginning to have a bad feeling about the patrol, his eyes taking in the gloomy jungle all around them, the persistent rain coming down with no let up. By the time evening arrived, the long line of men had been fighting their way through some bad jungle terrain, up and down ravines and small hills, crossing swollen rivers, the hard trek sapping their strength. The men were tired and irritable, soaked to the bone, the cold water finding every available route down their necks.

Reaching a small clearing, Pierce halted them and the men flopped down on the wet ground unceremoniously, welcoming the respite, dropping the rucksacks and working on the blood sucking leeches they had acquired along the way.

Pierce waited until everybody was in the small perimeter and then he approached Ashworth and Gallagher.

"Lee, see if you can get something on the damn radio," he said, hoping that they could. He needed to find out where his men were and why the delay.

"Paul and I will inspect the men while you try the radio," he said, dropping his pack in place, glancing at the dark sky above. It would be completely dark in about an hour and if he had two men behind him in the jungle, they would not be able to find him. It would be tomorrow before they could catch up with them and he desperately needed a radio. The bad feelings he had all day now intensified and Pierce shook his head irritably. The rain had not let up at all, coming down now in a downpour, masking any noise, making it hard to see more than a few feet in front. In weather like this men tended to get depressed, not paying much attention to their surroundings, making them easy targets for an enemy that was somewhere around and eager to inflict damage.

"Lets go, Paul," he said, hefting the M-14 in his hand. They made their way, talking softly to the men, Pierce's singsong Vietnamese a mere whisper. They found Tranh and he joined them, making sure all the men were ready, vigilant. This was Victor Charlie's (VC) weather and Captain Pierce had a feeling that they were close by.

* * * *

U Minh Forest
371st Main Force Vietcong Battalion

Senior Colonel Le Quang Hue, of the North Vietnamese Army, listened attentively to the VC (Viet Cong) soldier reporting to him. The enemy was in place and Hue's face lit up with pleasure. He dismissed the soldier with a peremptory wave of his hand and stood still, glancing at the sliver of sky above him, his staff waiting impatiently for his orders. All around him, more than a thousand VC soldiers were dispersed around the jungle, forming an L-shaped ambush. The men were dressed in black pajamas, rubber sandals on their feet and for a such a large group of men, were exceedingly quiet, waiting tensely for the order to attack the enemy not two hundred meters away. They had taken care of the flankers and their point man quietly, now they just had to wait for the order to attack the enemy they had shadowed all day.

Colonel Hue glanced around satisfied at the way things had turned out for him. Two days prior, he had pushed his men through the jungle at a steady pace, on his way to annihilate the Special Forces camp that had been a thorn in his side for months. Before the coming of the Americans with the funny green hats, the countryside had been theirs, to come and go as they pleased in their fight against the puppet regime of South Vietnam. But since the camp had been built, the enemy had inflicted many loses upon his people, even fighting them at night, confusing them and making their morale weak.

He had approached the Special Forces camp in the early hours of the evening, hoping for a night attack, only to find the enemy exiting the compound, a long line of armed Vietnamese civilians marching out. He had spotted the green berets on three men, Americans for sure and his mind had immediately started to formulate a plan. He could storm the compound now, something that would cost him quite a number of his men due to the superiority of American artillery and air power, but if he followed the men heading into the jungle now, he could form a trap for them and kill them all. Or he could do his best to capture the three Americans in the group alive and then Hanoi would be grateful to him. Hue's eyes closed to slits, his swarthy face etched in pensive lines.

For a long moment he remained standing still and then his mind made up, he had ordered the men to retreat and eventually, he was following the unsuspecting patrol. When the patrol had stopped for the night, he had done the same and in the morning had continued to follow them, searching for a place that would give him the advantage in a firefight. Sometime in the morning, his flankers came in contact with two civilians, one carrying a radio and by the time he had finished with them, he had all the information he needed on the combat patrol moving slowly ahead of him. The men in front of him were without a radio and therefore, unable to get help. The rain that had started early in the morning had continued for most of the day, helping him to mask his movements and the noise. Slowly, he bypassed the patrol and then he had sent his men forward, his officers and non-coms getting the men ready for the ambush, until everything was ready and the battalion was in place, waiting for their pray to show up.

Colonel Hue pulled his pith helmet from his head and made his way up front slowly, the fine hair of his head plastered to his forehead, the rain running down his face. His eyes centered on the men crouching over the 88mm mortar emplacement and a grin flickered across his face.

He glanced around one more time, realizing that in an hour it would be completely dark and slowly, he raised his hand, putting a whistle to his mouth. The eyes hardened, closing to slits and then the shrill sound of the whistle rendered the evening and his hand chopped down into the air.

* * * *

Captain Pierce cocked his head to one side, his eyebrows raised in question, believing he had heard something coming from the darkness of the surrounding jungle. They had just finished their inspection, making their way quietly, waiting for the point man and the flankers to come in with a report of the area ahead of them. And then all hell broke loose.

The "swish" and "thump" sound of a mortar round broke over the noise of the rain coming down and for a brief second Pierce thought he was hearing things. His eyes bulged in his face and with a sinking realization he knew that they had been suckered into a trap.

"Innn…coming," he yelled at the top of his lungs, the sound shrill in the confines of the small clearing. And then he was pushing Paul down, diving to the jungle floor, his face smacking the wet ground hard. A brilliant explosion rendered the evening and red hot metal fragments sang a deadly song all around them. Flares started to come down, turning night into brilliant daylight, the shadows dancing in the jungle. From the corner of his eyes he saw movement and Pierce snapped his head around, his eyes registering on a man running toward him, one of his CDIG men, his hands trying to push back the greasy mass of intestines spilling from his stomach. The Vietnamese tripped and went down face first, the screams of pain and terror emanating from his mouth reverberating in the jungle. He tried to get up, the blood gushing from the wounds inflicted by the sharp mortar fragments a vivid red, soaking his clothes. Pierce started toward him, but before he was able to reach him, the man went down again, his face striking the wet earth. His body jerked spasmodically for a moment longer and then it remained still, dead.

The sound of small arms firing and more mortar rounds could be heard now and in seconds a ferocious firefight erupted all around them, the roar of the ensuing battle washing over them. The sound of men wounded and dying reverberated all over the place and bullets searched for them like angry hornets. Paul Gallagher crawled on the wet ground, the mud getting in his mouth, the smell of wet earth and rotten vegetation gagging him. He spit out a mouthful of dirt, his hands working feverishly on the rifle. He felt himself trembling, adrenalin coursing through his veins like he was on fire, his gut a mass of melted fear threatening to choke him. He swallowed hard, wiping his face, searching for the elusive figures darting in the jungle toward them, trying to breach the small perimeter. The flashes from the rifle muzzles could be seen all over them and the volume of fire directed toward the defenders in the small perimeter was incredible. He heard a loud moaning; something like a keening sound, and with amazement he realized the sound was coming from his mouth.

"Oh God…oh God, please don't let me die…don't let me die," he whispered over and over, feeling the rifle bucking in his hands, clicking on empty, reloading.

"There must be at least a thousand men out there," he heard a calm, strong voice next to him and realized it was Pierce. Paul took the calm in the voice and the soft talk and he realized that if Pierce was scared, he sure as hell had it under control. He breathed a sigh of relief and then a strong hand was grabbing him, the fingers digging into him. "Steady my friend, steady," Pierce said softly and Paul shook his head ferociously, his teeth biting his lip until the taste of blood was strong in his mouth.

He took a deep breath, feeling the rush of adrenalin coursing through his veins and a sensation of peace took hold of him while he fired mechanically now, regaining control. It would not do to lose control on a firefight, he thought fleetingly, and besides that, the CIDG were counting on them for advice and support.

In the fast encroaching darkness, a grin flickered on Captain Pierce's face; Lt. Gallagher would do just fine, he thought, his eyes catching glimpses of men dashing around them in the jungle. A dark figure loomed in front of him, muzzle flashes hunting for him and he fire, the rifle clicking on empty. The Viet Cong soldier came at him in a rush and Pierce stood up swiftly, the butt of the rifle coming up, connecting with the man's face, crumpling him. He reloaded the rifle and continued to pour fire into the jungle. All around them men fought and died, their cries of pain and rage intermingled with the incredible noise, the smell of cordite, blood and human feces permeating the air around them. Somewhere behind them, an RPG (Rifle Propelled Grenade) round smashed against a tree, sending slivers of hot metal flying in every direction. Men screamed in pain and agony as the hot metal slapped into them, the horrible wounds gushing blood and watery fluids.

"Stay here," he told Paul and immediately stood up, bending down at the waist to make a smaller target. If he could find Tranh, together they could get the men to rush small sections at a time, attempting to push the encircling enemy back. It would be dark soon and if they could hold the enemy at bay for a few more minutes, darkness would be their ally, giving them some breathing room. The perimeter they were holding was too small and the men were bunched together, making them easy targets to hand grenades and mortar rounds, Captain Pierce thought. They needed to expand their field of fire and increase the size of the perimeter, but that would be difficult with the amount of fire they were receiving. They were pinned down, and any man that stood up, was cut down immediately. He could sense, more than anything else, his men putting up a stiff resistance, remembering their training and the advice given to them by the Special Forces men and he smiled inwardly, feeling good about them. The men would not give in easily and whoever was out there would find out that they were about to pay a heavy price for what they wanted.

He moved as fast as he could, sensing more than feeling, bullets searching hungrily for him. A mortar round exploded behind him and the force of the explosion picked him up boldly, slamming him hard against the ground, knocking the wind out of him. For a moment he was stunned, his ears ringing loudly, his head swimming from the impact. He shook his head to dispel the swirling darkness, the bright lights jumping in front of his eyes. He pushed himself up and then red-hot pain hit him in the back. He screamed at the incredible intensity of the pain, biting his lips and then he felt the wetness running down his back. He had been hit, mortar fragments more than likely, he thought, and for a second, his mind was blurred with the feeling he was about to die. He fell back on the ground. As his hearing came back, he laid still, taking inventory of his body. He moved his legs and arms and once again tried to get up. He got to a sitting position and finally found his legs. He was trembling all over, but realized that even though he had been hit, it wasn't too bad, flesh wounds more than likely. He fumbled around, searching for his rifle in the darkness. Finding it he checked the magazine, it was empty. He threw it down, snatching the Swedish K submachine gun from around his neck. He looked around, bewildered, realizing that the fight had somehow, slowed down, the firing not as fast or as intense as it had been. He was surprised to find that it was completely dark, the Vietcong slowing down their attack. He breathed hard, getting air deep into his lungs, the pain in his back now a dull, pulsating ache.

"Tranh…Tranh," he yelled, hoping that the little man was okay. A dark figure lifted from the earth, not ten feet away from him and Tranh was there. Flares started to go up in the night again, their brilliant light pushing the shadows away. Firing started again and grenades and mortar rounds came in, reverberating in the perimeter.

"Check the men, Tranh…tell them to save their ammo and the flares."

Tranh nodded his head and like a ghost in the night he disappeared to comply with the directive.

Pierce whirled around, his eyes trying to make out things around him. He yelled again, calling for Paul and Ashworth. The rain that had pestered them all day was slowing down some, but the sky was completely dark, visibility almost nil, the rumble of thunder and the strikes of lighting adding to the confusion. He forced his sluggish body to move, breathing deeply of the hot, humid air, his powerful chest rising and falling with each raggedy breath. Thunder, like the clashing of bowling pins rumbled overhead, the roar of it reminding Alton of a pack of hunting lions. Twin streaks of lighting flickered right above him, the eerie light illuminating the clearing, shadows dancing in the ethereal light given by the thunderbolts.

He heard footsteps approaching and Ashworth was there, followed immediately by Paul.

"Everybody okay?" he asked, his hand going to the small of his back, feeling the slippery blood, the pain intensifying now. He stifled a grunt of pain, feeling the sweat running down his back, mixing with the blood.

"I took a bullet in my leg, but nothing major," Ashworth said, the pain in his voice making him a liar. The bullet had not hit bone, but it was still there.

"Come on," Pierce said and the three of them started moving. Another flare went up and they hurried to find a tree to get behind. Sporadic rifle fire could be heard here and there and Pierce knew they were in deep trouble. By the light of the dancing flares, Pierce looked at his men, seeing the stress marked clearly on their faces. They were in a bad situation and they knew it. Blood, bright and red, covered Gallagher's right shoulder and the pain could be seen on his handsome, young face.

"You okay?" Pierce asked, his eyes fixed on him. Gallagher made a deprecating gesture with his left hand, shaking his head in the affirmative.

Paul Gallagher glanced at his friend and then he saw the blood covering his shirt.

"Mine is just a scratch, but it looks like you're hit badly." he said, glancing at Ashworth who took a step toward them, his hand opening the medical bag.

"Lay on your stomach and let me see," he ordered and Pierce turned around. Strong hands pulled at his shirt and something ripped behind him, the pain lancing through him.

Ashworth gave a low whistle and glanced at Paul. "Get the flashlight and hold it for me," he requested, his hands busy with his medical bag.

For the next few minutes Ashworth worked in silence, while the sweat covered Pierce's face, waves of intense pain coming and going, making him nauseous.

"You have several pieces of fragment in your back Captain. I bandaged them the best I could, but I need to cut them out as soon as possible," Ashworth said.

Pierce sat down again, shaking his head, wrapping the wet shirt around him, grunting with the effort.

"You want something for the pain? Ashworth asked.

"Later…not now," he said, biting his lips at the pain coursing through him. There was no time now for his injuries. They were in trouble and his men were dying by the score.

After checking on Gallagher's wound, the three friends took stock of their position and shortly afterward Tranh appeared, making his report. More than fifty men were dead or wounded and their probes searching for a possible escape route had been sent back reeling. There was no way out of the trap. The Viet Cong had chosen their ground well and now the whole company was pinned down, with no clear avenue of escape.

They were trapped, Pierce thought, with a sizable unit of Viet Cong surrounding the perimeter and with no hopes of getting artillery or chopper support. And even with a radio available, the weather was rotten, so there would be no help coming.

"What about the radio, Lee?" Pierce asked.

"No good. I tried to get through, but…nothing comes back." He stopped then, shrugging his shoulders.

All three men were silent, each one immersed in his own thoughts, the silence finally broken by Pierce, his voice resigned to the fact that there wasn't a damn thing they could do different now.

"Do the best you can. Lee, see about the wounded." He was silent then, his mind working all the angles.

"Paul, you and me and Tranh, lets see what we can do," he continued. "They know they've got us and it's not going to be long before their leader sends them in."

Paul heard the words of his friend and his face drained of all color. This was it, he thought, thinking that he didn't want to die in this God forsaken place, so far away from his wife and parents.

He shook his head to dispel the thoughts of impending doom running wild in his mind and then a small smile flickered across his face, his left hand closing into a fist. He might die in this stinking jungle, he thought, but they would pay a good price for it. He shook his head at the absurdity of his thoughts at such a moment, knowing well that he was not ready to die, not now and not in this piece of real estate anyway.

In the company of Tranh and Pierce, they made the rounds in the small clearing, talking softly to the men, cautioning them to save the ammo, whispering a word of encouragement here and there, getting them ready for the hand to hand combat that was coming. While they covered the perimeter, Ashworth moved around the clearing stiffly, tending to their wounds the best way he could. He had forty two weeks of very intensive medical training, courtesy of the Special Forces specialized individual military occupation (MOS) given at Ft. Bragg, but here his supplies and equipment were limited and most of the wounded were bleeding to death or had suffered so many wounds that it was just about impossible to do any better. Regardless, he did his best. That's what he had been trained for and he gave it all he had. Moving from man to man, he checked all the wounded, while all over the small perimeter firing continued. His hands were slippery with blood and his own wound was giving him incredible pain, but he continued until he had covered the whole perimeter. Some of the wounded men were too far gone to need medical attention, their wounds gaping holes where the intestines were ruptured or limbs were missing. By the time he got to them, they had bleed to death or close to it, most of them in shock, their lifeblood seeping slowly into the ground.

All through the night, the Viet Cong probed the small perimeter, at times short, but furious firefights erupting at different places, keeping the men trapped in the small clearing on edge all night, waiting for the inevitable. At one point in time Captain Pierce toyed with the idea of he, Paul and Ashworth sneaking out of the trap. The three of them could do it fairly easily in the cover of darkness, he knew that, but the thought that so many of his men would die without proper leadership made him stay in place. It would be better to die fighting like a man, helping the Vietnamese, even if all of them would find death at the hands of the Viet Cong, he thought, smiling grimly at their predicament.

Time and again the jungle reverberated with the sound of mortars and grenades, automatic rifle fires and RPG's (Rifle Propelled Grenades) going off in all directions until finally an eerie silence fell on the jungle and Pierce knew that the enemy was getting ready to come at them, all at once.

"Get ready Paul, they're coming," he said softly, shifting his body around, feeling the stiffness on his legs and back. They had remained alert all through the night, fighting the pain of their wounds, adrenalin keeping them in a high state of readiness. Shortly after Ashworth had checked his back, he had realized that his legs were bleeding also and when he had checked, had found out that several pieces of fragments had lodge in his calves too. They were painful wounds, getting stiff and cold, making him bite his lips while walking to stop himself from screaming.

The rain that had fallen most of the night, stopped now and the first glimmer of daylight showed itself in the sky above. Pierce darted a quick look above, noticing that the dark clouds were almost gone, the wind pushing them away like fast galloping horses. Long tendrils of fog drifted around the small clearing, adding to the surreal atmosphere of the perimeter. Pierce closed his eyes to slits, trying his best to catch a glimpse of what was coming from the jungle, but it was to no avail. Whatever was there was waiting patiently for the right moment to strike.

For long minutes nothing moved, not a sound could be heard and then the gates of hell opened up and the small clearing became the site of a frantic, ferocious fight where quarter was not asked or given, men killing each other in a frenzy of death and destruction.

The cries of men engaged in mortal combat, grenades going off, and the sound of rifle fire filled Paul's senses until everything was a blur and he fought on instinct, his rifle spitting lead until it was empty, reversing it and smashing the faces that came rushing at him, intent on killing him. Hundreds of black clad men were swarming all over them, the rapidly rising sun shining on a tangled mass of men, their faces etched in a snarl of pain and rage.

Paul glanced around quickly, his eyes catching a glimpse of Pierce, two Viet Cong closing in on him. One man thrust a bayonet toward him while the other came in low, swinging the rifle like a club. Pierce sidestepped the bayonet thrust, and the Swedish K opened up, spitting bullets, catching the VC on the side, the man going down screaming. Pierce moved nimbly, the butt stroke from the other enemy soldier barely missing his head. He swung the Swedish K, striking the man on the face, crumpling him to the ground. But he had lost too much time, giving the other men coming at him an opening. The enemy rifles crashed on his head and Pierce went down, a swarm of black clad figures engulfing him. With a primordial scream, Gallagher move toward his friend, smashing men around, feeling blows raining on him, tripping and falling headlong on the ground. He shook his head to dispel the dizziness threatening to overwhelm him and glanced up, seeing the Viet Cong coming toward him. He pushed his battered body up, bar-ing his teeth in a snarl of agony as the rifles came crashing down on him. He pushed again, getting to his knees and then a blow to his right shoulder sent pain coursing through him like molten lava and he went down again, his face smacking the wet ground with incredible force, the swirling darkness engulfing him until the lights went out completely and he knew no more.

Ashworth saw his friends go down and he thought them dead. Like an incarnation from hell he ran toward them, rage and pain etched on his black face, dodging the enemy as best he could. While he ran, he realized that the VC were not trying to kill him, they wanted him alive and were willing to risk the death of many of them in order to get him. He stumbled once, almost going down on the bum leg, Regaining his balance he glanced around him, the Thompson spitting fire, men going down, their dying cries reverberating loudly. The Thompson finally clicked on empty and he threw the machine gun away, his hand snatching the Colt from its holster. All around him the scream of men dying in mortal pain reached his ears, the sound a nightmare of horrendous proportions. Smashing men aside, emptying his pistol on the VC hemming him from all sides, he attempted to get close to his fallen friends. He tripped and went down and this time was unable to get up. The Viet Cong soldiers were on him instantly, smashing his body with their rifle butts, pinning him down until movement was just an illusion. A man in uniform stepped in front of him, smiling and the rifle in his hand came down on his face, the pain incredibly sharp. He spit blood and swallowed hard, feeling the soft rain on his face again. He lifted his eyes to the heavens seeing the rifle coming down again, this time on his head and he went limp, falling, falling into a well of darkness until finally the darkness grew intense and he knew no more

* * * *

Paul Gallagher woke up to a world of incredible pain, the sensation that he was moving strong in him, his whole body stiff, sore. He remained with his eyes closed, taking inventory of his battered body. When he opened his eyes he had to close them again, the brilliant light making him moan in pain. He had a terrible headache and his left shoulder was a throbbing lump of flesh, but otherwise, he was okay. He tried to move his arms, but for some reason they would not move and he desisted.

He opened his eyes slowly again, everything swimming in front of him and he shook his head slowly, the pain pounding in his head, forcing him to close his eyes. He blinked repeatedly, finally opening them again and this time was able to keep them that way. For long seconds his befuddled brain was not able to absorb what his eyes were telling him and then everything became crystal clear and he stood still with his mouth open. He snapped his head around, finding himself in a bamboo cage, his arms tied behind his back, and four Viet Cong soldiers carrying him. He swiveled his head to see behind him, catching a glimpse of another form lying in a similar bamboo cage coming after him several feet away, another group of Viet Cong soldiers staggering with the load. Here and there, wounded Viet Cong soldiers passed his cage, their pain dulled eyes glancing over him.

"What…what the hell is going on?" he asked himself softly, wishing that his brain could function clearly.

The cage where he was riding stopped swinging suddenly and the next second it was dropped unceremoniously on the jungle floor. The flimsy door was ripped open and eager hands reached for him and he was dragged out, several Vietcong standing over him, rifles ready. He looked around, seeing the same thing happening just behind him and he waited, watching the body of another man being dragged out. His heart leaped in his chest at the sight of Pierce and again when he saw Ashworth limping painfully toward them, a rope around his neck. Rough hands reached for him, pulling him up. In a matter of minutes all three men were standing next to each other and Paul smiled ruefully at them, opening his mouth to say something.

"Pierce"...he started, never finishing. The blow from the Viet Cong next to him caught him across the mouth, busting his lips, tasting the salty blood. With a cry of rage and pain, he stumbled forward, tears clouding his sight. At the first move, two other Viet Cong soldiers jumped at him, the blows raining on him until his body slumped forward, crashing on the jungle floor. For the next minute kicks, fist and rifle blows came down on Paul and then as suddenly as they had started they stopped, the men laughing at the wretched form on the ground puking his guts out.

When the beating started, Ashworth was the closest to him and he screamed at them, lunging toward the soldiers. A Viet Cong next to him yanked hard on the rope, at the same time swinging a bamboo stick, hitting Ashworth on the head, the blow staggered him, sending him to his knees. In rapid succession, more blows descended on him until a voice next to him put an end to the beating.

A slight built man approached then, a smile of satisfaction on his face. He was dressed in the uniform of a North Vietnamese officer, a Senior Colonel by his shoulder rank, a riding crop in his hands and a pith helmet on his head. Stopping close to the three men, he took the pith helmet off, wiping the sweat running down his face and forehead with a handkerchief. The clothes were clean, his boots polished and his black hair was freshly combed and oiled. His eyes, the color of burnt almonds, were bright, intelligent and at the same time hard and uncompromising. His lips were one straight, thin cruel line as he glanced at the captive men in front of him.

He looked at the three men closely, the smile on his face one of pure pleasure. "I'm Colonel Hue," he said, in heavily accented English, the riding crop hitting his right leg for emphasis. A cigarette dangled from a corner of his lips, the smoke curling upward. "And you gentlemen,...are my prisoners of war."

Saying that, he glanced at Paul who was slowly coming up. The Colonel took a step toward him, his leg moving swiftly, kicking him in the stomach, and sending the man face down on the ground again. Animal sounds escaped from Paul's lips as he curled himself small on the ground.

Senior Colonel Hue laughed then, a cruel, mirthless laugh and he looked at Pierce, fixing his cold, reptilian eyes on him first and then on Ashworth, his eyebrow raised in question.

"I'm Captain Pierce and I demand that you follow the rules of the Geneva Convention Colonel," Pierce said.

Colonel Hue looked at him like he was looking at an insect. A grin flickered across the Colonel's face and suddenly the right arm shot forward and out, the riding crop crashing on Pierce's face with such force that the skin broke, blood seeping slowly from the cut.

"Shut up," Colonel Hue said, his voice rough, almost yelling now, raising the crop above his head again. Not a cry escaped from Pierce's mouth, but his eyes became hooded, an unholy light in them.

"We are going to have a grand time," Hue said softly, the liquid brown eyes closed to slits, lowering the arm.

He looked at the Vietcong guards standing close by and nodded his head. Gallagher was lifted from the ground roughly and the ties of the three men were cut. The Colonel said something in rapid fire Vietnamese and eager hands started taking their clothes off, pulling their boots off their feet, taking all their personal gear off them, finally leaving them with just their underwear. The VC searched their pocket, appropriating anything they wanted. One of them came across the envelope in Gallagher's shirt and he handed it to Colonel Hue, who took it. The man opened the envelope, reading the contents slowly, his face impassive.

"You are...Gallagher?" he asked softly in his accented English, smiling now, his eyes centering on Paul.

"That's me...and that's my letter," Paul said, holding his side, taking a step toward Hue and reaching for the letter.

Immediately the VC converged on him, talking loudly and making threatening gestures with the rifles and the ever-present bamboo sticks.

"Ah...ah," Hue said smiling, his hand keeping the letter away from Paul.

Pierce and Ashworth looked at the situation unfolding in front of them wondering what the hell was going on now. Pierce saw Paul's face become cloudy, his eyes hard and cold, and he knew his friend was about to do something that would get him kill. He didn't know what was in the letter or why it was so important to Paul, but whatever it was, it was going to cost him his life. He took a step toward him, his hand reaching for Paul.

"Steady Paul...steady my friend," he said softly, watching the interplay between the two men. For a moment he thought that Paul would not respond, but finally he felt his friend's body relax, taking a step back.

"So you are going to be a father?" Hue said and finally Pierce understood.

"Lord in heavens...have mercy," he said softly, shaking his head, wondering what else would be coming their way.

Paul Gallagher looked at the man in front of him and the bile rose to his mouth, the bitter taste choking him. Hatred, an emotion that was almost alien to him, surged in his mind and if he had been able to, Hue would have died then and there, torn to pieces by his hands. Every fiber of his body was tense and he wished for nothing more than to erase the smirk off the Vietnamese face, to pound his head in the dirt, to kill the man.

Colonel Hue fixed his cold eyes on Gallagher, laughing now, putting the letter in his pocket.

Once again, he gave an order and the VC guards moved. Tying a rope around their necks and tying their hands, they made the three Americans get in a single file, Captain Pierce first, followed by Gallagher and then Ashworth, walking barefoot, the guards talking excitedly, pulling at the cords around their necks.

Slowly the line moved, the three prisoners of war absorbing the pain of their wounded bodies. Paul Gallagher squared his shoulders and then he closed his eyes, taking a deep breath, his mind centering on the events that had brought him to this point.

CHAPTER 2

United States Military Academy
West Point, New York
May 1962

Second Lt. Paul W. Gallagher fidgeted nervously in his seat, his hand going to the tie at his neck, pulling at it in an effort to alleviate the pressure on his throat. Today was graduation day after four years at West Point, having earned a bachelor of science degree and in a few short minutes the man whom he most admired in the world would be at the podium delivering the closing ceremonial speech. The mess hall of the United States Military Academy was packed with hundreds of students, proud parents and well-wishers, all waiting expectantly for the General to make his appearance. His parents and his fiancé were there and he was eager to join them.

It was warm in the mess hall and Paul Gallagher, wishing for an end to the ceremonies, could feel the sweat running under his tunic. He was a tall, deeply suntanned young man of twenty-three with short black hair and laughing blue eyes and he was really looking forward to whatever the feature had in store for him. He had excelled at boxing during his years at the Academy and at the leadership courses and now was looking forward to other endeavors, other adventures. He had grown up during the years of World War II and was barely two years old when his father had returned from the Pacific theater, wounded and with a chest full of medals and the young boy had decided that when he was all grown up, he would be a soldier. He had excelled during his high school years and with the help of his father and some influential friends of the family, he had gone to West Point. Now he was an officer and a gentleman in the United States Army, a proud soldier and guardian of freedom.

Little did he knew then that the lessons learned in West Point would stand him well in the not too distant future, helping him to overcome an incredible ordeal, an ordeal that would change his life forever.

When the door at the end of the mess hall opened, Paul W. Gallagher held his breath while he watched the tall, aristocratic man making his way to the front.

"Attention," someone behind the General shouted and the assembly of graduates came smartly to their feet.

General Douglas MacArthur strode to the small podium. Reaching it, his eyes took in the cadets and for a brief second, a smile was etched on his rugged face.

Paul sat now, unmoving, all his attention riveted on the man giving the speech. He heard words like "Duty, Honor, Country," the motto of the Academy, and then General MacArthur hit his stride.

"Those three hallowed words reverently dictate what you aught to be, what you can be, what you will be. They are your rallying point—to build courage when courage seems to fail; to regain faith when there seems little cause for faith; to create hope when hope becomes forlorn."

There were other words spoken during that hot afternoon, but for Paul W. Gallagher, it was the three first words that were imprinted forever in his mind. He had read them before, had listened to other cadets talking about them, but never before had he been as keenly aware of what those three words really meant. But now he did and for some unexplainable reason his heart beat strongly with emotions.

After MacArthur finished it was finally almost over and the Cadets made their way to the parade grounds where thirty minutes later with a great shout, the Cadets stood in place and the white hats went up high in the air. One phase of his life was over, another about to start.

Second Lt. Gallagher made his way among the throng of people, looking for his fiancé and his parents. Finally spotting them, he made his way toward them, wondering who all the people around his parents were and when he came closer he stopped cold. Among several men in uniform and the superintendent of the Academy stood a man, tall and distinguish looking, his eyes covered by sunglasses, General (Retired) Douglas MacArthur, talking to his father like they were old friends.

Like a man in a dream, he approached, until finally he was there. His father look up, seeing his son standing with his mouth open, his eyes fixed on MacArthur. A smile came across William F.Gallagher and he extended a hand to his son.

"Lt. Gallagher come meet General MacArthur," his father said, an impish smile on the weathered face, the black patch covering his left eye, a 'memento' from World War II, making him look like a pirate in an action movie. He was dressed in his Sunday best, as Carol Gallagher used to say, a three-piece suit, gray in color that accentuated the tall, slightly built frame of the man. His eyes were a clear blue and his sun and wind weathered face gave you the impression of strength and character. He was a man with an immense love for the land, for his country and for his God, patriotic to the end.

Paul W. Gallagher came to attention, snapping a parade perfect salute to the General, shaking hands, wondering how in the hell his father knew the man. They talked softly for a few more minutes and then the General took his leave. Paul stood in awe at what had just transpired.

Seeing the man leaving, he turned around and looked at his father and mother. "I didn't know you knew the General," he said, waiting expectantly for his father to acknowledge the fact.

"I do," his father said simply. "We served together during the Second World War."

Paul Gallagher fixed his eyes on his father and shook his head, an amused look etched on his handsome face. The old man sure is something, he told himself, wondering how he had pulled that one off.

Chapter 3

Fort Bening, Ga.
Jump School, Third week
June 1962

The C-119 plane, fondly called "Boxcar Bertha" due to her lumbering appearance, rumbled loudly through the sky, fifteen hundred feet above ground, the wind rushing in through the open door. The Jump-master looked out, checking the landing zone below. Pulling himself back inside the plane, he glanced at the paratroopers who crowded the airplane. A single red light could be seen above the door and the long stick of paratroopers move stiffly down the length of the aircraft, doing their best to ameliorate the heaviness of the parachute equipment strapped on their backs. This was their fifth jump; the last jump for his class before graduation and Lt. Gallagher was looking forward to it. He was getting a three-week leave before departing for Ft. Bragg and Special Forces training and he was eager to see his parents and wife again. H e had gotten married shortly after West Point, refusing to wait any longer. He was deeply in love with Susan Connelly, his high school sweetheart, and they had decided that as soon as he was finished with West Point they would marry. They had done just that and had gone to live with his parents at the farm. Later on there would be time to decide where they would settle down, but for now they were taking it one day at a time. He smiled inwardly at his thoughts, thinking that everything was going smoothly, all his hopes and plans working out to perfection so far.

The loud voice of the grizzled Jumpmaster, screaming to make himself heard above the roar of the propellers brought him out of his thoughts.

"Check your equipment," the man roared, his eyes glancing at the group of men, making sure they were doing exactly as they were told. The plane smelled of sweat and fear, mixed with oil and fuel fumes and Paul could hardly wait for the order to jump.

Every one of the jumpers checked their equipment, making sure the static line was routed properly and all the belts were snug and tight. This was serious business and there was no room for mistakes.

The Jumpmaster glanced up and down the line, his eyes scanning the faces of the men on the "sticks." He nodded his head, satisfied, he looked out the door again.

"Hook your static line," he yelled again and as one, the stick of paratroopers hooked the static line to the steel cable just above their heads, making sure the wire that ensured the hook was locked was pushed through the hole.

"Two minutes," the Jumpmaster screamed, signaling the first man on the stick to come forward, his eyes darting to the hook.

The seconds went by slowly and then the Jumpmaster screamed again. "Stand by the door."

The first man on the stick moved up, standing in front of the door, the incredible sound of the wind rushing through the open door masking any noise or talk inside the plane.

The red light flickered for a second, changing to green and the first man on the stick went out the door, the rest following swiftly. When it was his turn, he went out fast, counting the seconds until the T-10 army parachute opened up, jerking him upward, the incredible feeling of falling through the air intensify by the adrenalin rush that coursed through his body. With his heart beating a wild crescendo and his stomach tied in a knot he glanced up, checking the parachute, making sure everything was right. In a few minutes he was down, making a parachute-landing fall that his instructors would be proud off. He stood up beginning to recover his parachute, happy that another step in his career had been accomplished.

He carried his parachute with him, finally reaching the rendezvous point, waiting for the rest of the troops to get there.

A few minutes later one of the black hat instructors called to attention and Colonel Miller, Airborne School Commandant, Fort Benning, Ga. made his appearance, walking down the men in formation, pinning the silver badge of the paratroopers to their chests. It was a short ceremony, with the Colonel wishing them good luck and God's speed and soon afterward the class had being dismissed.

A couple of hours later, the newly minted paratrooper, Second Lt. Paul Gallagher, proudly displaying his Paratrooper Silver Wings, was on his way to Waterloo, Iowa, where his wife Susan would pick him up for the rest of the trip home to his parent's farm on the outskirts of Mason City, Iowa. It was quite late in the night when he was finally able to get aboard the plane that would take him home and once he was settle, he slept for most of the ride.

Several hours later, he was there, his mind numb from the ride, but exited at the prospect of seeing his wife and parents. The first rays of sunshine were pushing the shadows away when he exited the plane that had brought him home and he stretched his body, his eyes searching for Susan. She was nowhere to be seen and he felt some mild annoyance at that. He glanced at his watch noticing the time, six in the morning, and decided that Susan was probably still in bed. She was a sleepy head and could sleep through an earthquake. He made his way to the baggage check and was in the process of grabbing one of his bags from the conveyor when he heard his name called. He turned around swiftly, just in time to catch in his arms the red haired woman coming toward him. With a cry of delight, Susan entangled her arms around the neck of her husband and planted a wet kiss on his lips, much to the glee of the people around them. She was of slight build with flaming red hair and green eyes. At twenty-three years old, she had known Paul Gallagher all her life, growing up in the same farming community next to Mason City where his parents had a farm. While he had been at West Point she had gone to veterinary school. She had graduated just before he went to Ft. Benning, Ga. for jump school.

Paul returned the kiss and then disentangled her arms from his neck, pushing her gently away. He glanced around, making sure nobody was paying them any attention and then he said softly, "Behave yourself, you wanton woman."

His eyes were bright and full of life and he looked at her, thinking that she was more beautiful than he remembered, taking in the lovely face, the full, red lips, and the green eyes with the mischievous look in them. She was a farm girl, with not an ounce of fat on her hard, well proportioned body, her breasts large and firm and he sighed deeply, his mind running wild with thoughts of that young, hard body in bed with him.

Susan saw the look in his eyes and she laughed a laugh full of merriment and then she turned her head slightly to the side in what was a characteristic gesture for her, looking at him long and hard. He was dressed in his Class A uniform, pants bloused in his jump boots and he cut a dashing figure. He was tall and tan and she was deeply and unequivocally in love with him.

He finished getting his bags, hefting the duffel bag on his shoulder. He looked at Susan, a warm, tired smile on his face and said, "Take me home sweetheart."

They walked to the car, a 1960 Chevy his father had obtained for them when Paul was in his last year at West Point. He dumped the bags in the back and slid his butt in the passenger side, his eyes taking in the sky above. It was a beautiful summer day and with Susan next to him, nothing could be better, he thought, glancing at the people rushing in and out of the airport doors, everybody in a hurry to get somewhere.

She started the car and a few minutes later they were out of the parking lot, heading for home. They rode in silence, their company enough for the moment, Susan enjoying the gentle pressure of Paul's hand on her naked thigh while she drove. She was wearing a white, summer dress and with the windows open, the wind was hiking it above her knees. The gentle pressure of Paul's fingers intensified and soon the hand was traveling in small circles, caressing the warm flesh, going higher and higher, until his fingers found the edge of her panties and he stopped. She turned her head to him, an impish smile on her radiant face, a row of perfect white teeth showing from her parted lips. Her breath was coming in shallow pants and she marveled at his ability to awaken the demons in her so easily. She turned the car onto a dirt road that would take them home the back way and she looked at him again, her eyes sparkling like a handful of diamonds in the sunshine.

"You want to play, cowboy?" she asked, her voice deep and husky now with the force of her passions.

Paul looked at her and laughed, shaking his head in the affirmative, his fingers going under the panties. She parted her legs to make it easy for him, a small sound escaping her lips when his fingers found the warm, moist spot they sought. She closed her legs, trapping his fingers where they were, sweat droplets forming on her upper lip. She drove fast now, the only car on the dirt track. There was an old parking lane that they had used when they were young and foolish, beginning to experiment with each other and now Susan found it, sending the car into a tight turn, too fast. She expertly corrected the vehicle and in a few more minutes had found the small, secluded spot. She put the car in park and with a last look at Paul, stepped out of the car. He did the same and by then she had the trunk open and a blanket in her hands. He glanced around, feeling the warm, gentle breeze on his skin and the sun on his face. Behind him, the clear waters of a small pond, surrounded by tall trees could be seen and the sky was cloudless and blue, the wind softly murmuring among the leaves.

"Well, I can see you are ready," he said, a grin flickering across his handsome face.

She didn't answer, only walked a few paces to the edge of the pond and spread the blanket over the spring grass.

After that and without a word, she reached behind her, pulled the zipper of the dress down and let it fall to the ground. She did the same with the bra, her large breast standing proud and erect, the nipples growing swiftly as the wind caressed them. Her skin was deeply tanned and her body was strong and hard, well muscled. She then turned to him, her fingers hooked on the edge of her panties; the green eyes speaking volumes to him.

She smiled at him and the panties came down, exposing the red triangular patch of hair insinuating itself just below the hard planes of her belly. Her legs were long and well muscled, the result of long walks and daily swimming workouts. Paul felt his breath catch in his throat at the sight of her. God, but she is one beautiful woman, he thought, his eyes never leaving her, feeling every beat of his heart as he stood a few feet away from her, drinking the loveliness that was her.

She whirled around, and sat down on the blanket completely naked, her arms outstretched toward him.

He looked at her for a long second and then he went down on his knees next to her, his eyes drinking her in, the lump in his throat about to choke him.

"I love you," he said softly, his strong arms taking her, his lips kissing her soft mouth in a long, lingering caress, until his body shuddered with his pent up emotions and she arched her back toward him, meeting his need with hers, her lips calling his name over and over. His tongue found her open mouth, tasting the sweetness of her and the heat, the velvety softness making him crazy. She pushed him gently away from her and then her hands were busy, taking his shirt off, her mouth still covering his, her heart about to jump out of her chest. His body was hard and lean like a Greek athlete, the daily workouts during his training melting every ounce of fat from him and she marveled at the hardness and symmetry of the muscles under her hands and at the same time the softness of his body. He helped her with the belt and the pants and then the sun was shinning on his naked buttocks, her strong hands pulling him down on top of her, reaching for his swollen member and guiding him into her. The sense of being engulfed in a hot vacuum washed over him and he quickly thrust himself deep inside her. Susan met him halfway, caught in her incredible need, her eyes closed in a rictus of ecstasy. He lowered his mouth to the dark tips of her nipples, taking one in his mouth, sucking it to stiffness, listening to her muffled cries of pleasure. Her hands pushed his head down, thrusting the nipple further into his mouth, his lips closing on it. He felt himself melting into her, the sensations almost overpowering in their intensity, until the world around him exploded in brilliant light and he was falling, falling, the cries of the woman he loved so dearly reverberating in his ear.

Two hours later they made their appearance at the old, rambling house, their radiant faces telling his mother Carol, exactly what they had been up to before reaching the house.

He spent three weeks helping his father and brothers around the farm, two thousands acres of wheat and pasture, with over two hundred head of Black Angus cows running around the place. It was hard, backbreaking work, but he was used to it and, like his father use to say, "Hard work never killed anybody, it just makes you stronger."

When the three weeks were over, way too soon as far as he was concerned, he said his good byes and headed for Ft. Bragg and Special Forces training. Another chapter of his life was about to begin.

Chapter 4

Headquarters
U.S. Army Special Warfare School
Fort Bragg, N.C.
Office of the Commanding General
July 5, 1962

Brigadier General Winfield Woods was in his office going over manpower requisitions when a slight knock on the door brought his attention back. He threw the paper he had been reading down on the desk, welcoming the respite that the knock on the door represented.

"Enter," he said and Command Sgt. Major Wilhelm stepped in, an Army 201 file in his hand. The man was tall, thin as a rail, a pencil line mustache on his upper lips. He was, as far as General Woods was concerned, one of the best Command Sgt. Majors he had ever seen and he was pleased that he had been able to obtain him. The Sgt. Major was dressed in his army fatigues, tailored and starched to perfection. On his left side there was a CIB (Combat Infantry Badge) with a silver star, representing a second award and the badge of the airborne. He was a professional soldier, with almost twenty years of service and had seen action in the Second World War, in Korea and Viet Nam.

"There is a young Second Lt. outside Sir, reporting for duty," he said now, a grin flickering on his face.

"Well Sgt. Major, show him in please," General Woods said. Sgt. Major Wilhelm nodded his head and stepped out, returning shortly with the young man.

Second Lt. Paul W. Gallagher took two steps forward, stopped in front of the desk and rendered a perfect salute to his superior officer.

"Lt. Paul W. Gallagher reporting for duty, Sir." Brigadier General Woods stood up, his eyes appraising the young man in front of him, returning his salute.

Paul Gallagher kept his eyes to the front, at the same time paying special attention to the General in front of him. The man was of medium height, with short, black hair that was beginning to show strands of silver. His eyes were the color of steel, dark gray, sharp and penetrating and at the same time showing kindness. He was dressed in his class A Greens and Lt. Gallagher glanced at the incredible array of badges and ribbons on the man's chest. The CIB (Combat Infantry Badge) was there and also the Paratrooper's badge. A Purple Heart could be seen, together with a Silver Star, the Legion of Merit and the Korea Service Medal. There were a few others that Paul couldn't recognize at the moment and then his eyes caught the first ribbon just below the CIB. The ribbon was blue in color, with five white stars and he recognized it immediately, the Medal of Honor. "Well I'll be..." Gallagher said to himself, impressed with the man and what the ribbons represented. You didn't see very many Medals of Honor around; you really had to earn that one.

The General came around his desk and shook the Lieutenant's hand, at the same time taking the file from Sgt. Major Wilhelm.

"Bring refreshments, Sandy," Woods said. "Coffee Lieutenant?"

"Coffee is fine, Sir," Gallagher said.

"Take a seat son, while I look at you orders."

General Woods opened the file and started reading. Shortly afterward, Sgt. Major Wilhelm came in with a tray in his hands. He offered coffee to Gallagher, fix the General a cup and put it in front of him. After fixing his own coffee, Sgt. Major Wilhelm sat down, waiting for the General to finish. At one point in his reading the General stopped, fixing his eyes on Paul, a frown etched on his face.

"They sure are relaxed around here," Paul thought, sipping the hot brew, waiting. Woods finished reading, dropped the file on the coffee table and turned his eyes toward Lt. Gallagher.

"We are glad you are here son. We need people like you in Special Forces and we hope you decide to stay for a while." He paused then, sipping his coffee.

"Thank you…sir", Lt Gallagher replied. "I intent to".

"Have you heard of Viet Nam," the General asked suddenly, catching Paul by surprise with the question.

"Yes Sir…some." He had seen the evening news, the commentator talking about advisors and the U.S. helping the Republic of South Vietnam to remain a democracy in that part of the world. That and some historical facts that he had learned while in his history classes at the Point were the extent of his knowledge.

"We are going to be involved in a very conventional war in that part of the world, soon, very soon," the General said, standing up and pacing the small office. "A lot of people think that we should go in there with all the power of the Armed forces, in other words, a full conventional war. Some of us think that is a mistake, that this war should be fought unconventionally, just like we have been doing so far." He paused again, stopping in front of a glass-paneled window, lost in thought.

"We are not ready for a conventional war in a country like that," he continued, "but like always, we will do our best. Right now we have several groups of Special Forces over there and a lot more on the way soon, working with the indigenous population and we will be okay as long as that is what we do." He paused again, shaking his head slowly and for a long moment the General's eyes were hooded, a pensive frown etched deeply on his sunburned face.

"I have my misgivings about that little conflict, but I'm just a General and we don't make policy, we just fight the wars that the politicians saddle us with," he said. He shook his head again and turned toward Paul, who had followed the little speech, wondering what it was all about or why the General had confided in him. Viet Nam was just a name for him until now, but apparently this General thought that it was going to be something big. General Woods stopped talking then, a rueful smile on his face.

"I better read about this place," Paul thought, waiting for the General to continued.

"You will start your officers training tomorrow. Sgt. Major Wilhelm will assist you with anything you need and I wish you good luck."

Paul stood up, realizing the meeting was over. He snapped to attention and saluted the General, did an about face and headed for the door. He was about to pull the door open when the General's voice stopped him cold.

"Are you by any chance Bill Gallagher's son?"

Paul whirled around, fixing his eyes on Woods, the surprise on his face evident. "Well…yes sir…I am," Gallagher mumbled, wondering how the General had known that. "I had the pleasure of meeting your father, a long time ago", Woods said. He stopped talking, a far away look in his eyes now. He shook his head like a man wanting to dispel memories and took a deep breath.

"He is a good man," he continued, "And by the way, how is he doing?"

"He's doing good sir…thank you, Sir," Paul said, his head spinning. Now, how in the hell had his father come to know this man, he asked himself, shaking his head. Obviously there were things about his father's life that he didn't know. He was going to have a talk with his father about all this, he thought, turning around and exiting the office. First MacArthur and now General Woods, all on a first name basis with him.

The next day his training started in earnest. Besides the physical and mental training, his days were a flurry of activities, especially the first twenty-one days of the assessment and selection process. It had been explained to him that it was necessary to pass this assessment in order to continued with the training and he had exerted himself, finishing the selection process and showing his commitment to Special Forces. From weapons to engineering, demolition and land navigation, to communications and intelligence and small unit tactics and then there was military free fall parachuting or HALO, (high altitude, low opening). The training continued with several weeks of specialized training in his chosen military occupation, 18 Alpha or officers training, until finally the coveted Green Beret was perched atop his head. But he was to find out that his training didn't end there. Within a week of finishing at Ft. Bragg, he was on his way to Language School where he was about to do his best to learn Vietnamese. He had been looking at the country more and more and he knew without a shadow of a doubt that soon, he would be on his way there. A nasty little war was brewing in that part of the world and Special Forces was the one that would take most of the brunt. They were trained in guerrilla warfare and their A-teams were capable of conducting operations in remote areas, and they could develop, organize, train and equip the indigenous population better than any conventional unit.

Once Language School was over in July 1963, Paul returned to Ft. Bragg, waiting for orders and just like he had predicted, he was assigned to Viet Nam. But first he had a thirty-day leave and as soon as he was able, he headed for home, thoughts of Susan making him smile. He really missed her and at times he wondered why he had chosen Special Forces, knowing that the time spent together with his loved ones was severely curtailed because of his chosen field. Several of his friends at the Academy had expressed concern for him when they had found out his assignment choice. They believed that Special Forces was a fad, something that would not last long and that a career officer would hurt his chances for advancement and promotion by getting himself assigned to such an outfit. And maybe they were right, Paul had thought then, but just briefly.

There was something about Special Forces that stirred deep emotions in Paul Gallagher's heart and somehow he knew that was where he belonged. He had been sure that he was making the right decision then and now, more than ever, he believed he was doing the right thing. He had spent the last year in training and his skills had been honed to a razor's edge. He was ready in mind, spirit and physically for anything that might come his way and he was eagerly looking forward to whatever the future might bring.

He was due back at Ft. Bragg the first week of September and then he would be on his way to Viet Nam with a detachment of Special Forces. He was really looking forward to putting into practice everything he had learned and eager to see the country and get a chance to meet the people.

He had kept his eyes and ears glued to the news about the place, realizing that the little known country was in the news more and more as time passed and he remembered General Woods' words when he first met him. This was going to be a dirty, nasty, little conflict. But for now, he was going home, to his parents and Susan and that was all that matters.

Chapter 5

Mason City, Iowa
August 1963

Susan Gallagher slowly sipped the cup of sweet tea in her hand, her mind a myriad of thoughts revolving around her husband. She was sitting on the porch of the big, farmhouse, waiting for Paul to finish getting dressed. Today was the last day of his leave and he was due to catch a plane back to Ft. Bragg, N.C. in a matter of hours. And sometime next week he will be in harm's way, she thought bitterly. Next year is going to be hard without him, she said to herself, sighing deeply. Paul was headed to a far off country, Viet Nam, somewhere in Indochina, a place she had never heard of until recently. The place would be her nightmare until the man she loved more than anything in the world was back home and in her arms. She closed her eyes and the handsome face appeared, smiling, the blue eyes bright and full of laughter, the image so clear she gave a small gasp and opened her eyes. She stood up, shaking her head, the red hair shining in the brilliant sunlight. It was summer time and the sky was an incredible blue, the sun shining bright in a cloudless sky, but despite that, her body was cold.

She glanced at her wristwatch. Two hours before he was out of her life. Slowly, the realization that something bad was going to happen to their lives intruded in her thoughts and Susan shook her head, attempting to dispel the bad feeling, her body shivering despite the heat of the day.

Get a hold of yourself, girl, she told herself, shaking her head to dispel the bad thoughts. She heard footsteps coming her way and swiveled her head around. Paul, his mother and father were exiting the front door, coming toward her, the two younger brothers, Charlie, seventeen, and Ralph, eighteen, a step behind them, everybody talking at the same time.

Paul Gallagher embraced and kissed his mother tenderly and then he turned to his father. William Gallagher looked at his son, pride etched deeply on his sunburned face and he took a step toward him and gathered his oldest son in his arms. In a rare show of emotion, Susan heard the words coming out of his mouth, the eyes bright and wet.

"Take care my, son," he said softly, "and do your duty with honor." He swallowed hard, feeling the unaccustomed lump in his throat. "Remember that we love you".

Paul took a step back, his eyes also bright and wet, extending his hand to his father. They shook hands, Paul feeling the strength in the old man's grip.

"I will, Dad. Love you," he said, almost in whisper and was gone.

William Gallagher saw him go and he wondered when he would see his son again. He was not a man given to second guessing his government, but he had been listening to the news commentators lately, had done some research on Viet Nam himself and had come to the conclusion that there was nothing to be gained by the United States involving itself in a conventional war in that particular place. What they had going in Viet Nam was nothing more than a civil war and the United States really didn't have any business sending men over there. He had thought long and hard about it and didn't think that the U.S. Government really had a clear policy about South Vietnam.

While the United States had Korea, the French had their Dien Bien Phu in Indochina and now Kennedy was in the process of getting the

U.S. deeply involved in another morass. Everybody was concerned about the domino theory and communism, running around scare that another country thousands of miles away would fall into communist hands and somehow the United States would look like a paper tiger. He shook his head in consternation, thinking that his son and a bunch of other good men were going to be involved in one hell of a mess soon and probably for nothing.

He had fought in World War II, but there the lines had been clear, there was no doubt that they were fighting to make the world a better place to live, free of tyrants and psychopaths. But this Viet Nam thing was different and Bill Gallagher had his doubts. He would support the Government and its views, he knew that, because even if the policies were wrong and the people in the government made mistakes, this was still his country, right or wrong and he would never turn his back on it. He had worn the uniform of a United Sates Marine with pride and had shed his blood and tears in far away places all for the sake of freedom and he had never regretted it. His country had asked for him to come and join the fight and he had done so, just like his son was doing now. But somehow, to him, this was different. He had a feeling that the people of the United States would not support this war. He had faith in Kennedy nonetheless and felt that somehow the President would see that the U.S. would not get embroiled in a war in that place, that somehow he would see the light and pull the men out in time.

He watched his son get in the car with his wife while the family stayed on the porch. Bill Gallagher watched his son and suddenly his body shuddered, feeling cold all over. Beads of sweat broke out on his forehead and he had to hold on to the veranda for support, wondering what was going on. He shook his head to clear his sight, his heart beating fast. As mysteriously as it had come, whatever it was, disappear, leaving him weak and trembling. He kept himself in tight control lest his wife see him in such a state, trying his best to come to terms with the feeling. He had had the same thing happened to him, long ago on a battlefield, just before he charged a nest of machinegun emplacements, the place where he had won the Medal of Honor. And now, whatever this thing was, had come back, making him wonder what was going to happen to his son.

A few minutes later, the car taking his son away from him was on its way, the couple making the trip in silence, the impending separation weighing heavily on the lovers. Finally they made it to the airport and with a heavy heart, they went into the terminal, sat down and waited for the plane call. They made small talk for a while, neither one really speaking about what was in their hearts until the plane call came and Paul stood up. He looked at her long and hard, like a man trying his best to engrave a face in his mind and then he pulled her to him, holding tight, his heart breaking with the pain of the impending separation.

"I love you girl…so very much," he said in her ear, softly.

"I love you," she said, her voice small and quivering.

The plane call came again and Paul bent down to retrieve his duffle bag.

"Be careful, please," she said, her eyes fixed on him, tears starting to fall down her cheeks. Her hand went to his face, her fingers caressing him in a loving, touching way.

"I will…I promised," he said, closing his eyes for a second. He felt the fingers touch his cheek, featherlike and he opened his eyes, breathing deeply. He kissed her lips tenderly, softly, wishing the moment would last forever.

For a moment longer they held each other's eyes and then Paul smiled sadly and whirled around, walking away.

Susan Gallagher stood in place, her heart breaking, and the awful premonition that she would never see him again haunting her thoughts.

She watched the tall, proud figure of the man she loved walking away, until he climbed in the plane and she couldn't see him any more. She retraced hers steps to the car, opened the door and sat down. Her pent up emotions finally broke and heart-rending sobs racked her slender body. For a long time she cried and when the tears finally subside, she cleaned her face, absorbed the pain and lifted her chin high. She started the car, put it in gear and backed out of the parking lot. She looked at herself in the mirror and shook her head.

"Never again," she said softly, "never again." There would be no more crying on her part, no more thoughts of a life without Paul. Her husband was a soldier, an officer in the U.S. Army and she knew that no matter what, she would always be at his side. She was as patriotic as any one else and the fact that Paul had decided on a career in the Army was something that gave her immense pride and at the same time filled her with fear of the unknown, the perils and dangers that he would face in a strange country. But she knew she had to be brave and besides, why was she thinking that something awful was going to happen? She shook her head, mystified at the thoughts running through her mind. Something was wrong, but what, she wondered?

Whatever it was, it left her with a sense of foreboding clouding her mind and oppressing her heart. She shook her head like a person wanting to get rid of bad thoughts and unconsciously her hand went to her belly. It was hard and ridge with muscles, but she wondered how much longer it would be that way. Her period was late and she had a feeling that pretty soon a new life would be kicking inside of her.

Chapter 6

U.S. Army Special Warfare School
Ft. Bragg, N.C.
August 1963

He arrived at Ft. Bragg that night, his body tired and stale after the long plane ride. He had gone straight to bed after calling Susan, but he had been unable to sleep, the conversation that they had running through his head. It had not been a very good call at all and it was obvious that Susan was doing her best to be cheerful about the whole situation, but the pain was still there and something else too. He had tried his best to get her to talk to him, but it was to no avail, she denied anything was wrong. He understood how she felt, hell he was feeling the same way, but he had a job to do and a duty to confirm to. Finally, in the early hours of the morning he slept and when the time came to depart, he was ready. They had made their way to Pope Air Force Base, on the outskirts of Ft. Bragg and after the paperwork was finished, they had boarded the plane. The trip to Vietnam took over twenty-four long, monotonous hours in a C-130 transport, with stops in Alaska and Japan and finally they were there; Paul Gallagher and eleven other Special Forces personnel. His first impression of the country was one of incredible heat and humidity, coupled with a smell that was a mixture of old sweat and rank jungle vegetation, intermingled with the smell of cooking fires and the noxious fumes of thousands of cars, trucks and motor scooters. And then there was the unbelievable noise. A cacophony of voices from a sea of humanity mixed with cars and bicycles, horns, trucks and scooters rumbling by and vendors hawking their wares on every street. They had been met by an NCO who provided transportation to a shack close to the runway and after several minutes, the group of men were loaded again, this time into helicopters and within an hour they were standing in front of Colonel (full bird) Brown, Special Forces commander in Saigon. The reception was short lived and soon thereafter, the group was heading for their specific assignments, once again being transported by helicopters. From above, the country was lush and green, rice paddies giving way to dense jungle areas, here and there intersected by a lonely farmers hutch, sometimes a few together.

Paul had found out that he and the Sgt. First Class by the name of Lee Ashworth, were going to be assigned to the same camp and he had made attempts to engage the man in friendly conversation. Ashworth was a career NCO, and had two tours in Vietnam already, something that fascinated Paul immensely. When he had found out that Ashworth was a veteran of that far off place, he had pestered the NCO to no end. Eventually both men made it to their destination, camp 28 in Chong Thien Province, the Mekong Delta area of the Republic of South Vietnam. Paul had met Captain Pierce then, the detachment Commander and at the same time had found out that he had been promoted to first lieutenant. That had been a pleasant surprise for him, thinking that things were beginning to look good in his chosen career.

Slowly he had learned the many ways of the people around him, and the enemy that they hunted in the dark, forbidding jungles and had come to appreciate the professionalism displayed by Pierce and Ashworth and the rest of the Special Forces men that comprised the lonely camp.

He had become part of the team and he really enjoyed the work, dealing with the Vietnamese people, helping them to fight the aggressors as he saw them, trying his best to follow his country's mandate in their effort to stop communism. He found out that he really liked the people and their simple ways and he went out of his way to learn all he could about them and their beliefs, knowing that the more he knew about the people he was suppose to be helping, the easier it would be for all concern.

After a while, he realized that this was the right way to fight the war and that the job they had been instructed to carry out by President Kennedy was important. Paul Gallagher was young and optimistic and he relished the thought of helping people make their own destiny. It was a heady experience, one that he came to realized, was very important to him. There was more to this war than killing Vietcong, he told himself many times during the course of his work. There was also the satisfaction of making friends and helping people with their everyday lives, providing medical assistance and the myriad of other things that Special Forces were trained to do in order to win the confidence and the friendship of the local population.

Paul Gallagher had immersed himself in the work with unabashed pride, until the death of the President, John Fitzgerald Kennedy in November of 1963 cast a pall over the entire effort of the Special Forces in Vietnam. But they had transcended that and once more they had dedicated their efforts to win the people and the war.

CHAPTER 7

Somewhere in the U Minh Forest
Mekong Delta
Republic of South Vietnam
December 13, 1963

And now this, Paul thought, putting one foot in front of the other, his mind rebelling at the thought that he and his friends were now prisoners of war. His thoughts went back to his parents and Susan—the anguish they were about to suffer when they learn of their predicament and his heart leaped in his chest, the rage and desperation building in him. He moved like a man a hundred years old, wondering what the future would bring for them. They had been trained at Ft. Bragg for something like this and he hoped with all his heart that he would not fail. They might kill me, Paul told himself, gritting his teeth, fighting the sharp edge of desperation edging into his mind, but they won't get anything out of me. And then he smiled ruefully at his thoughts. Brave thoughts, but in reality he was scared to death, not knowing what was going to happen to them, the quandary in which he found himself filled his mind with terror. He knew deep inside himself that he was not a coward, that he could face death with impunity if need be. But right now he was weak from loss of blood and depressed because of his family and his brain was not working right, making him susceptible to fear. He breathed deeply of the humid air and shook his head, willing the thoughts away, concentrating on the present.

All three of them were wounded and his shoulder was on fire, his throat parched and sore. He tried hard to work up some saliva in his mouth to wash away the gritty scum, but was unable to do so. He shook his head like a lion, sweat drops falling from his forehead, sparkling like diamonds in the sunlight. He glanced back once, catching a glimpse of Ashworth staggering behind him. In front of him he could see Pierce grimly putting one foot in front of the other, his legs and back wet from the blood seeping from his wounds. Paul knew that mortar fragments peppered his legs and that it was probably hell for him to walk. But he knew Pierce and the man would not complain about anything, even if it cost him his life. He was not about to let the enemy get anything on him and Paul made the resolution then and there that he would do his best to honor his friend and superior officer and try to followed his lead no matter what happened to them. He looked around the dense forest trying his best to deduce where they were or the direction they were heading, but the jungle was so dense that daylight barely filtered through the triple canopy, denying him the opportunity to see the sun or to guess where they were.

All day long the long line of men walked, without respite or slowing down. When one of them tripped on the underbrush and fell, the Viet Cong were on them in a flash, the bamboo sticks coming down, the kicks searching for the stomach until slowly and painfully, the Americans dragged their beaten bodies up, biting their lips, absorbing the pain and resuming the trek, their minds hoping for an end to the agony.

When night finally came, the Viet Cong halted in place, dropping the prisoner's in a huddle. They cut the ties that bound their hands and all three of them had to grit their teeth at the pain resulting from the blood rushing through the veins. The rope had cut furrows on their skin, cutting their circulation and when it was restored, it was an incredible agony, something more to add to their misery.

For many long minutes they lay on the jungle floor, unable to speak or hardly move. One Viet Cong soldier was their guard now, while the others were busy preparing an evening meal, small fires going up, and the smell of food reaching them. The Viet Cong soldier guarding them was a young man and soon was tired of keeping an eye on the Americans, more interested in the food that was being prepared and the conversation going around than in the prisoners.

Pierce watched him closely, hardly moving and when the VC walked a few paces away from them, he seized the opportunity to speak to his men without incurring the ire of the guard.

"Lee, Paul," he whispered urgently. Both men raised their heads, glancing in his direction. Darkness had descended on the jungle and the small VC cooking fires barely disturbed the darkness surrounding them. Even as close to each other as they were, Pierce was barely visible.

"We need to keep our mouth shut boys," he said, his voice a mere whisper. "Don't give them anything they can used against us or our country."

Ashworth and Paul nodded their heads in the darkness, knowing well what was expected of them. Pierce cleared his throat and continued.

"Escape if you can, alone if you have to," he said, watching the guard who was coming back now. The VC came close to them, grunting something in Vietnamese, sending a kick toward the nearest man who was Ashworth, hitting him about the chest. That done he laughed, and dropped a canteen of water at their feet and a canteen cup of something that smelled awful and sat down closed to them. A small lamp was produced from his pack, lighted and put on the ground and then he watched the three prisoners with interest.

The three men split the water and the food in three equal parts and when they were finished, they were still hungry and thirsty. The food was something that stank, like rotten fish and rice mixed together, but they were starving and soon it was gone. As soon as they were finished, the guard tied their hands again, hard ties that would once more cut off the circulation, inflicting pain and torture. Leg irons were put on their feet and the Viet Cong instructed them to lie down.

That done, the guard left them alone and went back to the rest of the men and the food. They listened to their talk and their jokes, until the guard finally returned and kicked them some more before he lay on the ground to sleep, covering himself with a mosquito net.

The three men huddled together, fighting the biting insects that crawled over them the best way they could, finding some comfort in their proximity, wondering what was in store for them. Pierces' back was really hurting him now, the loss of blood made him weak, the fever racking his body. Lee's leg was also painful and swollen while Paul's shoulder was a throbbing mass, blood and watery fluids seeped from it slowly.

Despite their mental and physical exhaustion, sleep was hard to come by until the early morning hours when their exhausted bodies fell into a troubled sleep.

Soon they were awakened by yells and kicks from the guard and once more, the ties that bound their hands were loosened. The pain coursing through them brought sweat drops to their faces. They were stiff, their bodies covered by bruises, their faces swollen by the insect bites, their eyes almost shut. But they didn't complain and when Colonel Hue made his appearance, Pierce started on him.

"Colonel, my men need medical attention," he said, clearing his throat, wishing he had some water to wash the scum in his mouth. Colonel Hue turned his cold eyes on him briefly regarding him with a look of pure disgust. He wrinkled his nose at the smell coming from them, saying; "We will furnish your men with medical attention when you decide to tell me what I want."

"You can't do that, Colonel. The Geneva Convention is very explicit about medical attention for prisoners of war."

This time the eyes became bright and warm, a grin flickering on the Colonel's face.

"I can do as I please, Captain," he said softly, the riding crop swishing against his leg. "You and your men are nothing but war criminals." He stopped then, his hands going to his tunic pocket, a cigarette coming out. He lit the cigarette, his eyes never leaving Pierce, taking the smoke deep into his lungs, exhaling slowly and then he continued, "But if you help me, I'll help you." The voice was soft now, almost gentle, with almost a hypnotic quality to it.

"All you're getting from me, you pompous ass, is my name, date of birth and rank," Pierce said, tired now of the game. It was obvious that Hue was not going to play by the rules and the sooner he realized that the Americans were not going to give him anything, the better it would be for everybody concerned.

For a few seconds Colonel Hue stood still, unable to believe that the man lying on the ground had dared to talk to him like that. The swarthy face became pale, the eyes hooded and when he spoke, spittle flew from his lips, the rage surging up and consuming him.

"You are a fool," he snapped angrily, the smoldering eyes full of rage. He swiveled his head around and in rapid fire Vietnamese he gave his orders. Pierce heard the words and understood what the man was saying, giving him a chance to prepare himself for what was coming. VC soldiers swarmed over him, picking him up boldly from the ground. Pierce was a powerful man and now he squirmed and thrashed around, making the guard's job harder, until he was dropped back on the jungle floor and the bamboo sticks were brought out. The sound of the bamboo sticks hitting human flesh was loud in the confines of the small clearing and Pierce made himself small, grunting with the effort of not crying out in pain. For long seconds the blows rained on him, stopping abruptly. Paul and Lee surged forward, only to be stopped by the remaining VC, their rifles trained on then, and smiles on their faces. They knew without a doubt that if they moved another inch, the guards would be on them in a flash, accomplishing nothing.

Hands reached for Pierce again and this time he was forced face down on the ground, his underwear ripped, exposing his buttocks.

While four men held his hands, two more held his legs and then the Colonel came forward, his right boot on Pierce's neck, pushing his face down in the dirt.

"I'll teach you a lesson you won't forget," he said through gritted teeth, reaching for a bamboo stick from one of the VC next to him. The pole was about four feet long, completely round and shinny. The wood was hard and when it came in contact with human flesh it would inflict an incredibly painful, burning sensation.

Colonel Hue smile now and the hand holding the stick came down with tremendous force. Once, twice, the bamboo stick came down, until Pierces buttocks were a bright red and the blood started seeping through. The Colonel was in a fury, screaming obscenities, the sweat flying from his face at each stroke. Pierce squirmed and thrashed around, the muscles in his back rigid, the face contorted in an incredible snarl of pain. The muscles in his neck stood taut as rope, the veins bulging with the incredible effort not to cry. He bit his lips to stop himself from screaming and when the pain was too much to hold, he started yelling, cursing the man administering the whipping in Vietnamese, until Hue realized what the man was saying and he stopped, incredulous at the fact that the man was speaking Vietnamese, calling him names instead of crying, making him lose face in front of his people.

He started ranting and raving, in English while Pierce kept talking in Vietnamese, until Hue spit at him, throwing the stick on the ground.

"I'll have you shot," he said, furious, at a loss for words.

He bent down swiftly, his hand lifting Pierce's face roughly from the ground, his eyes clouded with an inner rage that was unholy.

"You will give me what I want or I'll kill all of you." Saying that, he let Pierce's face drop and strode away, the VC laughing at the event. Paul and Lee were let loose and they rushed to their friend, who was shaking violently from the beating.

Lee checked his buttocks, raw and bleeding, but his medical supplies were in the hands of the VC and there wasn't anything he could do.

The Viet Cong guard barked an order and Paul and Ashworth looked at each other, lifting Pierce's body tenderly, starting to walk. Pierce was almost unconscious and the wounds on his back had open up again, the flesh hot to the touch. Lee Ashworth shook his head in disgust, knowing well that if they didn't get medical attention soon, their wounds would get infected and they would die a slow, painful death, their bodies ravished by the poisons inside.

Like lost souls in purgatory the three men walked, their bodies rebelling at the treatment, but their minds refusing to believe that everything was lost. Somehow they would make it. They had to make it. They had the training and they had each other and they knew they could persevere against all odds, no matter what. And surely the United States Army would do anything possible to get them back as soon as possible. All they had to do was concentrate on staying alive, denying the enemy the use of their knowledge. They would not give up hope and they would not give the enemy the satisfaction of seeing them squirm or bend down to their request.

CHAPTER 8

Somewhere in the U Minh Forest
Mekong Delta
Republic of South Vietnam
December 14, 1963

Tranh Kinh moved slowly in the semi-darkness of the jungle, his body craving sleep, or a chance to slow down and rest. It would be daylight in a few minutes and he listened intently at his back trail, expecting company any moment now. Bright, red blood, mixed with watery fluids seeped steadily from a shoulder wound and from a bullet hole to his left side. He had been walking all day and most of the night, playing hide and seek with a band of Viet Cong soldiers hot on his trail, his feverish body craving solace and water. But the small man had a mission to accomplish and he swallowed the pain and discomfort and continued his trek. He was headed for camp A-28, and right behind him were several Viet Cong soldiers intent on catching him.

He had waited until the VC at the ambush site started their main assault, fighting like a possessed demon until he saw the end coming, the Special Forces men going down and then he had dressed himself in black pajamas, taking the clothes from a dead VC and making his escape. He had waited until he saw the three Americans go down, hoping to make it back to the camp with the news. He had been shot twice just before his escape, but the wounds were more painful than serious and he managed to staunch the flow of blood. In the incredible pandemonium that had existed at the time, Tranh Kinh had slipped into the jungle unnoticed, or at least he had thought so until later on during his trek back to the compound he realized that somebody was trailing him. The wounds had slowed him down some, but the fiery little man was determined to get there and come back with reinforcements. He didn't know if the Americans were dead or alive, but he had to try. Captain Pierce was his friend and he would do anything to try and save him

He slowed down some now, his keen hearing searching the trail behind him for any noise of the pursuers and finally he was rewarded by the sound of men approaching fast. He reached inside his bag, his hand coming out with two Claymore antipersonnel mines. Working by touch alone, he prepared the mines, setting them down, right in the middle of the trail, covering his work with brush and leaves. With a little luck, Tranh thought, I might just get them all. The VC were in a hurry to catch him and were overconfident. The prey was one lone man and they were eight seasoned fighters. They weren't expecting any trouble out of a wounded man. He played the wires and squatted down behind a tree to wait, the seconds going by slowly, and the sunlight intensifying. He waited, fighting the urge to close his eyes and rest, knowing that if he did, he would never wake up again. Finally his sharp hearing told him that something was moving on the trail and he tensed his body in anticipation, licking his dry lips. He blinked his eyes rapidly, his hand wiping the sweat from his face and then they were there. Tranh's face lit up with a wolfish smile and momentarily his pain was forgotten, eager now to finish off the hated enemy. They were bunched together on the trail, their heads bent toward the ground, following the telltale signs of his blood, talking to each other. Tranh let them get close, really close and then he pressed the levers, sending eight men to hell in a bright flash of orange, the explosion was loud, reverberating in the jungle for long seconds, the cries of men mortally wounded adding to the confusion.

Tranh Kinh stood up holding his side and walked slowly toward the pitiful remains of the VC. The hundreds of small dart like projectiles in the mines had shredded the men to pieces and with a last look at the place where the VC had stood, he whirled around and headed in the direction of the camp.

By early morning he was there, his eyes clouded, almost dead from the loss of blood. His tongue was swollen from lack of water and his face was etched in pain. He came in stumbling through the wire and eager hands went out to him, a runner dashing toward the command bunker with the news.

Sgt. Miller saw him coming, heard the commotion among the men and he rushed to them, his heart beating wildly. He had tried in vain, all night to get something on the radio from the patrol, but try as he did, nothing came in, just a garbled signal and he had worried himself sick, wondering what the hell was going on. Two CIDG had come in the early hours of the evening, requesting a new radio and batteries, dropping off a letter from Captain Pierce and immediately departing to catch up with the unit. But somehow the radio had never made it to them, and sometime during the night, Miller had heard a garble up transmission, men yelling and cursing, unable to make any sense of it. He had tried to latch on to the transmission, but was unable to, knowing damn well that Pierce was in trouble. Where, he didn't know. He had advised Colonel Brown, Special Forces commander in Saigon, about the radio trouble and his inability to get a response from Captain Pierce and the Colonel was on his way in.

And now this, Miller thought, running all out toward the figure lying on the ground.

His heart seemed to stop for a moment when he recognized the form of Tranh Kinh, and he kneeled down, reaching for him. The man was almost dead, barely holding on.

"What happened," Miller asked softly, his voice gentle, reaching for a canteen of water at his side, uncapping it and wetting Tranh's lips. The eyes opened and focused on him. The little man coughed, blood seeping from his lips and he smiled bravely at Miller. "VC trap…beaucoup VC in the jungle…all dead," he said and another coughing fit took hold of him. When the coughing subsided, Tranh lowered his head, wiped his mouth feebly with the back of his hand, the blood smearing his chin.

"Captain Pierce…where is captain Pierce?" Miller asked, his eyes taking in the wounds that covered the CIDG scout.

"Don't know…don't know," Tranh said and his head went down, his eyes closed and his breathing labored.

"Get him to the medical hutch," Miller said, standing up, starting to run back to the command post.

He made it inside and reached for the radio. "Alpha six, this is Charlie—Bravo-niner, do you read me? Over."

The response was fast and clear and Miller realized that Colonel brown was close by.

"This is Alpha six, Charlie-Bravo-niner, read you loud and clear, over."

"Alpha six, we have one Charlie-India-Delta-Golf that has just returned. We have news from Alpha-1, over."

"Roger Charlie-Bravo-niner. Will be circling the zone in minutes. Over and out."

Several minutes later, Miller could hear the sound of rotors outside and the Colonel's Huey came into view. In seconds the chopper was down and a tall, slender built man with a receding hairline stepped out, the eagle on his shoulder indicating he was a full bird Colonel. A Green Beret was in his hands and the man walked fast, covering the distance to the command post in seconds.

Sgt. Miller saw him coming and came to attention, snapping a salute.

"What do you have for me?" he asked, returning the salute, giving Sgt. Miller a blue-eyed stare full of concern.

"One of the CIDG, sir. He just got back, wounded, but we might be able to save his life."

Colonel Raymond Brown nodded his head, a frown on his face. "Anything about Pierce and his men?" he asked.

"No sir. We have to wait and see about Tranh Kinh."

"Damn it…damn it all to hell," Colonel Brown said, agitated. He was fond of Captain Pierce—a first class soldier and a hell of an asset to his command. And now this, he thought bitterly.

"Get on the horn and get base camp to send me an A-team," he said. "I'll be in the medical hutch."

Sgt. Miller came to attention, saying, "Yes sir," whirling around and getting on the radio.

Colonel Brown walked outside, making his way to the small hutch that served as a medical station for the group and went in.

A small generator could be heard outside, providing electrical power to the hutch and in the feeble light, Colonel Brown saw a small man lying on a table, a Special Forces medic working on him. The medic look up when the Colonel walked in, his eyes glancing at him for a second, and then getting back to work on the wounded man.

"How is he?" Brown asked gently, approaching the litter.

"He will be okay if we can get him out of here and to a decent hospital," the medic said, finishing bandaging the man, checking on the IV hooked on his arm. His eyes were open and his breathing was regular and now he turned his head toward Colonel Brown.

"You can use my chopper to transport him," the colonel said, bending over the prostrated figure.

"Thank you…sir", the medic said

"Can he talk?" Colonel Brown asked.

"Yes sir, but not for long. I just put a drip bag on him and he will be out shortly." Colonel Brown inched his face forward, looking intently at the man and in rapid fire Vietnamese he started talking. The man on the table looked at him for a few seconds, the pain etched deeply on his face and then he answered. They talked for a few minutes and then the Colonel stood up, his hand reaching for the man, touching his shoulder and squeezing it gently.

He turned toward the medic and nodded his head. In turn the medic called for help from several Vietnamese standing outside the hutch and shortly after Tranh Kinh was picked up and taken to the chopper. In a few minutes the bird was airborne with its cargo, heading for the nearest hospital.

Colonel Brown stood still for a moment, his forehead creased in thought and finally he made his way into the commo bunker. Sgt. Miller was there working the radio. He heard the Colonel come in and he swiveled his head.

"We have an inbound Huey with an A-Team arriving in twenty minutes, sir." Brown grunted his approval, walking toward the hot plate with the coffee pot on it. He found a clean cup and poured some of the strong black brew and sipped it slowly. In the few minutes he had spent with Kinh, he had found out that the CIDG force with Pierce had been exterminated and that Pierce and his men, Ashworth and Lt. Gallagher, were either captured or killed on the spot.

He ran his fingers through his short, thinning hair, thinking about the possibility of his men been captured and he shuddered despite the heat.

"Sgt. Miller," he called and the buck Sgt. stood up, coming toward him.

"Sir," he said, waiting.

"Show me the last coordinates that you have and exactly where they were going," he said, bending his tall frame over the map resting on a table.

Miller did as he was asked and Colonel Brown shook his head. "That is some rough terrain there," he said softly, almost to himself.

At that moment, the sounds of rotors could be heard and Colonel Brown stepped outside, watching as a Huey disgorged an A-team, the men ready for anything coming their way.

A young man, of medium height, separated himself from the group and walked fast toward Colonel Brown, stopping in front of him, coming to attention and saluting.

Brown returned the salute and then shook hands with the man, a captain in rank. "How are you Sandy?" he asked.

"Fine, Colonel," Captain Sandy Fisher replied, his eyes fixed on him. Something was wrong, deadly wrong, he thought, watching the shape the "old man" was in. What's up sir?' he asked.

Brown steered him away from the chopper, talking softly.

"Sandy, Captain Pierce is missing and so is Ashworth and Gallagher," he started. "They were caught in an ambush, the CIDG were eliminated completely. They are either dead or prisoners of war, so we have to go and see what we can find."

Sandy Fisher looked at Colonel Brown, shaking his head at the news. He knew Pierce, knew him to be a warrior and a no nonsense man, the same as Ashworth and Gallagher. In their small group, everybody knew everybody else and when something like that happened the whole community banded together.

"I'll give you the coordinates and the approximate area where the ambush took place," Colonel Brown continued. "See what you can find."

"Yes sir," came the replay from Fisher.

Within minutes the team was ready to go and shortly afterwards the chopper's rotors started moving. The pilot took the bird up, put the nose down and sped away. Colonel Brown saw them go hoping that they would come back with good news, his heart telling him that there would be no good news regardless of what was found.

He paced around the perimeter of the camp, too keyed up to be still, listening to the cries of the families who had lost a loved one on the ill fated patrol, thinking that pretty soon he would have to give the bad news to his superiors and in a couple of days somebody would be making their way to Pierce's family and Gallagher's with the grim news of their disappearance. He knew his men and he knew that Ashworth was a single man, no family anywhere, just the Army, but Pierce's father was Major General Pierce, and he also knew that Gallagher was married and his parents lived somewhere in Iowa. He cursed long and hard under his breath, dreading the coming news. This was war and people get killed and disappeared in war, he knew that, but this, it wasn't easy. He stood still for a long moment, he glanced at the beautiful blue sky overhead and his lips moved in a silent prayer, hoping that the gods of war would be kind to his men, wherever they might be. He glanced around one more time and slowly made his way into the command bunker, patiently waiting now for word of his men.

Two hours later, the Huey was back and Sandy Fisher approached the commo bunker. Colonel Brown came out to meet him, his eyes scanning the serious face of Captain Fisher.

He sighed deeply, steeling himself for the bad news that he knew was coming. "Well?" he asked.

"We found the place of the ambush, sir, but no sign of Pierce and his men," Fisher said. He paused then, his right hand coming up with an object. "Except for this, sir." Fisher raised his hand and Colonel Brown saw the Green Beret with the silver tracks of a captain on it, dirty and stained with blood. He reached for it slowly, his fingers closing on the soft cloth of the beret. He nodded his head, his right hand wiping away the sweat running down his face and his eyes came back to Captain Fisher.

"There must have been an incredible fight," Fisher continued, "but again, nothing concerning Captain Pierce or Lt. Gallagher and Ashworth."

Which meant one of two things, Brown thought. The Americans were either taken prisoner or killed and dispose of. Tranh Kinh had seen them go down, but couldn't confirm that they were dead and more than likely they had been captured. It was a hell of a situation, not knowing anything about his men, or what had actually happened to them. Colonel Brown felt like his hands were tied, unable to do anything for the welfare of his men.

Fisher, who was standing close to him, brought him out of his reverie. "Is that all sir?"

"It is for now, Sandy. We will have to go back in the morning with a foot patrol and do a thorough examination of the area, but for now, that it is." He paused, his brow creased in thought, mulling over his options.

"You are in charge here now, Sandy," he continued slowly. "Bring your detachment in and see about the fortifications on the camp. If this VC Battalion that we have been talking about is the one that annihilated Pierce's men, then I'm sure they will hit this place soon. I'll see about some reinforcements for you as soon as I get back to Saigon."

Fisher nodded his head, his face showing the emotions coursing through him. Some of their own were missing and they would do whatever was necessary to get them back or find out what had happened to them.

Sandy Fisher came to attention, saluting Colonel Brown and with a heavy heart, went on his way. He had known Elton Pierce for a while now, he was his friend and he sure would miss him. The man was a soldier, one imbued with a sense of personal pride and honor in his chosen profession and a damn good man to have around when the going was tough.

"This is going to be one hell of a Christmas present for a lot of people," he thought, walking toward the chopper, dreading the next few hours.

They would assemble a force and go back in the morning, scouring the countryside around the perimeter of the battle for any sign or evidence of what had happened and to make sure that Pierce and his men were nowhere around, dead or wounded. There was also the gruesome task of recovering the bodies of the CIDG forces that were killed during the fight and transporting them back to the camp for proper burial.

Captain Fisher's thoughts went back to Pierce and his men and he shuddered at the prospect that the Viet Cong had their hands on them. He knew well the cruelty exhibited by the enemy when Americans fell into their hands and nothing good was going to come out of it if they were prisoners.

Sandy Fisher stopped next to the chopper and then he swiveled his head around, in the general direction where the firefight had taken place.

"May the God in heavens have pity on you, guys," he whispered softly, his throat constricted. For a few seconds longer he remained standing still, his face hard, and a troubled look in his eyes. He roughly wiped away the wetness in his eyes with the back of his hand and with a shake of his head, turned around and jumped swiftly into the chopper, joining his men already there.

There was work to do now. Later there would be time to mourn their dead and missing.

CHAPTER 9

Mason City, Iowa
December 13, 1963

William Gallagher woke up with a start, his heart beating furiously in his chest. He felt the sweat running down his face and he wondered if he was going to have a heart attack. But no, it wasn't that he soon realized, breathing deeply, trying to control the racing heart pounding painfully against his ribs. Something had intruded in his sleep, some nightmare and now he sat on his bed, the sleeping form of Carol, his wife, next to him. He wiped the sweat from his face and pulled the covers off of him, getting out of the bed slowly. The figure of his wife moved slightly and a sleepy voice said: "What…what is it, Bill?"

"Nothing, honey. Just go back to sleep." Carol turned over, half asleep and William Gallagher glanced at the clock on the small table. Four o'clock, almost time to get up, he thought. He reached for his slippers and the robe on the end of the bed and made his way out of the bedroom, feeling his heart go back to its normal beat. It was cold and drafty in the old house during the winter and he headed for the kitchen, turning the gas stove on and putting water on to heat for coffee. The old house was silent, the clock on the kitchen wall ticking the seconds slowly. The heater in the basement kicked on, the sound loud in the stillness of the morning and Bill listened to it, his ears attuned to the noise. The heater was old and he thought that pretty soon he needed to do something about it. The whole house needed some work and for a while he had toyed with the idea of tearing it down and starting new, but that idea didn't last long. The house had been in his family for generations and through the years rooms had been added here and there, making it large and comfortable. The memories encase in the walls of the old house were something precious to him and as far as he was concerned the house would stand as it was until he was dead and gone.

While the water was heating, he made his way to the small room, next to the kitchen that served as his office, sitting down and turning the small desk lamp on. He stifled a yawn, wondering what had intruded in his sleep, an uneasy sensation still with him and his eye drifted to the small glass enclosure hanging on the wall, a shadow box, the medal in it reflecting the light from the small lamp.

A small light blue ribbon with five stars on it, two on top and three below, was also in the glass enclosure and the medal hung just below that. The Navy Medal of Honor was a bronze star with oak clusters on the points, attached to a light blue, silk ribbon bearing thirteen white stars by an anchor. In the center of the star was the head of Minerva, Roman goddess of righteous war and wisdom. William Gallagher thought that he had never seen anything that had so much meaning for him as that medal on the wall. The sound of water boiling in the teakettle brought him out of his reverie and he stood up, walked to the kitchen and fixed the coffee. He liked his strong and black, with two teaspoons of sugar. After that he sipped the strong brew as he wandered back to the small office. Sitting down he sighed deeply, realizing that whatever had interrupted his sleep was still bothering him. What is going on? he asked himself softly, unable to answer the question.

His eyes strayed to the wall again and his mind took him back to the day he had received the Medal and the events that had lead up to it.

He had been born on January 1, 1912, on the outskirts of Mason City, Iowa, on his parents farm and together with three other brothers and two sisters, had helped their parents to plowed the land and harvest the crops on the farm that had been in the family for generations.

There were more than two thousands acres of land then and it had taken everybody's sweat and hard work to make a go of it. He had been almost twenty years old when the Great Depression hit. Things were bad, with hardly any money, but living on a farm was really a blessing in those days. They had plenty to eat and by selling produce in the city, they were able to save some pennies, everybody pitched in, running errands, doing what was necessary to survive. Hunting and fishing supplemented their food and all in all, Bill Gallagher would say that the Depression was really a blessing for them. It had united the family in more ways than one, making them dependant on no one but themselves, the land holding the family together, sustaining them trough the hard times.

He had married his high school sweetheart, Carol Gibson, in nineteen thirty-nine when he was twenty-six years old and she was twenty-four. He brought her to the farm and a year later, in nineteen forty, his son Paul W. Gallagher was born.

He had followed the war in Europe closely, just like most Americans at the time, knowing that it was just a matter of time before Roosevelt had his way and the United States would enter the war. Then Japan made the incredible mistake of attacking Pearl Harbor in Hawaii and the war was on.

When the United States declared war against Japan and then Germany, William Gallagher was almost twenty-eight years old, a clear-headed young man who believed in doing his duty for his country. Together with two of his brothers, they enlisted—William in the Marines and his brothers in the Army. It wasn't long after that that he found himself island hoping in the Pacific, engage in a brutal fight with the Japanese. It was there in nineteen forty-three that he had lost his left eye during an assault against enemy positions and was sent home with an honorable discharge to recuperate. He had come home to find his mother dead of a brain tumor and his father barely hanging on to the farm. It was also the time they had received notice that his two brothers had been killed in action, one in a B-24 bomber shot down during a bombing raid in Germany and the other killed by friendly fire. They had mourned their dead; coping with the tragedy of loved ones gone. Three months later he had received a letter from the War Department, requesting his presence at a White House ceremony, something about him getting a medal. They had made the trip to Washington by train, he and Carol and his ailing father and when he had found out the real reason for the trip, he was dumfounded. He had done his duty for his country and he never thought that he had acted any different than any other GI on that particular piece of real estate that day. But other people had thought differently, among them General Douglas MacArthur and his former Commanding Officer who had put him up for the Medal of Honor.

Bill Gallagher sighed deeply, the haunting memories of that long ago battle still fresh in his mind.

He had awakened at a field hospital, his body in constant pain from the wounds, his left eye covered by bandages. After a short while he realized that he was not alone. In the diffused light of the tent, he could see other GI's laying on cots, their bodies bloody, the grunts of pain and small talk permeating the small enclosure, nurses rushing in and out. At some point in time there had been a commotion at the entrance to the tent and several officers and doctor's came in. There was one man, taller than all the rest of them, coming toward the men lying on the cots and Bill Gallagher realized that the man was General Douglas MacArthur no less. The General had come in to pin Purple Hearts on each and every one of the men lying there. He talked to most of them, reassuring them like a father would a son and complementing them for their valor and courage in the face of overwhelming odds. When it was his turn, Gallagher was surprise to see his commanding officer there, next to MacArthur, recounting his exploits with the machinegun nest. MacArthur had come close, wanting to hear the story from the man who had been there, embarrassing him to no end. They had talked for quite a while, but eventually Gallagher had drifted into sleep. When he awoke again, he was on his way to a ship; he found a Purple Heart stuck to his pillow and a note. He had unfolded the paper and there, in MacArthur's scribbled handwriting, he had read the line; "Thank you for a job well done, Marine," and at the bottom, the signature of the General.

The ceremony had taken place at the South lawn of the White House and President Truman had placed the Medal of Honor around his neck.

"Congratulations, son. Your country is proud of you," the President of the United States had said then and William Gallagher just shook his head, emotions about to overtake him. There had been another Medal of Honor given that day, to a young Army infantry Lieutenant by the name of Winfield Woods for conspicuous gallantry above and beyond the call of duty. Afterwards, the two of them with their families had gone out to celebrate, finding out that the two of them had a lot in common besides a deep abiding love for their country and a sense of duty.

And now the old fire dragon was his son's commanding officer, Bill thought, amused at how life has a way of creating coincidences. He sipped his rapidly cooling coffee and his hand went to the glass surface, his fingers touching it.

Like he had done a hundred times before, he read the caption just below.

> Rank and Organization: Sgt. (Then Corporal), U.S. Marine Corps. Born: 1st January 1912, Mason City, Iowa. Accredited to: Iowa.
>
> Citation: *For conspicuous gallantry and intrepidity at the risk of his life above and beyond the call of duty while serving as Acting Scout Sgt. with the 4th Battalion, 15th Marine, 6th Marine Division, during action against Japanese forces on Tarawa Shima during April 15, 1943.*
>
> *Undaunted by a powerful, organized opposition encountered during a fierce assault waged by his company against machinegun emplacements, Sgt. Gallagher single handedly assaulted two enemy emplacements. Attacking prepared enemy positions on a hill, which*

> *could only be approached through meager cover, his company was pinned down by machinegun fire, mortars and artillery barrages. Although painfully wounded on his left side, Sgt. Gallagher refused to be evacuated to the rear and on his own initiative crawled forward alone until he reached a position near the machinegun emplacement. Hurling grenades, he boldly assaulted the position, destroyed the gun and killed several Japanese soldiers who were trying to escape. When he rejoined the company, a second machinegun opened up and again the intrepid soldier went forward utterly disregarding his own safety. He stormed the position and was wounded again, but was successful in destroying the machinegun emplacement, killing three enemy soldiers with rifle fire. When a grenade thrown by the enemy landed next to several of his comrades, Sgt. Gallagher pick up the grenade and with complete disregard for his own life hurled the grenade back to the enemy position. He fought with his company until the position was finally taken, receiving another wound to his left eye from a grenade fragment and refusing medical care until the action was over.*
>
> *"Sgt. Gallagher's valiant spirit in the face of such overwhelming odds reflects the highest credit upon himself and upon the U.S. Naval Service."*

William Gallagher sighed deeply and reclined back on the hard chair. He had done his duty to the best of his ability, he thought. He was no hero, just a man doing his job. He was grateful for the medal and what it represented, but he knew well that countless other men and women had sacrificed and given their lives during the war so others could live. He had learned that lesson well and if he had won the medal, it wasn't just for him, but for the others as well, the ones that paid the ultimate sacrifice for the principles of liberty and freedom. In his quiet, unassuming way he had become the hero to his small community and he was respected and well liked by all who knew him.

After the ceremony they had returned home to their daily tasks, picking up their lives where they had left off. He had gone to night school, earned a college degree and worked long hours during the day to keep the farm going after his father died. Slowly things had improved and soon they were expanding and making a good living.

His sisters had married farmers and his youngest brother had gone to college to become a veterinarian, had come back to Mason City to practice, got married and had three children.

Bill sipped the remainder of the coffee and stood up, running his fingers through his thinning hair. He walked into the kitchen, poured the dregs of the coffee in the sink, washed his cup and put it on the drain board. He walked toward the back door and opened it, feeling the cold air come in. He shivered in his flimsy robe and his eyes glanced at the sun about to make its appearance over the distant horizon. Slowly the first glimmer of daylight appeared, bathing the land with the sun's rays. The sky was an incredible blue and the birds chirp their morning song. Everything is peaceful and quiet, Bill thought, except my heart. He breathed deeply of the morning air, shaking his head to wish away the memories.

He went back inside, closing the door, brooding about whatever it was that had intruded into his subconscious and he shuddered. Something was wrong with Paul. With a certainty that was uncanny, he had the awful premonition that his first-born was in serious trouble. Something was definitely wrong.

He walked back into the kitchen, glancing at his watch, realizing it was time to get dressed and start the workday. He thought about another cup of coffee and was in the process of fixing it when footsteps behind him made him turn, wondering who was up this early. He swiveled his head, glancing at the hallway, seeing Susan walking slowly. His daughter in-law, Susan, was still dressed in her pajamas and a robe and the hour was early even for her.

"What are you doing up, child?" he asked noticing the pallor of her face. He liked his daughter-in-law, always had. Admired her spunk and her outlook on life and was glad when Paul had decided that she was the right girl for him.

"Couldn't sleep, Dad," she said, her voice small, like a child just waking up. She shook her head irritably and continued, "Something woke me up, this terrible feeling that something is wrong with Paul."

She hugged herself with her arms, her eyes haunted and she look deep into William Gallagher's eyes, seeing the same worry and concern she was feeling. An incredible feeling of loss had insinuated itself into her being, leaving her desolate and confused.

"You too, Dad?" she said, her eyes opening wide at the realization that she was not alone in her feelings.

"I…I don't know, Susie," he answered her, using the appellative that he always had used with her when they were alone.

"I think that we are just worried about our boy and we are letting our emotions get the best of us", he said softly.

Susan looked at him long and hard, trying to find something in his voice that would tell her that he didn't believe a word he was saying, but Bill Gallagher had put the mask on now and whatever he was feeling, would stay with him. She shook her head and went back to her room to get dressed. She had plenty of work to do and if she couldn't sleep, she might as well get to it. Undressing, she heading for the shower, her mind trying its best to put the misgivings away.

In the meantime, Bill Gallagher had finished his second cup of coffee and had also gotten dressed. It was time to go to work and there was no use fretting about it until something definitive comes up, he told himself, hoping that he was wrong and his boy was perfectly safe, or as safe as he could be in the middle of a war on the other side of the world.

He immersed himself in his work; keeping the ever-growing feelings to himself that something was not right, wondering what tomorrow would bring. There was no sense in worrying Carol about something he couldn't put his finger on and he kept his mouth shut, hoping that Susan would do the same thing.

CHAPTER 10

U.S. Army Special Warfare School
Office of the Commanding General
Ft. Bragg, N.C.
December 14, 1963

Brigadier General Woods stood up, stretching his body, stale after so many hours sitting on the chair. He was not the type to spend his whole days enclosed in an office doing paperwork and whenever he was forced to do so, he would get into a pissy mood. He was much better talking to his officers and men, watching them during training exercises, making sure the soldiers were taken care of. He walked to the small bathroom in his office, emptied his bladder and washed his hands. Too much damn coffee, he told himself, remembering what the base doctor had told him about his prostate. Caffeine was not good for him. He finished washing his hands and his face, glancing at his watch and deciding to call it a day. He walked out of the room to find Sgt. Major Wilhelm waiting for him, a look of consternation etched on his face. The Sgt. Major was rattled, and that was something new for General Woods. Wondering what was going on now, he stopped in his tracks, his eyebrows going up in a silent question

"The Pentagon is…is on the line, General," Wilhelm said, his eyes clouded.

Woods grunted and reached for the blinking line. "This is General Woods," he said. He listened to the person on the other end of the line and his face went deadly pale at the news he received. He reached for a piece of paper and a pen on his desk, scribbled something on it and hung up the phone. He sighed deeply and shook his head at the news he had just received. Three of his men were believed to be either missing in action or killed—Pierce, Gallagher and Ashworth.

"Damn it," he said, whirling around and facing Sgt. Major Wilhelm. "Did they tell you?"

"Yes sir," he said, obviously shaken. Special Forces was a close brotherhood and when something like this happened, emotions ran high.

Woods was silent for a while, his face etched in conflicting emotions, and then, like a man who had just made up his mind about something important, he said, "Get my aide de camp. Tell him we are taking a trip to Iowa, tonight." He stopped then, thinking about his wife and the engagement they had tonight. It was going to be postponed and she would be pissed, but she would understand. "I'll call my wife and you get an overnight bag, you are coming with us," he continued.

"Yes sir," Wilhelm said softly, coming to attention, saluting and departing to carry out his orders.

When Wilhelm was gone, the old warrior stood still, surveying the office. He shook his head, sighing deeply, and his thoughts went to his men, lost or killed in a far away place. He had lost men before, but to him it was always the same, a feeling that he had lost a part of himself. The war in Viet Nam was really heating up now and he knew without a shadow of a doubt that many more of his elite troops would be put in harm's way and that many more lives would be lost in that far away place. And the interesting thing was that as far as General Woods was concern, the country where they were fighting was not worth the life of one of his men. What was going on in Viet Nam now was a civil war and the United States didn't have any business there, he thought grimly, rehashing the thoughts in his mind as he had done a thousand times before. Not that he would express those feelings to anybody or refuse to serve, but Viet Nam and the U.S. involvement there was a political decision. Backing up a man like Diem, who in the personal opinion of General Woods was nothing but a dictator, was in complete contradiction to what the United States always stood for; integrity and respect for human life. The man was a butcher, a dictator with no real feelings for the masses and he didn't deserve the help of the United Sates.

General Woods sighed deeply, shaking his head to dispel the thoughts, trying to keep a tight grip on his feelings. He closed his eyes, feeling the unaccustomed wetness in then and his lips moved in a silent payer to God above. He opened his eyes and looked around, walking to the door like a man a hundred years old. He was going to see an old friend, bringing bad news like a thief in the night.

Chapter II

Mason City, Iowa
December 15, 1963

The day was bright and clear, the wind slicing through the old barn like there was no door in front. Bill Gallagher was bending over the motor of a tractor, a number of tools spread all over the place. The huge machine had broken down the day before and now he was in the process of getting it fixed. It was cold inside the barn and still colder outside, the temperature somewhere in the low teens. The small kerosene heater next to him was not doing much to warm the frigid air and Bill could feel the cold seeping slowly into his body.

I should have listened to Carol, he thought, with a shrug of his still powerful shoulders, his hand putting pressure on the wrench. She had wanted to send the tractor to be repaired, but Bill liked doing the work himself and had balked at the idea. It wasn't that they couldn't afford it, he was more than well off, but he still liked to mess around with machinery and do most of the repairs himself. And he was going to pay for it, just like Carol had said.

He stood up, stretching his body, feeling the kinks in his back and the pain growing. He dropped the wrench in place, muttering something about stubborn tractors and made his way out the door, the cold wind going through him, making him shiver in his work clothes. It was barely eight o'clock in the morning, but he had been at it for the better part of two hours now, while his two boys had seen to the cows and then had gone to school. A cup of hot tea would be nice just about now, he thought, patting his belly, walking fast toward the house. His stomach was still a mess and he had eaten very little in the past two days and maybe the hot tea would help to settle it. The feelings of the previous day were still with him and now he raised his head, noticing the strange car making its way up his driveway. The driveway was at least half a mile long and Bill watched the car intently, fascinated, something inside of him knowing that whoever was in that car, was bringing bad news. He shook his head, irritated at himself and then he made his way through the back door into the house. Going to the front porch, he waited. The car made its way and soon, three men stepped out.

Military men, Bill thought, seeing the Army green uniforms, the star of a General on one of them.

He opened the door and stepped out, his hands in his pockets, waiting, looking intently at the three men making their way up the steps. There was something familiar about the General and Bill centered his eyes on him, recognition finally downing on him.

"Well I'll be…if it isn't old Winfield," he said, going toward his old friend, shaking his hand, noticing the strength in it.

"It's been a long time," he said simply.

"Yes it has," Woods said, hating himself for what he was about to do.

General Woods shook his hand and then he introduced the other two men.

"This is my 'aide de camp', Lt. Walker," he said, and the tall, skinny officer shook his hand.

"And this is Sgt. Major Wilhelm." Bill shook his hand also, liking the man immediately.

Bill fixed his eyes on General Woods saying, "I presume this is an official visit, so come on in out of the cold and I'll get some coffee."

Woods nodded his head and all of then followed Bill Gallagher into the den, sitting themselves down, grateful for the roaring fire in the fireplace. Bill busied himself making coffee and shortly afterward, a tray containing a pot of coffee, cream and sugar was in front of the men. The General had removed his tunic and loosened his tie. He fixed his own coffee, sipping the hot liquid gratefully.

He put the cup down and now he looked at Bill, coming straight to the point. "Bill, your boy Paul…was involved in a combat patrol a few days ago. The patrol was ambushed and…and Paul is…is missing." He paused for a second, seeing the emotions playing in his old friend's face. He liked Bill, always had, ever since they had become friends a long time ago at the receiving ceremonies for their respective Medals of Honor on the White House lawn.

For a moment, silence engulfed the group of men all eyes centered on Bill Gallagher. He put the coffee cup down now, his eyes hooded and his shoulders slumped forward. Suddenly he felt old, old and used up and his head nodded slowly, his world crumbling around him with every word from Woods. He was glad that Carol and Susan weren't there at the time, having gone to spend time with his ailing sister. But they would be back today and Bill knew their world would be turned upside down too. "I knew it Winfield…I knew it," he said softly, his gut seething, turning to jelly, making him weak.

He leaned back in his chair, closing his eyes, trying his best to control his emotions. With a tremendous effort, he opened his eyes, giving his friend a blue-eyed stare that said it all, waiting for him to continue.

"Two other men with him, Captain Pierce and Sgt. Ashworth, are also missing and we presume they are in the same situation." He cleared his throat, standing up and beginning to pace the den. It was obvious that he was agitated, mourning the loss of his men.

"We will do everything possible to find out what really happened, but right now we have precious little information to give you. They are missing and that's about all we know so far."

Bill Gallagher remained sitting, his face impassive, his mind absorbing the words, trying to remain calm in the face of the overwhelming news he had just received. His son was dead or worse than that, a prisoner of war and he rebelled at the unfairness of it all. His son was going to be a father and now the child probably would never see his father or get to know him. He shook his head sadly, but slowly the feeling that his son was alive intruded in his mind and finally he raised his eyes to the group of men in the small den, saying, "I don't know how I know this, but he is alive, Winfield, and somehow he will come back to us."

General Woods looked at his friend closely, knowing that receiving news like he had just delivered were enough to cloud anybody's judgment. But there was something in Bill Gallagher's eyes that made him pause and he shook his head. "I hope so, my friend…I hope so," he said, wishing he had the same feelings that Bill had.

"You will get official word of this, probably by tomorrow, but I wanted to tell you personally," he said, wishing there was more that he could share with the old soldier.

"I understand, Winfield, and I'm thankful for your consideration," Bill responded. He wanted to be left alone with his thoughts, wanted to hold on to the small hope that his son was not dead.

An hour later the men were gone and Bill Gallagher stood on the porch of the old, rambling house, watching the car make its way down the road, his mind a jumble of thoughts. He shuddered once, not because of the cold, feeling the wetness brimming in his eyes. He wiped them angrily, his mind rebelling at the thought of his son gone, or a prisoner, almost giving in to self-pity. But the inner faith of the man came to the surface and he held himself in tight control. The good Lord would see to his son and no matter what he would never lose hope.

He went in the kitchen and made more coffee, sitting down to wait for the women to come home, hating the pain he was about to impart to the people he loved.

Half an hour later, he heard their voices outside, their steps echoing loudly on the hard wood floor.

They came in the kitchen, bringing the cold with them, chattering about clothes and the baby until Carol noticed the way Bill was looking at them and her heart skipped a beat. She had been married to him for over twenty-five years now and she knew him better than he knew himself, could read him with a precision that was uncanny. She had seen his mood the day before and had waited patiently for him to come and talked to her like he always had when something important was on his mind, but he had not done so and she had wondered about it. His eyes were clouded; his face etched into hard lines, unmoving, the straight line of his lips telling her that something bad had happened. "What is it, Bill?" she asked softly, her heart beating wildly and Susan, who had gone to the counter to get a cup of the hot coffee, looked at him, something in Carol's voice alerting her to the situation. The bad feeling she had all day resurface and she fixed her eyes on Bill Gallagher, who stood up, coming closer to them. His eyes became soft and moist, but were unable to disguise the incredible pain that was there, his heart breaking.

"It's Paul…our son is…" he stopped, unable to continue. He took a deep breath and tried again, seeing the conflicting emotions on Carol's face. "Our son is…missing in Viet Nam, or he is dead," he finally said, the words rushing out of his mouth.

Both women looked at him, disbelief etched on their faces and then the whole import of what he had just said finally got through to them. Susan screamed, the cup in her hand falling to the floor, shattering in a million pieces while Carol just looked at him, shaking her head. A heart-wrenching sob came from her throat and silent tears rolled down her weathered cheeks, her face etched into a mask of pain and disbelief.

"My son, oh merciful God…my son," she said, feeling the hot tears scalding her face. She came into his arms and Susan did the same, their cries of pain and anguish breaking his heart in pieces. It was so damn unfair, he told himself, thinking about the new life that was going to be born, his father missing, or worse yet, dead.

An animal sound escaped from his lips and he swallowed hard, feeling the lump in his throat. He wanted to cry with them, wanted to lower his head on his wife's breast and take comfort from her, but he couldn't cry, not now, he told himself. He needed to be strong for them, keep their hopes up. Later on there will be time for crying, but not now. He embraced the women tightly, feeling their bodies shudder with their pent up emotions and he closed his eyes, his lips calling to the God that had sustained him during all the hard years of his life to do so one more time.

CHAPTER 12

Key West, Florida
December 15, 1963

Major General Robert W. Pierce (Retired) shaded his eyes away from the smoke coming from the grill in front of him. The wind had picked up some late in the evening, making grilling the steaks and chicken a continual fight with the smoke. He turned the meat over, adding sauce, checking on the chicken breast, listening to the friendly chatter going on behind him between the friends who had been invited to his wife's birthday party. There were almost twenty people in the backyard enjoying the balmy weather of the Florida Keys and helping themselves to his food and liquor.

He glanced at the rapidly setting sun, watching the light play in the sky, the clouds a tapestry of color painted by the dying sun. A cacophony of noise from the nocturnal insects could be heard, the sound giving notice that nighttime was almost upon them.

He looked around making sure everything was taken care of. He noticed the well-manicured lawn and the imposing house. They had just acquired the place and the General had splurged a little bit, buying a house that was too big for just the two of them, but enjoying the smile on his wife's face when he first suggested that they buy the place. It was a two-story brick building with a swimming pool in the back, recently painted, and nestled among tall pine trees, the nearest neighbor half a mile down the road. He gave a satisfied sigh, a grin flickering on his ruddy face as he saw his housekeeper approaching.

The General was of stocky build with a deep chest and a bull neck. He was sixty-two years old and had just retired from the Army two months ago. He had to admit that it was a lot harder getting used to being a civilian than he had thought, after spending the major part of his life in the Army serving his country. But Alma, his wife of forty-two years, was not in the best of health and when the doctor told him that she was deteriorating fast, he had put his papers in to retire, trying to make up for all the time away from each other and all the lost opportunities. Her heart was fragile and he took care of her to the best of his abilities, dreading the moment of truth when she would be gone from his life.

He checked on the meat again, almost done, reaching for the drink next to the grill. He was not a drinker; never had been, but occasionally he liked his Jack Daniels. He took a sip, his eyes glancing at the housekeeper, who came to his side, her demeanor telling him that something was afoot.

"There are two gentlemen waiting for you in the study, General," she said quietly. "They said it was an urgent matter."

"What?" General Pierce asked, wondering who the hell had come calling at such a time.

"They are military men, sir," Mrs. Graham said, her hands twisting her apron nervously. She had been in the Pierce household for a long time and was Alma's constant companion and she knew something about Army men coming to the house.

General Pierce frowned, handing the cooking tongs to Mrs. Graham. "Take care of this, will you please," he said. He turned around, making his way into he house through the rear. He stole a glance toward his wife, seeing her in conversation with the neighbors and he hurried inside, his mind wondering who had come calling. When the Army sends you unexpected visits, he knew, something terribly wrong had happened. His only son was in Viet Nam, in the middle of some stinking conflict that was getting bigger and bigger by the day and he surmised that whoever was in the house had something to do with him. He walked fast now, his heart beating painfully against his ribs. Reaching the study he pushed the door open, his eyes registering surprise at the two officers standing in the room. He stopped in mid-stride, puzzle now. The two men were dressed in Army class A greens, one a Colonel and on the shoulders of the other one, the two stars of a Major General could be seen. He was a tall man, with a strong square face and piercing blue eyes. His black hair was salt and pepper and he had known General Pierce for the last thirty years, beginning when both of them were brand new first lieutenants scare to death crawling in the sand at Normandy. Medals and badges covered the left side of his chest, the Combat Infantry Badge with a star denoting a subsequent award being the first one on top. Just below that stretched line after line of ribbons, the first one a ribbon in red, white and blue. It was the Distinguished Service Cross, the nations seconds highest award, just below the Medal of Honor. There was also a Purple Heart, a Silver Star and a host of other medals and badges, including the Master's wings of a paratrooper.

"Jesus…Walter," Pierce said, his heart now beating fast. "What are you doing so far from the Pentagon?"

Major General Walter Donovan was the director of planning and strategy at the Pentagon. Something must have gone terribly wrong for him to be here, Pierce thought briefly. He had been a Major General in the Army, Pierce said to himself and suddenly there was one of his best friends in his house, another Major General. Then it dawned on him. They send a General to see a General when somebody dies. Then he knew. His son Alton…was dead. A sinking feeling hit him in his gut and his mouth became dry, his heart racing. "My son…" he started, stopping, not wanting to hear what was coming, his knees almost crumbling with sudden weakness.

General Donovan came to his side, nodding his head. He looked at his friend of so many years and his heart went out to him.

"He is missing in action…presumed captured by the enemy," he said gently, his hand coming to rest on his friend's shoulder, squeezing it lightly.

Good Lord Almighty, Pierce told himself softly, breathing a little easier now. Prisoner of war, not dead.

"What happened?" he asked, feeling his knees still trembling. He found a seat and dropped onto it unceremoniously, watching his friend intently.

"He and several men went out on a patrol. They were ambushed and the last we know, they have probably been taken prisoners."

An eyebrow went up on Pierce's face. "Probably?" he asked.

"Yes, Robert. We really don't know what happened, just that their bodies were not found at the site of the firefight," Donovan said. "Since the bodies were not found, we suppose that they are missing in action.

Pierce nodded his head, still absorbing the news.

"When I heard about it, I decide that you needed to hear this from a friend, so here I am." Donovan said, his eyes fixed on his friend's face.

"Thank you, Walter. I appreciate that," he answered, rubbing his face with his hands, standing up. He took a deep breath, managing to control himself, his mind running through all the options available, his brain absorbing the import of what he had just learned.

"I'm sorry gentlemen, I forgot my manners," he said, walking to the corner wet-bar in the study. "May I get you gentlemen anything?"

Major General Donovan glanced at his junior officer, who nodded his head and he turned toward Pierce. "Sure Robert, why not"

Pierce fixed the drinks automatically, scotch and soda for everybody and then he returned to his seat. He took a sip of the drink and grimaced at the taste, glancing at Donovan who was sitting next to him.

"The Army will do whatever we can to confirm his status and whatever information we can obtained, will be passed on to you," Donovan said, taking a drink. "By tomorrow you will receive official notice, but I want you to know that I'll personally become involved in this. I have friends who can help gather information and I'll keep you posted.

Pierce nodded his head, grateful for Donovan's words and then he said: "You mentioned other people…who?"

"Lt. Paul Gallagher was also taken, along with a medic, Sgt. First Class Lee Ashworth."

"So he is not alone," Pierce said softly, thankful that whatever happened, his son was not alone in that God forsaken place of Viet Nam. He thought about Gallagher and Ashworth and a silent prayer filled his mind for the two men.

They talked a while longer, old friends sharing the pain, Pierce asking questions, thirsty for information about his son, until finally the messengers were gone, leaving him with an emptiness in his heart. He sat quietly in the semidarkness of the study, his mind full of images of his son, feeling the tears running down his cheeks. He wiped them irritably, thinking that he shouldn't be crying, that he was a man unaccustomed to things like that, but he was also a father and he loved his child deeply and the pain in his heart was real, so terribly real.

How am I going to give this news to his mother, he thought wearily, knowing that the news would kill her. He sat there dejected; feeling like the whole world was coming down on his shoulders. His son was a prisoner of war or maybe dead by now. He shook his head, the feeling of hopelessness in the face of such calamity eating at him. He was a man accustomed to action, always one to take the bull by the horns, but here, he was immobilized, unable to help the one person in the world that meant the most to him, his son. He thought about his son's captivity and the men with him and for a brief instant his pain was assuage by the knowledge that they were some of the best trained men in the world, members of the most elite force in the Army. He knew his son and he knew that his boy would not give up easily. He was stubborn, just like his old man; a man who when he thought it was right, would not budge.

He stood up slowly, taking a deep breath, controlling himself. It would not do to let his wife see him like this; she would worry to death about him and she sure didn't needed that right now. He gulped down the drink, feeling the warmth of it working its way down to the pit of his stomach. He stood up, putting the empty glass down and with a forced smile on his face, he walked outside, rejoining the party.

He would wait until the guests were gone and find the way to break the news to his wife.

CHAPTER 13

Somewhere in the U Minh Forest
Republic of South Vietnam
December 16, 1963

For two days the three men walked, their battered bodies and painful wounds a living torment. On the second day, the VC threw them some filthy black pajamas, allowing them some comfort from the myriad of insects feasting on their sweat and blood at night. It was also on the second day that their eyes were blindfolded, a rope around their neck their only contact with their captives, until finally on the morning of the third day of captivity they reached a Viet Cong prison camp, deep in the U Minh forest. They were the first to use it, but soon they would find out that they wouldn't be the last. The compound was under the jungle canopy and unobservable from the air, allowing the VC to come and go as they pleased without fear of being discovered by a passing plane or helicopter. They could see Viet Cong soldiers coming and going, the men talking loudly among themselves, eyes settling on the prisoners as they went by.

For the moment they were put in a bamboo cage big enough to hold all three of them and for the first time since the last beating on Pierce, they were allowed to huddle together and talk. Ashworth took advantage of the brief respite to check all their wounds. They were in constant need of water and by repeatedly asking Ashworth was finally able to get some, enough to bathe their wounds and drink. It was scummy, stinking water but it was wet and they drank eagerly, their dehydrated bodies and parched throats relishing the few seconds of comfort. Paul's shoulder wound was the one in best shape, healing fairly well. The bullet had passed completely through without hitting any bones and while painful, the wound was clean and healing, a surprise to all of them. Ashworth's leg wound was the worst one, getting infected and giving him a tremendous amount of trouble. It was hot to the touch and beginning to smell bad. Pierce was also in bad shape, the fragments of shrapnel still imbedded in his back, causing him incredible pain, the metal infecting the wound. Ashworth did the best he could without any equipment or medicine, Colonel Hue refusing to give them any.

Sgt. Ashworth looked around the encampment, shaking his head at their predicament. The Viet Cong had dropped their equipment and were relaxing, some of them cooking food, the sound of their voices chattering loud in the small camp. One lone Viet Cong guard squatted down in front of the cage and kept his eyes on them, obviously bored with the assignment.

Pierce glanced around also, taking in the layout of the camp, the guards coming and going, his mind working on the possibility of escaping as soon as possible.

"Boys...don't give up," he said softly, almost a whisper. "We will get out of this...one way or the other."

Paul watched him, seeing the pain deep in his eyes and he marveled at the resilience of the man. There was no hesitation in Pierce, no doubt that they would live and make it out of the prison camp.

"Pretty soon they will start their interrogation guys," Pierce continued, glancing at the young guard near them. "So just give them garbage." He was referring to the fact that they should avoid giving the enemy any useful information and both Paul and Ashworth nodded their heads in assent.

Their respite didn't last long and when Colonel Hue made his appearance again he started barking orders. The VC guards came forward, opening the cage and separating the prisoners, each one to an individual bamboo cage. The cage was a completely Spartan affair, with a thatched roof above and the hard, bare ground for a sleeping pallet. The bamboo poles lining the walls were set about two inches apart, giving them enough room to observed what was going on outside. The cage was barely big enough to move around, their feet tied with chains now. The chain was long enough for them to reach the waste hole that had been dug out at the farthest corner of the small cage. The VC dropped a mosquito net on each one of them, leaving one guard to keep an eye on them while the rest went about their business in the camp. Senior Colonel Hue remained in place, his eyes fixed on the prisoners, an inscrutable look etched on his face. For long seconds, he stood still and then, with an enigmatic smile playing on his thin face, he whirled around, departing.

And so it started, the days of their capture stretching into long hours of pain and suffering, intermingled with days of hope for eventual released from the hell they had fallen into.

Three times a day they were fed a watery soup and a piece of mildewed bread or a handful of rice and salt, a starvation diet that was sure to kill them in due time. All three of them were weak from hunger and exposure to the elements, dehydrated for lack of water and the diarrhea that had accompanied their first bout of dysentery. Their wounds were painful, their bodies covered by insect bites and heat rash, adding to the discomfort they felt.

Lee Ashworth was the worst of them now, and slowly Pierce could see that if his man didn't get proper medical attention, he would die soon. The leg was completely infected now, the smell overpowering in its intensity, the fever racking his body and consuming the flesh until the man was nothing but a whimpering shell of his old self. Day after day he lay on the cage floor, his delirious mind begging for water, the sounds escaping from his mouth unintelligible babble. Without assistance, Ashworth lay on the hard ground, weak from hunger and the fever that consumed his remaining strength, urinating and defecating on himself. He was dying in front of Paul and Pierce and both men were going mad, frustrated at their inability to do something for him. They had tried their best to talk Colonel Hue into letting them take care of Ashworth, but to no avail.

Alton Pierce never let up on jumping Hue at every opportunity, insisting that they should be treated according to the Geneva Convention. He was the senior officer at the compound and he had taken it upon himself to see that his men were treated fairly, taking the brunt of the mistreatment himself. And by so doing, brought the wrath of Colonel Hue upon him.

He had been pestering the guards, talking to them in Vietnamese, requesting to talk to Hue, until finally one evening the Colonel made his appearance at Pierce's cage. The Colonel came striding by slowly, a cigarette dangling from his lips. As usual he was dressed neatly, the riding crop in his hand. The brown eyes fixed on Pierce and the nose wrinkled up in distaste at the smell emanating from the cages.

"I was advised that you wish to talk," Hue said, inhaling deeply from the American cigarette in his mouth, letting the smoke out slowly in Pierce's direction.

"Colonel, my men need medical care," he started, knowing well he was wasting his time. But Ashworth was in bad shape and he would do just about anything to help his men.

"Are you prepared to sign a confession about your criminal acts against the people of Viet Nam?" he asked, dropping the cigarette on the ground and stepping on it. Pierce glanced at the man's face, looking deep in the cold, hard eyes for any sign of pity, any sign that the man in front of him was a human being, with feelings for his fellow man. But all he saw was the cold, calculating eyes of a man determine to get what he wanted, the cruel sensuous lips smirking at him.

"We aren't criminals of war, Colonel," Pierce continued, restraining the anger in his voice, "and all we want is treatment as prisoners of war, according to the Geneva Convention."

Hue stepped closer to the cage, a grin flickering across his face, and the pencil line moustache on his upper lip quivering with some kind of repressed emotion.

"You give me what I want," he said softly, his eyes bright and eager, "and I'll give all your men food and clothes and medical attention."

Pierce shook his head, breathing deeply, tired of the game now. His back was giving him a tremendous amount of pain, his legs cramped, but he was not going to play games with Hue or sell his soul for special treatment for them. He knew that he could make things easier for all of them, stop the beatings, save Ashworth life and possibly theirs too. For a split second, his mind toyed with the idea of doing just that, but the thought disappeared as fast as it had come. He was an officer in the U.S. Army and regardless of what happened to him or his men; he couldn't betray himself or his country. He could not be a traitor any more that he could deny his faith in God. That was his decision and good or bad, he would have to live with it.

"The only thing you are getting from me is my name, rank and service number," he said.

For a moment longer, Hue fixed his cold, detach eyes on him and then a smile came to his face.

"I'll teach you a lesson today that you won't forget," he said. "And by the time we are finish, you will give me what I want," Hue said softly, almost in a whisper. He nodded his head in the direction of the guard and stepped away from the cage, the smile still on his face.

The guard said something in Vietnamese and several other VC soldiers came forward. The guards opened the cage, took the shackles off his legs and dragged Pierce out. Once outside, his clothes were ripped, while Pierce yelled at them, cursing them in their own language. Paul looked at the scene outside the cage and his heart raced like a galloping horse, afraid for his friend, wondering what was going to happened now.

Four men took hold of Pierce, dragging him with his back to the ground, while another Viet Cong soldier came forward, waiting, a bamboo cane in his hand. When they had him like they wanted, two Viet Cong soldiers held his legs up high, the soles of his feet about four feet up in the air, his shoulders pinned to the ground.

The VC in front of him stood to one side and at a nod from Hue, the bamboo cane came up and down, swishing in the air, the sound of the wood hitting human flesh loud. With incredible force, the cane hit Pierce on the sole of his feet, the blow extracting an inhuman cry from his lips. Over and over the cane came down until bright red blood seeped slowly to the jungle floor from Pierce's soles. Alton Pierce bit his lips, the metallic taste of blood in his mouth, his mind rebelling at the pain coursing through his body like molten lava. He twisted and contorted his body, his muscles taut with the effort of trying to get away from the burning pain, a snarl of pure rage etched deeply on his face. Sweat ran down his face in rivulets and he closed his eyes, willing the pain away. Like in a dream, he heard Paul cursing them, his screams reverberating in the jungle.

Another nod from Colonel Hue's head and the bamboo cane stopped, the VC sweating profusely with the exertion.

"Put him in the "special" cage," he ordered, lighting a cigarette, taking the smoke deep into his lungs, as was his habit, releasing it slowly.

Two VC soldiers took hold of Pierce's body by the arms, attempting to drag him away, but much to their surprise, he squirmed in their arms, pushing them aside and tottered to his feet. A rictus of pain was etched on his face, the blood seeping from his raw soles and for a minute, he swayed like a palm tree pushed by a strong wind, almost falling. With an incredible show of will power, the naked man squared his shoulders and took a step forward, absorbing the pain, the VC guards following after him shaking their heads.

Paul Gallagher saw him go to whatever the Colonel had in store for him, marveling at the man's courage, hoping that when it was his turn he would do as well. He was brought out of his reverie by the voice of Hue next to his cage, making him jump. "Soon it will be your turn," he said, his eyes laughing. Paul did not answer—just looked at the man disdainfully, a wave of repulsion washing over him.

Hue looked in Ashworth's direction, said something in rapid fire Vietnamese that Paul couldn't quite comprehend and whirled away.

Several minutes later, Ashworth's cage was opened and he was dragged outside, the inert form of the man whimpering softly. Seconds later Paul's cage was open and Ashworth was thrown inside unceremoniously, his body hitting the bamboo wall with a thud, a scream bursting from his mouth when the injured leg hit the ground.

"Oh, you bastards," Paul yelled, his hands gripping the bamboo wall with incredible force, feeling impotent, the rage burning inside of him.

He turned around and went to his friend, picking up his body and cradling his head on his lap. The stench emanating from Ashworth's leg was overpowering, making him nauseous, but he swallowed hard, his mind concentrating on doing his best to comfort the man. He laid him on the ground, and his hand worked on the dirty bandages covering the wound. It was obvious that the wound was infected and that blood poisoning was ravaging Ashworth's body. When Paul pulled the bandages away, he was aghast at the look of the wound. The flesh where the bullet had gone in was almost black, the thigh swelled almost twice its size. He touched the wound tentatively, feeling the heat emanating from it, and then pushed on the swollen flesh, eliciting a grunt of pain from Ashworth. He pressed harder and a stream of yellow pus burst out of the wound, the smell of rotten flesh overpowering. This time Ashworth scream and Paul pulled his hand back, unwilling to create any more pain for his friend. He re-bandaged the wound carefully, shaking his head. Ashworth was barely conscious, his body hot and the sweat running down in rivulets. Paul knew his friend was dying and he cursed his captors long and hard for being so inhuman and indifferent to their plight. He remained next to Ashworth for the rest of the day, talking to him softly, not at all sure that his friend was listening, giving him his own share of the putrid water when it came. When night finally settled over the camp, it turned cold, Ashworth's teeth shattering with the fever. Paul wrapped his arms around him, trying to warm him up as best he could. The shaking of the fragile body finally subsided sometime in the night. He continued to talk to him, holding the man in his arms, praying to the Almighty God for release. If his calculations were right, tomorrow was Christmas day and his mind went to his family and Susan. It is going to be one hell of a holiday, Paul thought wearily. The families probably didn't even know for sure they were alive and would be wondering about them.

Another fit of shaking took hold of Ashworth and Paul held him again. Ashworth was nothing but skin and bones by now and the poison in his blood would not take much longer to kill him, Paul told himself, wondering if Ashworth would not be the better of them if he was dead. At least there would be no more beatings for him and his spirit would find solace. With those thoughts in his mind, Paul's head came down on his chest and with his arms still wrapped around his friend, he went into a fitful sleep, the horrible nightmares hounding his dreams.

Chapter 14

The U Minh Forest
Viet Cong Prison Camp
December 24,1963

Alton Pierce walked slowly to the cage indicated by the VC, his feet pieces of raw meat. The pain was incredible and he had to excise all his will power not to scream. When the VC halted him, it was in front of a thatched bamboo cage that was about six feet long, three feet wide and four feet high. They made him get in, lying on his chest, snapping chains on his feet. The cage was so small that there was no room to turn, forcing him to stay flat on his chest. His body was taller than the cage also and he was forced to pull his legs up several inches, constricting his blood flow. The way the cage had been constructed, there was barely any light showing, making it dark and hot during the day. The temperatures were in the nineties during the day and coupled with almost one hundred percent humidity, the cage was an instrument of torture, wringing any available moisture that he had left in his body. After several hours in the cage, Alton Pierce couldn't feel his legs anymore and the thirst that assailed him was a torture in itself. Unable to move or change positions, his body eventually felt like a lump of raw meat, numb, time dragging by slowly, ever so slowly. He pushed his mind away, thinking about the training instilled in them back at Bragg. He had to disassociate his mind from the pain, or he would be a basket case soon, he thought. The Colonel was obviously going to wear him down in the hope Pierce would sign a confession and he had a feeling that this little cage would not be the last resort in Hue's repertoire. That night, when the guards finally let him out to use the latrine, his whole body was one solid ache. For long minutes Pierce lay on the jungle floor, his legs refusing to support him, the blood passing through his veins after so many hours of been constricted, a pure hell. When he finally made it to his feet, it was dark, with just several fires illuminating the area close to him. For some unknown reason, the guard in charge of him was not paying him any attention and Pierce moved slowly away, in the direction of the waste hole. He made it and went about his business, his eyes glancing in the direction of the guard who was still absorbed looking in another direction. Without thinking any more. Pierce went down to the ground, crawling away as fast as he could, hoping to get enough of a head start to get far enough to find a hiding hole somewhere. The sole of his feet were in too bad a shape for him to run and he had to content himself with a slow crawl. He had made it several yards into the jungle when he heard shrill voices, the VC guard finally realizing the prisoner was nowhere around. In a few seconds the VC were combing the area and Pierce went to ground, hiding himself as best he could, knowing that he would be discovered in seconds.

"Damn, just a few more minutes," he thought bitterly, listening to the rapidly approaching footsteps of the guards, seeing the flashing of lights all over the camp. A noise behind him made him swivel his head, to see the underbrush parting, the face of a Viet Cong soldier peering at him. The soldier yelled to someone behind him and the light of one powerful flashlight was shined on his face. Without ceremony, rough hands yanked him up, the rifle butts coming down on him, followed immediately by kicks. He went down in a heap, making himself small, rolling with the kicks and punches aimed at him. A rifle butt smashed against his head and he saw stars in front of his eyes. Another followed that stroke and finally Pierce went down for the last time, the darkness rushing at him.

Chapter 15

The U Minh Forest
Mekong Delta, South Vietnam
December 25, 1963

Paul Gallagher woke up in the early hours of the morning, his body numb from holding the same position with Ashworth's body all through the night. His buddy was cold now and Paul moved slightly trying to get into a better position. He wrinkled his nose in disgust at the smell emanating from the leg wound and he moved slowly. He untangled his arms from Ashworth, feeling the resistance when he tried to move him. Ashworth was cold and rigid. With his heart beating furiously in his mouth, Paul stood up, positioning Lee's body on the floor. There was enough light now to see and Paul bent down to his friend. For a moment, he remained still, his eyes taking in the body of his friend; the eyes wide open, staring into empty space. Lee Ashworth, that valiant soldier, was dead. Something broke inside of Paul and a sob burst from his mouth at the sight that had greeted his eyes. With infinite care, he cradled Ashworth's head, his hand closing the eyes that would not see another day, tears falling down his cheeks.

For a long time, Paul Gallagher remained still, a million thoughts crowding his head. The sound of the cage coming open brought him back to reality, seeing two VC standing in front of him. Without a word, they reach for Ashworth, but Paul held on to him, covering the body with his own. "Get the hell away from him," he yelled at the top of his lungs, first in English and then finding the words in Vietnamese. His face was contorted in rage, the eyes were those of a man who had lost his mind and for a second the VC stood still watching him. Finally with a shrug of their shoulders and laughing at the crazy man in the cage, they stepped back. Paul Gallagher dragged the body of his friend out of the small cage and with a supreme effort he picked him up. He looked at the VC guards and they motion for him to come out. He did and he followed them a short way into the jungle until they finally stopped, pointing at the ground, one of them throwing a shovel to him. Without a word, Paul put the body down, picking up the shovel and starting to dig, his mind trying to come to grips with the death of his friend.

When the grave was deep enough, the VC guard told him to stop. He climbed out of the hole and slowly, carefully he picked up Ashworth's body, placing him at the bottom of the shallow grave. He got out and picking up the shovel again, he covered the body with dirt, his hands moving automatically until the deed was done. When he was finished, he stood over the grave and silently, humbly, he prayed for his friend.

"May the good Lord in heaven bless you and keep you, my friend," he said softly, feeling the tears running down his face and the lump in his throat. One of the VC came toward him, pointing with his rifle, ordering him to move. Paul's eyes, hard and inscrutable, fixed on the Viet Cong and for one fleeting moment, Paul Gallagher thought that it would be so easy to end it all right then and there. The tableau held for another brief moment and then the Viet Cong soldier took a menacing step toward Paul, the rifle rising, the gesture unmistakable. Paul shook his head, sighing deeply and slowly controlled his feelings. He turned around and started walking back, passing close to the "special" cage where Pierce was laying unable to move or see anything of what was going on outside.

"Lee is dead," he said in passing the cage, loud enough for Pierce to hear it, continuing his walk.

He stepped into his cage, the guard shackling his leg again and finally leaving him alone, wondering what else would be coming their way. One of their own was dead due to the inhuman treatment and the lack of food, medical attention and water and with a shudder he thought about who would be the next one to die. His wound to the shoulder was healing properly, how he didn't know. But somehow, he had not developed any infection and so far the only thing that could be considered bad for him was the constant hunger pain in his stomach and the lack of vitamins. They had been put on a starvation diet, with most days, just a bowl of rice and a handful of salt, or some kind of watery soup and bread. He was also dehydrated, getting enough water only when it rained hard enough for the water to come down past the triple jungle canopy and slide down his thatched roof.

He lay back against the bamboo walls of his small cage, closing his eyes, wondering what was next. Pierce had tried to escape last night, he had listened to the guards screaming and yelling, hoping that he would have been successful, but that had not been the case. He had been beaten mercilessly for it and put back in the isolation cage again. He opened his eyes, blinking rapidly, his thoughts going to his friend. Paul knew that Pierce was playing a dangerous game. His Captain was trying his best to draw attention to himself in order for the sadistic Colonel Hue to leave the rest of his men alone, but it was a game he was going to loose one way or the other and probably with his life. But Pierce was a man who once set on a course of action, would not budge or give in. Here, that was surely a step closer to death.

He closed his eyes again, sighing deeply, lost in his thoughts about Ashworth and what his death meant to them. Hue had let him die, refusing medicine and care, just to show him and Pierce that he was the master of their fate and that he and he alone could give them life. But for that life to be given there was a price to be paid and as far as he was concerned, the price was to steep. He couldn't betray his country or his code of honor and he was sure that Pierce couldn't do it either. So death would be waiting for them just as surely as it had taken Ashworth. Paul shook his head slowly, shuddering, unwilling to think anymore about the fate awaiting them, refusing to believe that they would leave their bodies to rot somewhere in the jungles of Viet Nam. He tried to center his thoughts on Susan and his parents, but the wave of despair that engulfed him was too much to bear. He looked at his hands, seeing them tremble, realizing that the death of Ashworth had left a deep void in his heart. There was just the two of them now and the way things were going between Pierce and Colonel Hue, he didn't give much more than a plug nickel for their lives.

Paul Gallagher sighed deeply, shaking his head, wondering what was in stored for them, thinking that whatever it was, it certainly would come soon.

Chapter 16

Mason City, Iowa
January 2, 1964

Bill Gallagher stretched his long legs and rubbed his face with his hand, moving his buttocks around on the hard wooden chair, trying his best to find a comfortable spot. He glanced at his wristwatch, checking the time, shaking his head in consternation. The day was young, but he was already tired, the day stretching in front of him full of chores. He wasn't getting much sleep these days and his haggard face and hooded eyes told the story as eloquently as words. The old house was quiet at this time of the morning with his two sons taking care of the morning chores around the farm and his wife Carol somewhere in the house. Susan was gone to her sister's in San Francisco, having decided that she needed to keep herself busy. Her pregnancy was giving her some trouble and the doctor was concerned about the amount of stress she was feeling and had prescribed a long vacation.

Christmas had come and gone and also New Years with no news from his son. It had been over three weeks since the news had reached them of his disappearance and even now the Army wasn't sure what had happened to him or his companions. According to the Army, the Red Cross didn't list their names as prisoners and the information coming in was sketchy at best. General Woods had kept his promise to keep him informed, but the news was always the same. They were doing everything possible to find out their status or some kind of confirmation that their boys were prisoners of war and that was it.

According to Woods, several Teams had gone in scouring the area where the firefight took place, but no bodies of Americans were recovered at the site. Which in itself was good news, Bill thought, getting up from his chair, pushing the mountain of papers away from him. He had been going through the bills and the myriad of pamphlets and advertising junk, his mind just carrying him through the motions. Outside, the wind howled with increasing fury, the snow swirled, coming down hard. The weatherman had said that it would snow at least six inches by morning and the snowstorm was on its way to prove him right

He walked into the kitchen, fixed himself some coffee and came back to the small cubicle that was his office. He sat down heavily, dreading to go back to the task at hand. He shook his head slowly, thinking that he had never been a man to procrastinate regardless of what the job was and here he was now, morose, unable to get his mind and body working right, unsatisfied with the results from everything he did. But he didn't feel like working or much less going through bills and junk mail right now. He felt like he need to be doing something for his son, trying to find out what had really happened in that God forsaken country so far away from home.

If his son was dead, then he could deal with that. He would have died serving his country, in an honorable manner, but this uncertainty about his fate, the fact that they didn't know if he was dead or alive, prisoner or just missing was something that weighed heavily on his mind, making his days a living hell. There was no conclusion to something like this and Bill Gallagher was lost in a world of pain and uncertainty.

Footsteps behind him brought him out of his reverie and he glanced up, seeing his wife Carol coming to him. She had aged in the short weeks since the news had reached them, her eyes sad, the wrinkle lines deeper, and the timbre of her voice slow, just like Susan. The house that was always so full of life and laughter was now a somber place. She resented that, Bill knew it, but he also knew that eventually, their life would go back to normal, or as normal as it could be when your oldest son was missing and you didn't know if he was dead or what the feature held for you.

He stood up now, going to Carol, his arms opening up, nestling the dear face close to his heart. He was taller than she was and her head reached up to his chest. He kissed her gently on the top of her head, his powerful arms wrapped around her. Carol sighed deeply, shuddering, feeling the warmth of her husband's arms slowly engulfing her. She tilted her head in order to look at him better, her eyes fixed on him, the sadness and the pain that she was experiencing showing clearly.

"Is our boy going to be all right?" she asked, her voice small, almost a whisper, wanting reassurance.

Bill Gallagher looked at his wife tenderly, his eyes taking in the dear face. Gently, he touched her cheek, his finger tracing a line. "Yes sweetheart...he will be," he said with a conviction that he really didn't feel right now. But he loved this woman, the mother of his children and he would do anything, say whatever, in order to make her feel better.

"I know that he is alive and somehow, he will come back to us." And then, there was always hope, he thought. He was a Christian man, with a deep, unyielding love for God and in the end, it would be faith and hope that would sustained them and see them through the rough times.

He held her tightly, wanting to believe that his words were true and that their son was alive. But it was hard to hold on to the believe that their son was okay, the doubts infringing in his mind, feeling the slow hand of desperation engulf him in its cold embrace. He had never known pain so deep, for so long, and he knew that Carol was feeling the same way he did. The void in his heart was something alive, that left him weak and on the edge of going crazy. He had to fight the waves of fear and depression that washed over him at times, calling on his God to sustain him, realizing that day by day the fight to keep going, to keep believing was harder and harder.

He closed his eyes and held onto his wife, rocking slowly on his feet, talking softly, his hand caressing her hair, feeling like a condemned man on his last day on earth.

CHAPTER 17

Key West, Florida
January 1964

Major General Pierce (Retired) sat quietly on the front porch of his house, absentmindedly watching the sun go down. A gentle breeze whispered softly among the trees, accentuating the peace and quiet of his surroundings. The sky was a rainbow of colors, a shimmering attraction that, at any other time, would have sent him into the house looking for his camera. He was an ardent photographer, with a good eye for color and he prided himself in the pictures he had taken since he started the hobby. But this was not a good time for him. The sky above didn't hold his attention at all on this day; instead his thoughts were on his wife and his missing son.

The official notice had come in as stated by his friend, General Donovan, but it was just the same information he already had. It had taken him two days to develop the courage to give the news to Alma and just like he had suspected, the blow had been too much for her. Within days, her fragile heart had suffered another heart attack and she was now bedridden, barely conscious in a hospital bed. The doctor was not optimistic at all this time and General Pierce thought that he would go crazy at the cards fate had dealt him. Four days after receiving the official news concerning the fate of his son, he had received Alton's last letter to him, a letter full of life and hope for the future, wishing his parents a joyful holiday season. And that had been the same day he had been killed or captured. General Pierce had thought at the moment that fate had been unkind to his son.

His only son was dead or a prisoner of war and his beloved wife was dying. It is enough to makes a man go crazy, he thought, standing up, rubbing his face with his hands. He felt the roughness of two days without a shave, and not much sleep. He walked into the house, making his way slowly upstairs to the master bedroom. He had come to get a change of clothes and go back to the hospital to be close to Alma, the depressing thoughts weighting heavily on his mind. He had checked the mail and the calls on the phone, but as usual, there was no news about Alton. He was in weekly contact with General Donovan, but not even his friend had been able to get any new information about the men missing in action. He had tried everything and everybody he knew, calling on powerful friends and Senators alike and using all his influence at the Pentagon. Calls to the Red Cross had also been futile and in the end it was like the earth had parted and swallowed them, leaving nothing behind.

He pick up a small overnight case, put some items in it and made his way back downstairs to his car. He opened the back door and threw the case in the back seat. Getting in and staring the engine, he sat still or long seconds, a far away look in his eyes. A lone tear made its way down the right side of his face and a trembling hand wiped at it angrily.

Major General Pierce nodded his head slowly like a man with the weight of the world on his shoulders and with a deep sigh he drove away.

Chapter 18

Somewhere in the U Minh Forest
Mekong Delta, South Vietnam
February 1964

Time passed slowly at the VC prison camp, one day the same as another. For the next two weeks after Ashworth die, Colonel Hue left them alone and after ten days of confinement in the "special" cage, Pierce was let out. Two Viet Cong soldiers dragged him out of the cage unceremoniously, pushing him forward.

When Paul laid eyes on him he was aghast at the change that had been visited upon Pierce. He was gaunt, almost emaciated and the days of confinement in the oven like cage had melted every ounce of fat from his body. He was underweight and his rib cage stuck out markedly. He was naked and his body was covered with sores and the stench of fecal matter since the guards would not let him out of the "special" cage even to go to the waste hole any more after his botched escape attempt.

To Paul's surprise, the guards walked him to his cage, opened it and sent Pierce crashing through the door. Painfully, slowly, Alton Pierce dragged his abuse body to a sitting position, his hand wiping blood from his cracked lips. His eyes glanced at Paul, who had rushed to assist him and he smile a tired smile.

"How…how are you buddy?" he asked, leaning his back gingerly on the bamboo cage, his breath coming raggedly. His eyes were hooded, full of pain. "I'm holding up okay," Paul answered, his eyes covering Pierce's body, seeing the shape his Captain was in. His physical condition was bad and the man was a shadow of his former self. Not that I'm in any better shape, Paul thought, wishing he had a mirror to see his face. But the man was still 'game', his mind sound. It would take an incredible amount of punishment to break a man like Pierce, Paul told himself, shuddering at that fact. Every man had a breaking point, but knowing Pierce, this man was stubborn as they come. He would take everything the VC had in store for him, laugh at them and make them lose face. That would enrage the VC, especially Colonel Hue and the revenge extracted from Pierce would be dangerous.

"Man…oh man, that…that was rough," Pierce said softly, pushing his back against the wall, the effort bringing a grimace to his face. He was weak as a baby, every bone in his body hurting and his stomach tied up in knots. Stars danced in front of his eyes every time he tried to focus on something and there was a dull pain behind them.

They talked for a while, both men enjoying the camaraderie and the fact that they were together now, reinforcing their hopes and belief. They both knew that the months ahead of them would be like a trip to hell and that Colonel Hue would not desist in his efforts to obtain whatever he could get from them. A confession from them condemning the war or denouncing the United States of America as warmongers would be something that would increase his prestige and Pierce and Paul knew that the man would stop at nothing to get what he wanted. He would use food, torture, inhuman treatment and psychological methods to get what he desired from them, knowing well that sooner or later one of the two would break and give him what he wanted. He had all the time in the world to do it and nothing to stop him, Paul thought wearily, contemplating their situation as calmly as he could.

As far as the two prisoners of war were concerned, the most important factor in their captivity and their eventual release depended on them completely. Pierce and Paul had been trained by the best and they knew that they needed to keep their morale and their hopes high.

There couldn't be any doubt in their minds that they would make it. There were no ifs, ands, or buts about it. They would make it alive. Somehow they would find a way to escape and they would manage to get back home. Their psychological training had taught both of them that a man who thinks about giving up was a dead man, the same as the man who loses his will to live. They would strive to keep hope alive and their minds sharp, attuned to their surroundings or they would leave their bones in some dark hole in the jungle floor, food for the ants and insects. They had each other and the thoughts of family and friends to keep them sharp and they intended to use everything in their power to stay that way. There couldn't be any thoughts about giving up or they surely would die.

That night, just before he succumbed to sleep and the accompanying nightmares that haunted his dreams nightly, Paul thought about his wife, Susan, and the precious child that would be born to her soon, his father a prisoner in an obscure patch of jungle thousands of miles away. Thinking about the little soul that soon would enter the world, Paul felt a wave of depression washing over him, smashing his soul like the strong surf on a beach. He sat upright in his cage, his eyes tightly shut, feeling emotions about to overwhelm his self control.

"God…oh God…please…please," he mumbled gently, trying to control the tide about to engulf him in a dark embrace. He stood up, groping about blindly through his tears, his hand coming into contact with the bamboo poles on the wall. He glanced around, noticing the guard outside pacing slowly in the semidarkness broken only by a lantern hanging from a tree branch. The guard had stopped his pacing and was looking in his direction, probably alerted by his moving about. For long seconds the guard remained still, his eyes searching. Satisfied, he continued walking, disregarding the prisoners.

He sat down again, shaking his head, trying to find some comfort in his desperate situation. He closed his eyes again, striving to calm himself, his mind finally giving him some rest, taking him to the place where everything had started, listening to the words that would dictate his life and the course of action to follow. Like in a dream he heard the words again; "Duty, Honor, Country. Those three hallowed words reverently dictate what you ought to be, what you can be, what you will be. They are the rallying point to build courage when courage seems to fail; to regain faith when there seems little cause for faith; to create hope when hope becomes forlorn."

He heard those words reverberating in his brain and his mind brought forward the image of the man who had spoken them so long ago, General Douglas MacArthur and he was suddenly at peace with himself.

"Lord...Lord...help me," he said softly, the words as ephemeral as the wind whispering in the darkness. Just before sleep finally came, a thought intruded in his mind—Add God to those words and faith will carry you thru—and finally Paul Gallagher, exhausted in mind and spirit, slept.

Next to him in the darkness, Alton Pierce closed his eyes, feeling the wetness in them, wiping his eyes noiselessly, remaining still, and knowing that there was nothing he could do for his friend in his hour of need. Events, completely out of their control would dictate who would live and who would die. All they could do was wait, wait and pray that somehow the nightmare would eventually end.

Chapter 19

Mason City, Iowa
April 23rd, 1964

Paul Gallagher, Jr. came into the world as most children do, squalling. His ruddy face twisted into a pout of discomfort at the rude awakening from a warm and secure place into a cold, noisy world. Moments later, the cry subsided, the infant found a breast and starting to feed.

Susan Gallagher looked at the child and her heart twisted with a pang of incredible pain. At a time when she should be completely happy and secure in her motherhood, she was having trouble concentrating on the small bundle she held in her arms. The little thing looks just like Paul, she thought, her eyes fixed on the hungry infant who was now absorbed completely in the process of sucking milk from her left breast. She shook her head at the thoughts crowding in her mind, wishing that her husband were there now to see his son. But instead he is gone; she thought bitterly—life sure was hard at times, making you humble and thankful for what you had. All her dreams had been put on hold, the prospect of life without Paul casting a shadow over her own life.

She had counted the days and weeks and months since Paul had disappeared in Vietnam, her life put on hold, waiting for the call that would tell her she was a widow or that Paul was coming home. It was a nightmare, thinking about him, wondering where he was or if he was alive and what he would be going through. That was the hard part, the not knowing for sure if he was alive, and her mind conjuring all kinds of terrible things. Her heart refused to believe that the man she loved more than life itself was gone forever, that he might be dead somewhere in the vastness of the God forsaken place the Army had sent him.

She looked down at the baby and noticed that he was asleep. She kissed him gently, her fingers caressing the small face, marveling at the softness of it. A nurse came in then, chatting about this and that and eventually taking the baby out with her. Susan reclined back on the bed, her thoughts on Paul. Once again, her face was etched in disgust, thinking about the Army and their role in the whole mess. Despite the efforts of her father-in-law and some of his friends, the family still didn't have any clear idea concerning Paul's status. The Army personnel called at least once a month, but the information was always the same. Nothing new to report—which meant that the Army really didn't have any information or they were keeping silent about the men missing. She had called friends and written a million letters to Congressmen and Senators alike, but the responses had been full of nice words and short on substance. There was nothing anybody could do until the fate of the missing men was confirmed. If they were dead then the Government would strive to get their bodies back for a decent burial, if alive and imprisoned, then the Government would strive to get them back somehow.

Which is frustrating as hell, Susan thought, wishing she could get out of the damn bed and back on her feet. She was restless, wanting to get back to the farm where at least she could be doing something. But the doctor had wanted her to stay at least one day and she had acquiesced when Carol had also intervened. But this waiting is not doing me any good, Susan told herself, knowing that she had too much time on her hands to think about Paul. Deep in her heart, she knew he was alive and that sooner or later he would find the way to come back or to let them know where he was, but until then, her heart would be in pieces, her soul mourning the absence of her friend, her lover. She was a Christian girl and she had always managed to keep her faith intact, calling on her God to help her through the rough times, but these past few months she realized that her faith had really been tested to the limits.

Susan closed her eyes, sighing deeply, her mind wondering about the words spoken by her minister just a few days ago at Church, words that she thought were directed at her. The whole community had expressed their support for her and the family, friends going out of their way to be there for them, sharing the bad times and helping in any way they could and her minister had done his best to be there for her.

He had looked directly at her, like he knew what was going on in that head of hers, saying; "When there is no other place to turn, turn to your God. When there is no trusting the words of men, trust your God's words and when faith seems to abandon you, remember the faith that you have in God. It will sustain you and it will keep you because faith is the knowledge that our God is the force that compels this Universe and by faith alone we can move mountains." He was giving her a message. "Hang in there child, have faith and sooner or later your faith will see you through."

The sound of voices coming from outside her door gave her pause in her thinking and she opened her eyes, glancing up to see the boys and Carol and Bill Gallagher coming in the room, their faces, for once, shining with a smile. This was their first grandson and they were both happy at the momentous occasion. It was a bittersweet moment for them, having a new life springing forward and missing another at the same time.

They gather around her, the new uncles talking a mile a minute, while Bill and Carol came to her, the three human beings united in their grief and in their sorrow.

"We...we just saw the baby," Carol said, her voice braking. "He looks so much like...like Paul."

Susan looked at Bill Gallagher, his eye moist, and he in turn looked at her, fixing his eye on hers. She saw sadness and happiness intermingle together and at the same time she saw hope. He nodded his head slowly and she felt the strong, calloused hand grip hers, the tears flowing freely now on his weathered face.

"It's going to be okay…you'll see," he said softly, smiling through the tears. "He will come back."

She shook her head, feeling the wetness in her eyes and the lump in her throat. The man in front of her had a broken heart, but faith had sustained him, never once abandoning his hope that his son would come back alive.

Chapter 20

Prison Camp
U Minh Forest
Mekong Delta, South Vietnam
November 1964

Almost a year had passed since Paul Gallagher and Alton Pierce had been captured. The only way for them to keep track of time was by listening to the VC guards talking and they were almost sure that they were correct about the time that had elapsed. Both of the men were emaciated, the starvation diet and the lack of vitamins and proper medical attention taking a toll on them. The food was always the same, a green watery soup, boiling hot, and a piece of old, moldy bread. Sometimes, not very often, the guards would bring a handful of rice and salt. The water was foul also, with little creatures swimming in it most of the time, contributing to the dysentery and diarrhea that riddle their bodies.

At one point in time Hue had used food as a psychological weapon against them, giving Paul and Pierce a deeper look into the sadistic nature of the man.

Pierce had complained for days about the stinking, nasty food and finally Hue had shown up. He was immaculate as usual; a cigarette dangling from his lips, the smoke spiraling upwards in the air, making him close his left eye.

He came to stand next to the cage housing the two Americans, his face etched in disgust at the smell emanating from the prisoners cage and the waste hole.

He took a drag from the cigarette, inhaling the smoke deep into his lungs, letting it out slowly.

"So you don't like our food," he started, making it more of a statement than a question. His cold eyes survey the prisoners and there was a smirk on his face.

"This filth you are feeding us is not food Hue," Pierce said.

Colonel Hue nodded his head almost imperceptibly, like he was agreeing with Pierce. "You will be feed properly," he said softly, his eyes animated, like a man who had thought of something funny. He remained with his eyes fixed on the two Americans for a minute longer and then without preamble, he whirled away, the enigmatic smile still on his face.

Pierce and Paul watched him go and for a brief second Pierce wondered what Hue had in mind. He was about to find out.

When the evening meal came, the fare was definitely different. Besides the rice, there was meat, something like chicken, covered by some red gravy, hot enough to numb their lips. Like famished men, they attacked the food, only to start throwing up minutes later, the pain in their stomach incredibly intense. On a starvation diet for almost a year, their stomachs had shrunk to the size of a child and now, the rich food and the great quantity of it brought the expected results. They could not eat it. They retched and threw up until nothing else could come out, leaving them exhausted, their bodies convulsing on the floor.

A laugh made Pierce look up, to see Colonel Hue outside the cage, his face etched with pleasure.

"Don't like our food, Captain?" he said, the heavily accented voice full of laughter.

Pierce looked at him, refusing to answer, his eyes hard and cold. The bastard outside had probably put some kind of poison in the food and was enjoying their suffering now. Hue walked away, the laughter receding slowly.

The next day, the food was the same as usual, the watery soup and the molded bread. There was also some rotten fish, the worms crawling in them and for a while neither one of them could bring themselves to eat it. But it was protein and they needed it and soon enough, the fish went into the soup. The same thing happened to the snakes that crawled into their cage. Every time one of the creatures crawled in, Pierce or Gallagher would kill it, ripping the skin with their teeth, adding the white meat to the green liquid, forcing themselves to swallow it raw at first, eventually getting use to it. They had lost a tremendous amount of weight, their gums were always bleeding and their skin hung loose on their frame. The fight to stay alert and sharp was one that had to be fought everyday, the feeling that their chances of getting out of the prison camp alive were slim at best, insinuating into their minds. They were guarded around the clock, their legs chained to the walls of the cage and were only permitted to come out when Hue had some unpleasantness to deliver or there was some work to be done around the camp.

The guards came and went, the same as Hue. Pierce determined that the little Colonel was being kept busy running a war in the particular area where they were held prisoners. At times they could hear the sound of planes flying overhead and from time to time, the sound of helicopters passing by. The level of activity in the area had really escalated in the last few months and Pierce kept that in his mind, hoping that sooner or later their enemy would make a mistake and they could use it to their advantage. Escape was always on their minds and together they would talk, long into the night, making and discarding plans. It was a way for them to stay sharp, connected and in the long days coming they would need every ounce of faith and strength they could muster just to survive. There were some dark moments in their existence and at times they would feel depressed, their spirits down, but for the most part they endure well, swearing that they would never give up hope, waiting for a mistake from the guards or a slowing of vigilance from their captors. They would bide their time and somehow, they would make it. Thoughts of their family were the most powerful influence on their behavior and as far as Paul was concerned, his desire to see Susan again and to hold her in his arms was the main reason for his sanity and for his endurance. No matter what happened, as long as he had her, as long as he knew she was waiting for him, he could endure.

For Pierce, it was his indomitable spirit and the knowledge that if he gave up the struggle, he would be betraying his country and the code of honor of an officer in the United States Army. And then there was his father and the things he had learned from him. Since he was a child he had heard his father talk about honor and country and the duty of a soldier and he knew without a shadow of a doubt that if he gave the enemy anything, if he bowed down to their demands, regardless of the reason, then he would be betraying his country and betraying his father's teachings.

For him it had always been God and Country, followed closely by Honor and Duty, and no matter what, it would always be the same. As far as he was concerned, there was no room in him to deviate; it was straight through or nothing. Therefore, there was no way that he would give in to Hue or write anything bad about his country. He would endure or he would die and in doing so he would uphold that which was so dear to him, his faith in God and his honor.

Chapter 21

Key West, Florida
January 22,1965

Major General Robert W. Pierce stood still in front of the freshly dug grave, feeling the warm sunshine on his shoulders, the whispering sound of the wind among the tall pines that surrounded the cemetery his only companion. It was early in the morning and Robert Pierce had just buried his wife an hour earlier. All the friends and relatives were gone now and the old General was alone with his thoughts, standing in the same place where he had stood an hour ago. His eyes were red rimmed and tired, the result of two days with hardly any sleep. He sighed deeply, his eyes glancing around, feeling the coldness in his heart, his nostrils flaring at the smell of the freshly turned earth of the grave. It was hard for him to admit that his life companion was gone, but it was so. He had lost her the day he had told her about Alton missing in a war that she couldn't understand, just like he had predicted. No matter that he had been patient and careful about it, her fragile heart had not been able to withstand the pain and anxiety and she had finally gone in the hospital. The doctors had somehow managed to keep her alive, but the prognosis had been bad and Alma had never recovered completely. She had eventually come home, but was bedridden and when the next heart attack came, there was nothing anybody could do and Alma had die, her last breath on earth calling for her missing son.

Pierce glanced around, and his eyes registered the fact that he was all alone at the cemetery. The friends had come and gone, unable to do more than whisper innate things to a man that had a broken heart. Like a man in a dream, he walked away, feeling old beyond his years, the weariness seeping slowly into his body. Reaching his car, he opened the door slowly and got in. "And now what?" he asked himself. He didn't relish the thought of going back home to an empty house, full of memories of a dead wife and a missing son. He felt the wetness in his eyes again and marveled at the thought that for a man who had never cried in his life, he sure had been doing it a lot lately. But he couldn't help it, any more that he could help loving his son and wife as much as he did. He missed his child and he missed his wife and now he was at wits end, the agonizing pain engulfing him like nothing he had ever felt before.

He shook his head, started the engine and put the car in gear, driving slowly away, thoughts of his son overshadowing everything else. The pain of not knowing what had really happened to Alton was a bitter pill to swallow for him and therefore, there was no rest, no conclusion to his son's disappearance. But he would never give up hope, Pierce thought, not until his last breath on this earth. He would continue to wait and hope, his faith in the Almighty God would somehow sustain him.

Chapter 22

Close to the Cambodian Border
U Minh Forest
South Vietnam
February 1965

It was during the beginning of the second year of their captivity that the Viet Cong prison camp was moved to a different location, still in the U Minh Forest, but closer to the Cambodian border. Colonel Hue had come and accompanied by shouted orders, the camp was dismantled as fast as possible and within a matter of hours, they were walking single file on a jungle trail. Pierce was puzzled at the decision to move the camp, wondering at the reason Hue had it taken down. Maybe things were getting too hot in the area for Colonel Hue, Pierce thought while getting ready to depart. Once again, a rope was put around their necks and their hands were tied at their backs. Surprisingly, their eyes were not blindfolded and Paul kept his eyes wide open, orienting himself the best way he could. It was also during this trek that Paul and Pierce discovered, to their surprise, two other Americans marching in the group and Pierce surmised that they were new captives. One of them was obviously a young kid, no more than nineteen or twenty years old and the other one by all indications was a helicopter pilot. The young man appeared to be in bad shape and was being dragged along by the other man.

At the first opportunity, Pierce and Paul manage to get close enough to them to talk. They were the first Americans they had seen in over a year of captivity and they were hungry for contact. They couldn't wait to hear news from home.

The young kid was slumped on the ground, his eyes wild, haunted. His body shook like a tall reed in a strong wind and his face was swollen and badly cut. Blood dripped from a gash on his forehead and the nose was twisted slightly. The pilot, a warrant officer (WO) was in slightly better shape with some minor burns and Pierce concentrated on him.

"Who are you?" he asked, watching the VC guard standing close to them. Lately they had been able to talk some without the guards getting too physical with them, but then, you never knew what was going to trigger a response from them.

"I'm warrant officer Wilson, Skip Wilson," he said, his eyes taking in the skeletal figure of the man in front of him. He shook his head like a man wishing to forget about something, but his eyes remained fixed on Paul and Pierce. "And who the hell are you guys?"

"I'm Captain Pierce, this is Lt. Gallagher, 5th Special Forces," he said.

Wilson nodded his head, assimilating the information given and then he asked; "How long have you guys been prisoners…sir?"

"Don't know for sure…going on two years I guess," Pierce said, watching the pilot closely.

"Gracious Lord…two years?" How in the hell could you make it…sir?" he asked, his eyes wide at the words coming from Pierce

"You just do Wilson," Pierce said. "You…do the best you can, never forgetting who you are and what you represent."

Wilson just nodded his head in wonderment. This was all new to him and the shock of being captured was just too much to swallow. Add to that the fact that he had been blown out of the sky while flying his chopper two days ago and he was in a funk, his brain trying to absorb everything that had happened in such a short time. He had made it out of the burning wreckage of the chopper just in time, dragging his door gunner out, the kid now lying on the ground next to him. Everyone else had died, including his co-pilot. He had a nasty burn to his leg and numerous cuts and bruises, but nothing serious. And now this, he thought wearily, glancing at the two scarecrows sitting on the ground, their ribs showing, and their eyes glued to him. Bruises and scars, new and old could be seen on their bodies and Wilson shuddered at the implication. The rough voice of the man who said he was a captain brought him out of his reverie and he look up.

"What happened to you guys?" the captain asked, his sharp eyes fixed on the flyer.

"I was flying a mission for the ARVN and some Special Forces camp when we were fired upon and the chopper was hit bad. I had to land the crippled bird, but came down in some trees and wrecked. I made it out with just some burns and was able to rescue one man, my door gunner over there." He stopped for a second, his eyes clouded, like a man lost in memories. He shook his head and resumed. "Before I knew it, a bunch of black clad guys were swarming all over us and here we are."

Pierce nodded his head, feeling sorry for the two newcomers. They would meet Colonel Hue sooner or later and then their lives would be nothing but misery. They talked for a long time, Wilson bringing them up to speed on the war raging in Vietnam.

"Ever since Johnson took over from Kennedy there have been rumors of an Army build up and it appears that the U.S. is going to commit ground troops to this war."

They had been talking in whispers so as not to attract the attention of the guards and now they remained silent, Pierce and Gallagher absorbing the news.

A moan arose from the young man laying on the ground and Pierce moved to him. When he came closer he could see that the soldier was in bad shape and that he needed medical attention. He cradled his head and in Vietnamese asked the VC guard for water. The guard looked at him and shook his head in the negative. Pierce stood up and confronted the guard, speaking rapidly and gesturing.

Wilson followed the interaction, wondering what the hell was being said. The voices were getting loud now, attracting other guards and suddenly a man dressed in khakis came forward. He stopped in front of Pierce and his eyes glanced at the soldier on the ground.

He turned to Pierce and spoke in Vietnamese. Pierce answered him, his face angry. Wilson watched them, wondering what the hell was going on and finally he couldn't stand it anymore.

"What the fuck is that asshole talking about?" he asked, turning toward Gallagher. He was referring to Colonel Hue who was now observing the young man.

"Just be quiet, Wilson," Gallagher said softly, his eyes never leaving the scene playing in front of them. "Let Captain Pierce handled this."

At that time Hue kicked the prostrate figure on the ground and Wilson became enraged. Before Gallagher could stop him, the pilot had pushed forward stopping mere inches in front of Hue.

"You bastard," he said, spitting the words, his face contorted in rage. Before he had time to say anything else, the riding crop came up, lashing at Wilson's face. Once, twice, the crop came down, cutting bloody furrows on the man's face. Two guards jumped toward him and in seconds they had him pined to the ground.

"You Americans," Hue said with disgust, straightening his tunic, the wolfish smile on his face now. He nodded his head imperceptibly and the bamboo sticks made their appearances. Another nod of the head and Wilson was soon screaming and thrashing on the ground, the guards beating him almost senseless, the kicks and rifle butt strokes raining on him mercilessly.

Paul and Pierce had attempted to come forward, but the VC guards were on them in seconds, holding them back, the cold steel of their bayonets kept them at bay.

"Damn you, Hue," Pierce said, rage and desperation etched deeply on his face.

Colonel Hue smiled, his eyes taking in the group of Americans. The young man on the ground moaned softly again, attracting Hue's attention. He gave orders to the VC guards and two of them pick the soldier up roughly. The young man's head lolled from side to side, his legs refusing to hold him straight. Blood dripped from a cut to his forehead and his hands were burned, the flesh black, charred, watery fluids seeping from it.

Hue grasped the young soldier by the face, looking into his eyes, finally dropping the head. He gave an order and the body was turned loose, falling to the ground in a heap. Pierce was about to open his mouth when to his horror, he saw Hue's hand going to his side holster, pulling a pistol. Without further delay, he put the muzzle of the pistol close to the young man's head and pulled the trigger, blood and pieces of brain spilling over the ground. The report was loud, making Pierce flinch, his eyes open wide at the horror he was witnessing and he went berserk. With an inhuman cry, he attempted to get loose, dragging the guards down in his effort to get to Hue.

"Oooh...you son of a bitch," he cried, a feral look on his face making him look like an apparition from hell. He struggled to get free, but he was to weak to fight more than one guard and was easily pinned down.

Hue put the pistol in the holster, lighting a cigarette. He inhaled the smoke deeply and looked at Pierce coldly.

"Maybe now you will cooperate," he said, his voice gentle, almost a whisper. He let the smoke out slowly, waiting.

"Don't hold your breath,...you damn murderer," Pierce said, his teeth clenched, his befuddle brain attempting to come to terms with what he had just seen. An American prisoner of war had been summarily executed in his presence.

Colonel Hue nodded his head, his eyes fixed on Pierce a moment longer. "Pick him up," he said, indicating the figure of Wilson, who was groaning feebly on the ground.

"Wait a damn minute, Colonel," Pierce said, trying his best to concealed the trembling in his voice. "We...we need to bury this man."

"You are not burying anybody Captain...and if you insist, I'll kill you and your friend right here, right now," Hue said, his hand going to the pistol at his side again in a threatening gesture.

Pierce opened his mouth to say something, his handsome face contorted in a blind rage, but this time it was Paul who intervened.

"Let it go, Alton. This bastard is just looking for an excuse," he said, his blue eyes fixed on Colonel Hue who watched them for a moment longer. Seeing that the situation was once more under his control, he closed the flap of his holster and with a last glance at Gallagher and Pierce he whirled around and was gone.

The guards let Pierce go, gesticulating and pointing with their rifles and without any more preamble, the two Americans lifted the semi-unconscious body of Wilson, resuming their trek into the jungle.

While they walked, supporting the body of Skip Wilson, Paul thought about what he had just witnessed and he shuddered. What type of human being was Hue?" he asked himself in wonder. It was obvious that human life was not worth very much to these people and that they would go to any extreme to make the prisoners understand that they were the sole masters of their fate. He closed his eyes, shaking this head slowly to dismiss the horrible nightmare of the shooting of the young boy and he gave a silent prayer for him to the God above.

"We don't even know his name," he told himself, putting one step in front of the other mechanically, holding the heavy body of the unconscious pilot the best he could. The next day they reach a new VC camp, much larger than the previous one, with a multitude of VC and some regular North Vietnamese Army soldiers coming and going from it. The camp was well hidden from any plane or chopper passing overhead with everything camouflaged by the jungle vegetation.

This time Hue separated them, each one to a cage, imposing isolation on them. For a week, the routine was the same as it had been in the other camp and then one day Colonel Hue made his appearance at Pierce's cage, Paul and Wilson trailing behind, their hands tied.

Pierce saw him coming and he wondered what was about to take place. By now he knew that every time Hue showed his face, something bad happened and he was sure that this time would not be any different. And he was right.

Colonel Hue stopped at the door to the cage and at a nod from his head a VC guard open the door, ordering Pierce to step out.

Hue lighted one of his cigarettes, inhaling the smoke and letting it out slowly, while his eyes watched the three men coldly.

"You are war criminals," he started, flicking ashes on the ground, standing in front of the prisoners. "But the people's Government of Comrade Ho Chi Min allows us to be merciful with our criminals." He paused for a second, throwing the finished cigarette on the ground, the highly polished boot grinding the butt. He glanced at the men and continued talking; "You will attend political school from now on and you will be instructed in the history of our country and our fight for freedom from the imperialistic U.S. government. After the classes, we expect you to write a statement that you oppose the war in Vietnam."

Hue had barely finished talking when Pierce started laughing, the sound incongruous in the jungle setting.

Hue's eyes turned cold at the laugh and his face was etched in anger. "Why you laugh?" he asked.

"If you think that me or my men are going to listen to your stupid propaganda," he said softly, "you have something else coming."

"You refuse?"

"Damn right I do, Hue. You can probably force us to listen to it, but as far as me or my men believing any of that hogwash, you might as well forget it."

"Very well," Hue said and two guards detached themselves, taking hold of Pierce, pushing him roughly ahead. Paul and Skip Wilson did the same and soon enough more guards were brought forward, pushing and shoving the prisoners to a makeshift classroom. For hours the VC cadre and some officers took turns talking, instructing the prisoners in their history. But the guards and instructors were playing a losing battle with the three Americans. Within minutes of the lessons starting, all three of them were asleep, the guards hitting and punching them awake. This continued for hours, the bamboo sticks inflicting the punishment, and the Americans absorbing everything the VC dished out to them. Finally Hue declared that Pierce was not worthy of the Vietnamese lenient treatment and ordered Pierce to be taken away, putting him in isolation again. Hue knew that he didn't stand a chance of making any of the Americans confessed to war crimes as long as Pierce was setting an example for the others. He would keep Pierce in isolation and maybe the others would cooperate somehow. Paul and Wilson were taken to their cages and this time Paul was really concerned for his friend.

The next day Pierce was removed from his isolation cage, stripped completely and put in a special cage, laying flat on his back, his hands in irons, unable to move, defecating and urinating upon himself. His diet consisted of one bowl of rice and a handful of salt a day with one cup of fetid water. For ten days this continued until Paul thought that his friend was surely dead. At the end of the ten days Hue opened the cage and Pierce stumbled out, his body emaciated, covered with sores and almost dead of dehydration. VC guards dragged him to the isolation cage, threw him inside and left him alone. From his cage, Paul looked at his friend being dragged to the isolation cage again, knowing that Pierce was close to death. In passing, Pierce glanced at Paul, managing a weak smile and Paul knew he was trying to tell him he was okay. That night, just before darkness engulfed the camp completely, Paul saw Pierce being taken out of the isolation cage, his body dragged by the guards and thrown into his cage. He was unconscious and Paul prayed that his friend was okay.

The next morning Hue made his appearance again, walking toward the cage. From his cage, Paul was able to hear the Colonel screaming and yelling at Pierce and a grin flickered across his face. Pierce was giving the colonel an earful, in Vietnamese, making the man loose face with his own people again.

"I'm not confessing to any war crimes, Hue," he heard Pierce yelling. "I don't give a damn what you do to me. All you get is my name and serial number and my rank." Paul heard Hue, screaming also and then he saw him, stumbling in his haste to get out of the cage, Pierce right behind him dragged out by several VC guards.

This time there wasn't any special cage, but Pierce was made to sit on a stool, his hands tied to his ankles, the position bending his back painfully. The long day passed slowly with Pierce in the same position. Paul couldn't eat or sleep watching his friend intently, knowing well that Pierce would die first before giving Hue the satisfaction of breaking him.

The early morning hours saw him still unable to sleep, the daylight showing him that Pierce was still in the same place. He knew his friend had to be in incredible pain by now, but not a sound escaped from Pierce's lips. Colonel Hue made his appearance and the ties binding his wrist to his ankles were cut. Pierce's body refused to unbend for long minutes and the pain that he was experiencing must have been incredible. His forehead was bathed in sweat and his face was etched in a snarl of agony, his mouth open in a silent scream. The guards stood around, smiling at the man's antics while Hue stood to the side watching also.

Pierce unfolded his body slowly and like a man a hundred years old, he stood up, facing Hue. Paul gasped at the condition of his friend and then his eyes saw something that left him dumfounded. Pierce took a step toward Hue, lifted his middle finger and smiled.

Paul Gallagher was aghast at what he had seen, his mind knowing well that Hue would go berserk at the affront. And so it was.

With a cry of rage and consternation, Hue closed the space between he and Pierce in one step, the riding crop slashing furiously at the man. Over and over the crop came down until Pierce stumbled and went down, an animal scream renting the air. Hue stopped momentarily;

sweat running like a river down his face, his mouth open in a snarl of pure hate and rage at the insult given.

The damn American was making him lose face again, showing his people that he would not break, not even bend no matter what they do to him. Kicks rained on Pierce and then at a nod from Hue, the guards joined in, fists and kicks pummeling the body, rifle butts striking him about the head. The awful beating continued for a long time, with Paul and Skip yelling at Hue to stop it, but all to no avail. When it finally stopped, the inert figure of Captain Elton Pierce lay unmoving on the ground, blood seeping slowly from cuts on his head. From where he was Paul was unable to see if his friend was still alive and once again, his mind was full of desperation, the rage clouding his judgment, his heart beating wildly. Frustration built up in him at his inability to help his friend and he cursed and raved at Hue and his minions.

Colonel Hue walked over to Paul's cage and like a visitor to a zoo, his eyes surveyed the man inside. He lit another cigarette and his brown eyes fixed on Paul. "Perhaps you would not be so stubborn," he said, his voice almost a whisper, "and would give me what I want."

Paul didn't answer immediately, his mind a whirlwind of thoughts. When he did answered, it was like a man who had just reached an important decision. "I'm not giving you anything, Hue," he replied coldly. "Not now, not ever."

Colonel Hue remained impassive, watching Paul, wondering what it was about these Americans that made them so damn stubborn. He knew that Pierce was almost dead and by now he knew also that no matter what the torture or punishment, Pierce would not budge. The man had an incredible ability to resist no matter what amount of pain was introduce and would probably die before he would give anything to him. He took a drag from the cigarette, taking the smoke deep into his lungs, disgusted at the way things were going. He had expected to have a confession by now from one of the Americans, something his people up North could use against the imperialistic Americans and the puppet regime of the South, but so far he had failed in his attempts.

He had to get something from one of them and soon, he thought wearily. He wanted to get back to North Vietnam, to Hanoi, and he saw the confession from one of the Americans as his ticket back to Hanoi. He was a well-educated, refined man and he missed his comforts, especially the French wine and food that he had gotten use to in France. Educated at the Soborne, in Paris, he spoke French and English and despite his allegiance to the party and the Communist ideology, he didn't see anything wrong with wanting his creature comforts. Besides he was tired of running around the jungle, fighting the South Vietnamese and the Americans with just a bunch of farmers that didn't have any idea who Sartre was or by the same token, Mozart. He had fought the French in Dienbienphu and his dedication to the cause had brought him to the attention of General Giap. At first that was something to really be proud of, enjoying the recognition and the admiration of other officers. But then he had been chosen by Giap to advise and lead a battalion of VC in South Vietnam and had been doing so now for almost five years, fighting the corrupt government of South Vietnam first and then the Americans. He inched his body toward the cage and when he spoke again, his voice was just a whisper, slow and monotonous, almost hypnotic in its intensity.

"You and your captain can be free of all these punishment," he said, "if you just help me. Food and medicine will be delivered to you. No more beatings, no more torture."

He was silent for a second and then he continued: "All I want is cooperation from you, a confession saying you are sorry that you participate in this war."

For a moment, Paul's mind reflected on Hue's words and then he shook his head emphatically. "I'm not helping you get anything from us."

Hue's eyes centered on him and a grin flickered momentarily on his face. "I have the power of life or death over you and if you don't summit to my desires, I'll have you shot, your body left to rot on the jungle floor." He stopped then, his hand going to his tunic, his fingers plucking an envelope from it. "And you will never see your child."

Something caught in Paul's throat, an inhuman sound escaping from his lips at the words from Hue and at sight of the envelope.

"I' don't give a damn what you do, Hue," Paul said, enraged at the smiling face in front of him. Oh God, how he would love to have the smirking face close to him, he thought, emotions welling inside of him.

"You will be next," Colonel Hue said softly, "and by the time I'm finish, you will give me what I want."

"Don't bet on it," Paul said with more bravado than he was feeling. He had seen the handiwork of Hue and his mind shuddered at the thought of what he was about to face at his hands.

"You are a fool," Hue snapped angrily at Paul. Swiftly, he whirled around and was gone. VC guards picked up Pierce's body, dragging him away, out of Paul and Skip's sight and once again, Paul wondered what was coming.

Chapter 23

Somewhere Close to the Cambodian Border
U Minh Forest
South Vietnam
March 1965

Alton Pierce woke up to a world on incessant pain, the nausea welling in his throat. He shook his head slowly, bright stars jumped in front of his eyes. He tried to open his eyes and couldn't, finally realizing that they were swollen shut. He swallowed the bitter gal in his mouth and tried to relax his body, the pain something alive, eating at him.

He felt his brain slipping, like on a wet pavement, a dark fog enveloping his senses. The steady amount of pain that had been dished out to him was finally eroding his mind and his body. A sharp lance of pain went through him, the intensity making him whimper, and the nausea welling in his throat again. He opened his mouth and green fluid escape from his lips, the taste of the bile gagging him. The sharp pain from his back wound came back again and his whole body twisted at the unrelenting onslaught, thrashing around involuntarily. His eyes felt like they were about to explode and finally Alton Pierce quit resisting and mercifully, he fainted, his mind unable to cope any longer with the reality of pain.

When he woke up again, it was to find himself in the same situation as before. A tear made its way down the corner of his right eye and a sob caught in his throat. He was so tired of the pain, his constant companion as of late and his mind was rebelling at the mere thought that more would be forthcoming. He tried to think clearly, his brain refusing to stay sharp. He knew that the starvation diet, the lack of water, the inhuman treatment and the torture were taking its toll on him and his mind craved solace. But he also knew that if he gave up, then all the suffering would have been for nothing. He was not going to submit to Hue and he would not give him anything to use against his country. He tried to move his body to release the pain, but was unable to do so, his mind finally realizing that he was pinned down to the floor of a cage. His arms were tied at his back and thick irons were attached to his ankles. A rope was tied above the elbow joints, making it impossible for him to move his arms at all, the circulation cut, the arms turning black slowly.

Pierce tried to focus his reeling brain away from the pain. Somehow he had to escape reality, sending his mind away from the constant pain. He set his mind to think of other things beside the pain, detaching his mind, retreating into a world of his own making. Slowly, ever so slowly, the pain that was his constant companion started to let go, his brain finding solace in the thoughts about his family, friends he had known and places he had been, anything to get his brain away from thoughts of pain and torture. This worked for a while and then he was brought back to reality by a VC guard talking outside the cage, the door opening and the guard coming over to him. The VC dropped a bowl of something hot on the ground, together with a cup of water, releasing his bonds, dragging him out of the "special" cage, laughing at the man convulsing on the floor.

Muffled sounds of pain escape from Pierce's lips when circulation was restored and he cursed himself for being so weak. He clamped his mouth shut, willing his emaciated, tortured body to absorb the incredible pain, beads of sweat covering his forehead. After several minutes he was finally able to struggle to a sitting position, his mind numb, his scrawny chest rising and falling slowly. He reached for the stinking bowl of watery soup, forcing himself to swallow the stinking mess slowly, making it last as long as possible. When that was finished, he drank the filthy water and then lay back on the ground, taking stock of his position.

Hue was playing his game now, dishing out the torture everyday in order to break him. Thoughts about Hue brought a red haze to his eyes and Alton Pierce cursed him softly. The man was without a shred of dignity or integrity and definitely didn't play by the same rules as everybody else. The man didn't conform to the Geneva Convention rules for the treatment of prisoners and Lee Ashworth and that other poor boy were dead, Pierce thought, feeling the anger washing over him. Those two men could be alive today if only Hue had followed the rules of fair play. But Hue was not going to do that and he would continue to torture them in order to get what he wanted. Colonel Hue was a sadistic bastard who not only enjoyed inflicting pain for the sake of doing so, but also felt that he was justified in torturing prisoners of war because his country had declare them war criminals. That the torture would also bring him what he wanted was secondary. He would exert his control over the prisoners any way he chose and if in the process some were killed, so be it.

Pierce shook his head slowly, forcing himself to think clearly. This was war, yes, but even in war men didn't have to lose sight of their humanity or their sense of fair play. He was sure that if the roles were reverse, he would do the right thing, regardless of what the situation was. He was a soldier and an American officer, ruled by their code of conduct and also by the way he was brought up, but Colonel Hue was different, much different.

He would probably end up killing us all, Pierce told himself. Noise next to the cage brought him back to reality. The guard was coming and Pierce shrank back involuntarily, his body reacting to the next oncoming onslaught of pain. Once again the ties were put into place and Pierce was left in the same position as before. Slowly, he felt the pain return and once again, his brain started the process of escaping reality, sending his mind as far away as possible from the confines of the cage.

For ten days he was left in the cage, the only break in the continuous torture the daily feeding of the watery soup twice a day. Unable to move, he had defecated and urinated upon himself, the smell emanating from the cage revolting in the heat. Alton Pierce had managed to escape the reality of the torture, sending his mind adrift, but his body was showing the wearing effects of the torture. He was weak and filthy, his rib cage showing clearly, his stomach in constant pain due to hunger pangs. His hair was falling out and his eyes were dull, almost lifeless.

For the first time in ten days Paul was able to see his friend out of the especial cage and his heart was glad. He looked awful, but he was alive and Paul Gallagher gave a prayer to heaven at the sight of his friend. Pierce walked slowly passed the cage and his eyes glanced at Paul, a smile breaking his face. With that and a nod of his head he told Paul he was okay. Shuffling slowly back to his cage, he was pushed roughly in by the VC guard and left alone.

Pierce sat on the ground, lowering his battered body slowly, feeling like he was an old, old man. He leaned his back against the bamboo poles and closed his eyes, his mind marveling at the thought that there was no real pain now, just a dull ache emanating from every part of his body. During the long hours of torture, playing mind games to minimize the pain, he had come to realized that up to a certain point he was able to stand it, the mind conjuring all kinds of thoughts to relegate the pain to a subconscious level. That worked, but just up to a point, then the body would rebel and the pain would come crashing through his defenses, the body finally giving up, the mind once again taking control and sending him into an unconscious world.

He smelled himself and almost gagged, shaking his head at the foul odor. Lord, how I wish for some water to wash the stink off me, Pierce thought, knowing that it was just wishful thinking.

For minutes he sat still, unmoving, wondering what was next, knowing well that Hue would not leave him alone for long. His eyes glanced at the jungle close by and he heard the sound of birds flying by. The sunrays filtered down through the jungle canopy, creating a surreal world of shadows and lights and for a moment everything was quiet, peaceful.

He thought about his father and mother and wondered how they were dealing with all this. His father could handle it, he knew that, but his mother was different. She was sick and her heart was not the strongest anymore. Lord in heaven, how he missed them, he thought, his eyes wet, feeling the emotions welling inside of him.

Alton Pierce sighed deeply, enjoying the seconds of peace, refusing to let go into despair. Something inside of him told him that his days were numbered, that rest was close at hand. Captain Pierce bowed his head, closed his eyes and prayed, asking his God to sustain him one more time for the ordeal he knew would be the final showdown between he and Colonel Hue.

Chapter 24

Key West, Florida
March 1965

Major General Pierce (retired) hung up the phone, cursing softly. He had made the same call, to the same number, countless times since Alton's disappearance, but it was always the same. Nothing new to report, the voice of the young man at the other end of the line was one of almost complete boredom. Pierce stood up stiffly, massaging the right knee that had been giving him trouble lately, thinking that he would probably go crazy waiting to hear something from the Army concerning his son. Here it was almost two years later and the damn people at the Pentagon still didn't have any idea what the hell had happened to Alton and his men, if they were alive or dead or just prisoners of war somewhere in North Vietnam. They had just disappeared and were listed as missing in action and that was all.

General Donovan had kept his word and had done his best to get information, but he had encounter the same walls Pierce had and in the end had been left with a sour taste in his mouth at the inability of the Army or better said, of the U.S. government, to find out about their own men captured or killed in Vietnam during the early stages of the war. Not even the Red Cross had been able to locate them and so far the North Vietnamese government, if they had them, were not talking either.

It was frustrating, General Pierce thought, not knowing about his son. Time had not assuage his pain at all and he knew without a shadow of a doubt that no matter how long it took, he would continue to have hope that his son was alive. He could live with the fact that his only son had die fighting for his country. Hell, he was a soldier and death didn't hold any terrors for him in that respect. But the fact that nobody knew if his son was dead or alive was the all consuming fire in him. There was no way to put to rest something like that, he knew that and so he prayed for the day he would know for sure. He wanted to know desperately and at the same time he dreaded it. He had made several trips to Washington and the Pentagon, pestering his friends and acquaintances to no end, even going so far as to go straight to the Chief of Staff of the Army, an old friend, but everything had been for nothing. Nobody could give him what he wanted and while everybody was sorry, there was no news about the missing men.

All he could do now was pray, pray and hope and the rest was up to the Almighty God above.

* * * *

Mason City, Iowa
March 1965

Bill Gallagher surveyed the wheat fields with an experienced eye, glancing at the sky above for any indication of rain. Like any other farmer, his life and the crops he planted were closely related to weather and a bad season could spell disaster for him and his neighbors.

"But all that is in the hands of God," he told himself quietly, walking toward his tractor and climbing in. He put the huge machine in gear, listening absent mindlessly to the rumble of the engine, his thoughts far away now.

He sighed deeply at his train of thought, realizing that as usual, his mind was centered on one thing; his son Paul.

He crested a hill overlooking the house and he stopped, turning the engine off, listening to the pings from the rapidly cooling motor. The sky was a tapestry of colors, the evening sun almost over the horizon now, bathing the land with the last dying rays. The wind whispered softly and he shuddered briefly, shaking his head.

Bill Gallagher took a handkerchief from his overall pocket and wiped his weather-beaten face. At times like this he really missed his son, the pain of not knowing where he was or if he was dead or alive, eating at him like a cancer.

He felt the wetness in his eyes, something that happened more and more often these days and he wiped them with his strong, callused hand irritably. He was not a crying man, but the emotions surging in him when he thought about his son always made him want to cry. He loved all his children, but Paul was his first-born and the boy had always held a special place in his heart. He was so much like him that it was uncanny, the resemblance something more than just physical. His mind was tortured with constant thoughts about him and his heart was in agony at the idea that his son could be laying dead in some forgotten land, away from his family and those dear to him. The fact that they didn't have any idea what had happened to him was also a matter of torment for the family and even after almost two years of uncertainty, they were still unable to find peace.

The Army had kept them informed to the best of their ability, but just like them, they were in the dark about Paul and the other men with him.

Bill Gallagher remained sitting for long moments and just like most days, he raised his eyes to heaven and prayed silently for his son and his friends, dead or alive. After that, he turned the engine of the tractor back on and slowly he made his way to the house. He would continue to wait and in waiting he would trust his God. One way or the other, it would be right.

CHAPTER 25

The White House
Washington, DC
The Oval Office
March 1965

Lyndon Baines Johnson was alone in his office; even the perpetual presence of the Secret Service was gone. His eyes were closed as he sat with shoulders slumped forward, his strong fingers massaging his temples. He opened his eyes, red rimmed and tired, the result of a long nights spent reading reports and checking and rechecking figures and estimates with his staff about Vietnam. More and more that far off country was taking incredible chunks of his time, draining his energy as well as the coffers of the United States. The great hopes that he had envisioned for his domestic policies were put on hold while the damn war in South Vietnam swallowed everything else.

While he considered himself an expert in domestic issues, he was insecure as hell in foreign policy issues and the war that had being entrusted to him after Kennedy's assassination was something that he had no stomach for.

He didn't want to give the impression that he was soft on Communism, but South Vietnam, with its incredible appetite for men and equipment were really draining and stopping his favorite causes, his domestic programs. And regardless of what he wanted to accomplish in foreign policy, it continued to move toward an escalation of the war in South Vietnam. He didn't want an escalation, but he sure as hell didn't want to be labeled as the man who lost a so-called democracy to communism either and therefore, was caught in a quandary. He wanted a peaceful solution to the damn war, but deep inside of him knew that it wasn't possible and that North Vietnam would not accept anything short of taking over the whole country. And that he couldn't accept. He was not about to be accused as the man who betrayed Kennedy's commitment to South Vietnam.

The President stood up, loosening the tie around his neck, glancing at the papers in his hand for the ump-teenth time. It was a memo from McGeorge Bundy and just like the one a few weeks before; it represented the views of most of his principal staff concerning the present situation on the war in South Vietnam. This time the memo had been signed by Rusk, Bundy and McNamara and the consensual opinion was that without an escalation of manpower and equipment, South Vietnam would be lost to the enemy in a short period of time.

And so, the President of the United States told himself, I must commit ground forces to this war, and God help us all.

On March 8, 1965 the Marines of the 9th Expeditionary Brigade landed in Da Nang's Red Beach, Republic of South Vietnam, soon to be followed by the Army first combat unit, the 173rd Airborne Brigade. The war in Vietnam had just escalated and from then on, it would be fought as a conventional war.

Chapter 26

U Minh Forest
VC Prison Camp
Republic of South Vietnam
June 1965

Life in the VC prisoner's camp had not changed much for the captured men. The beatings were as regular as the rising sun and the torture and inhumane treatment were an everyday affair for them. Colonel Hue was absent quite often from the camp and at those times, their lives were slightly better, the guards leaving them alone for the most part. But when Hue came back, the indoctrination tactics continued and on most days, the guards had to beat the three prisoners in order to make them sit still and listen to the officers and cadre. More often than not, Pierce would end in the "special" cage for days at a time, while he laughed and curse the VC guards in their own language. Paul was always afraid that one day Hue would have enough and Pierce would end up dead. The brunt of the inhumane treatment was always directed toward Pierce. Wilson and Gallagher added their voices to curse and yell at the guards when the beatings started. It was obvious to Paul that Colonel Hue was determined to break Pierce and that if the man didn't bend or break soon he would kill him. It was like Hue had issued a challenge and Pierce had risen to the occasion, picking up the gauntlet. Paul had pleaded with his friend and superior officer not to antagonize the bastard, but Pierce's replay was always the same. "That bastard can go to hell, Paul," he would say, "because he is getting nothing from me. I would rather die than play his game."

And that's probably what would happen, Paul had told himself many a time, watching the deadly game played by the two men, one eager to break the American and get what he wanted, while Pierce refused to be bend or be broken by the sadistic Colonel. It was a situation that eventually would spell doom for Pierce and Paul watched the deadly ballet with mounting anxiety. This was a no win situation for Pierce, but Paul knew well that once Pierce's mind was made up, Hue would have to kill him just to save face.

For several days now Hue had been missing from the camp, the prisoners getting a respite from the beatings and the indoctrination, but the respite didn't last long. Among a great deal of shouting and commotion, Hue returned to the camp and it was obvious that the man was pissed. A crude bandage could be seen on his head, stained with dark blood, his clothes torn and filthy. It appeared that the Colonel had encountered a fight and he had been the looser. From the walls of the cage, Paul could see several wounded VC being dragged into the camp by their friends, and a grin flickered momentarily on his face. It seemed to Paul that someone had twisted the tiger's tail and got scratched in the process and that someone had been Hue.

Hue went directly to Pierce's cage and his voice rose with the occasion, spiting curses and invectives, blaming the Americans for whatever had happened to him.

"Damn his soul...here we go again," Paul said, loud enough to be heard by Skip Wilson in the next cage. The Viet Cong guard had turned his attention to the sounds of argument, walking a few paces away from the cages.

"I'm afraid so," Wilson said, wondering what the hell had transpired to get Hue in a pissing mood. He had come to know the sadistic Colonel well, just like Pierce had told him and he shuddered at the prospect of more beatings. He had shrunk to just about nothing on the starvation diet that was their daily fare, his stomach in constant pain, the diarrhea making him weak and the torture and beatings sapping his strength and his will to live. He had lost all his hair and his skin was wrinkled and flaky. He also had the sneaky suspicion that he had beriberi and a host of other jungle diseases. Lately his body ached terribly and the headaches were so bad that he thought his skull would split, the thoughts flashing in his mind that he had contracted malaria. On several occasions now, he had almost given up, wishing to end the pain, restraining himself only because of the example given by his superior officer, Captain Pierce and by Paul Gallagher. The captain was something else, one tough son of a bitch and it was obvious that he was giving the Colonel fits with his behavior. And the lieutenant was not far behind, Wilson thought, remembering some of his antics. He knew they were a special breed, men who took their oaths seriously, patriotic to no end and men who would not give an inch no matter what. Their code of conduct was something they lived for and honor was more, much more than just a word. But how in the hell the two men endured was a mystery to him. He had only been a prisoner for a short time and already he was wishing he were dead. Thoughts of torture made him tremble, his mind rebelling at the pain. He was no hero and he knew that sooner or later Colonel Hue would start on him and he would probably give the man whatever he wanted. Paul and Pierce had been at it for almost two years and they still found it in themselves to challenge the son of a bitch, Hue. Just like now, he thought, listening to the voices reaching him.

A few seconds later, Hue strode away from the cage holding Pierce and in moments Pierce followed. VC guards came toward their cages and he and Paul were taken out, pushed roughly by the guards. All three of them were lined up in front of Hue who looked at them like a hunter viewing his pray. The eternal cigarette dangle from his cruel lips and beads of sweat were visible on his face. The man looked a mess with his filthy stain and bloody clothes, and there was a deranged look in his eyes, also something like fear, Pierce thought, fixing his eyes on the man, wondering what had put Hue in such a funk.

When all three of the prisoners were in front of Hue, the man started a tirade, talking for long minutes about the American aggressors and the puppet regime of South Vietnam. The tirade ended with Hue screaming about war criminals and the penalty they would pay. When the man had finally calmed himself, his chest was rising and falling rapidly, his eyes still haunted.

When he spoke again, his voice had regained a semblance of control and he directed his words to Captain Pierce. "I'll give you until tomorrow to give me a confession admitting that you are war criminals," he said in a slow, ice voice, "or I'll kill you."

His eyes were centered on Pierce and for a second Paul Gallagher felt a chill run over him. The damn, crazy son of a bitch was not playing, Paul knew that and whatever had transpired in the jungle had pushed Hue dangerously close to the edge. He looked at the three prisoners and then he whirled around, walking away from them. Pierce saw him go and he shook his head.

"I'm not going to give him anything guys," he said, his voice firm, resolute, "and I expect you two to do the same."

"I believe he means business this time Alton," Paul said softly, his eyes following the rapidly disappearing figure of Colonel Hue.

"I don't care Paul. There is nothing he can do to me to make me change my mind."

Unknown to them, Colonel Hue had finally attacked the Special Forces camp, A-28, and had come out the loser. He had thought the camp would fall to him easily, but the defenders had put up a concerted effort and the fight had dragged on through the night. AC 47 'Spookies' had made their appearance during the night and the sky was lighted with the incredible stream of tracer bullets coming down on the attackers. In the early hours of the morning Hue saw reinforcements pouring in by helicopter and shortly afterwards, the airplanes made their appearance. Napalm bombs came rushing down, inflicting death and destruction on his men, the smell of burned human flesh clogging his nostrils. After the planes, the choppers had made their appearance again, his men having to retreat, dying by the score. A bullet had creased his head and several pieces of fragment had peppered his back and Hue considered himself lucky to be alive, escaping from the enemy. He had been livid with rage at the result of his attack and the loss of so many of his men at the hands of the Americans and had walked into the camp with revenge on his mind.

The VC guards pushed the prisoners into their respective cages and left them alone. The rest of the day and night passed without any further events, but Paul was not able to sleep at all. He knew that Pierce would never give in to Hue and that in the morning if Hue was still in the same frame of mind he would execute him.

The hours passed slowly until finally the first rays of daylight penetrated the gloomy interior of the jungle, the shadows lengthening, and the new day braking upon them full of uncertainty. The camp came slowly to life, the sound of men talking and the smell of food cooking permeating the air. A gentle breeze ruffled the leaves and everything was peaceful, dreamlike, belying the events that would transpire shortly.

Their food was brought in, as usual a watery soup and a chunk of old, stale bread. Paul tried to eat, but his stomach was in bad shape this morning and all he managed was a few sips of the hot brew before his insides were spewing it back out. He glanced in the direction of Skip Wilson, seeing the man lying on the ground, coiled into a fetal position. Paul was worry about him, realizing that the young man was ill, possibly with malaria or some other jungle disease. He pushed his food aside, his eyes alert to any movement in the camp, waiting impatiently for any sign of Colonel Hue.

While he waited, his mind in turmoil, Alton Pierce was doing the same thing. He had spent the night in prayer, thinking that if tomorrow was going to be his last day on this earth, then his soul needed to come to terms with his God. He had thought long and hard about

Hue's request, realizing that it would be easy to accede to his demands. But he also knew that there was no way that he could betray his country and give the enemy something to embarrass the United States. They were not criminals of war; they were soldiers, carrying on the duties set forth to them by their leaders. But he knew that all the rhetoric was nothing but communist propaganda and that the enemy would take anything they could get in order to use it against them. If he was to die today for holding fast against the enemy's request, then so be it. This was a matter of honor and he knew that his father and mother would be proud of him and besides he was an officer in the U.S. Army and if he let the enemy use him for propaganda reasons, the lives of American soldiers would be put in jeopardy.

A VC guard brought his food and he let it lay, realizing that he wasn't hungry. He was at peace with himself, ready for whatever was in store for him. His thoughts went to his parents again and a smile came to his face, remembering the "old man" and his mother. His father was his hero and he owed him for his stubbornness and for his sense of honor. He had sat enthralled as a young man, listening to his father talk about his experiences during the Second War and then Korea. The old man had not tried to embellish anything, talking frankly about losing men in combat and the pain that was the lot of the field commanders when the letters were written to the folks back home, telling then about their loses.

Who would write his parents? Pierce thought, shaking his head at the way his thoughts were going. His parents probably didn't even knew if he was alive or dead and if he was killed here, unless some kind of miracle happened, they would never know his fate either.

He stood up, glancing at the VC guard in front of the cage. He was a new one, a young man, almost a kid and it dawned on Pierce that of late he had seen new guards around a lot. Also the sound of airplanes and helicopters flying overhead had increased within the last month or so. Maybe the war was heating up, Pierce told himself. The corner of his eye caught movement and he snapped his head around. Colonel Hue was coming.

This time the man looked his usual self, clean and well dressed, the skin of his face shining, hair combed. The Colonel made his way, finally stopping in front of Captain Pierce's cage. For a long moment the Colonel didn't say anything, just stood there with an inscrutable look on his face, his eyes taking the man in the cage. "Captain Pierce," he finally said, taking a step toward the cage, his face now mere inches from the bamboo poles. He was so close that Pierce could smell him, a mixture of some kind of cologne and other smells that were alien to him. Pierce shook his head at the incongruence of the moment. The man in front of him was clean, recently washed, and smelling of cologne, all in a jungle setting and with him smelling like a garbage dump. The sound of Hue's voice brought him out of his reverie and he listen to the words. Hue was speaking Vietnamese, probably for the benefit of the VC guards next to him, Pierce thought.

"Have you thought about my request?" Hue asked softly, his liquid brown eyes fixed on Pierce. His nose wrinkled in distaste as usual, at the odor emanating from Pierce and the waste hole in the cage and a grin flickered on Alton's face. The damn Colonel sure was a sensitive man, he thought, enjoying the man's discomfort, even if it was slight.

"I have, Colonel," Pierce said. "And the answer is the same as always. We are not signing a damn thing."

The unholy light that Pierce had seen in Colonel Hue's eyes before made its appearance again, the swarthy skin paling.

"How can you be so…so stubborn?" Hue said, the words rushing out. "This time I'll kill you."

"I believe you Hue, but I would rather be dead than betray my country."

For long seconds Hue remained transfixed, his eyes opening and closing rapidly. Was the American bluffing him, or was the man really ready to die. Surely nobody wanted to die for a piece of paper and a few words written on it. Or would they? Hue was baffled. He had thought all along that Pierce would probably crumple at the end, that the man would give him what he wanted instead of dying. But no, the damn American was calling his bluff, the smirk on his face showing Hue that he didn't give a damn about what could happened to him. He let the white rage take hold of him slowly, until his whole body was trembling with the force of his emotions. If he didn't do what he had said he would, the whole camp would be laughing at him behind his back, shamed by the American again.

"Very well," he said through clenched teeth. "Come."

At a nod from his head, the VC guards opened the cage and Pierce was pushed out, his hands tied. Hue started walking, followed closely by Pierce and then the VC guards. As soon as he started walking, he started singing softly, the haunting words of the national anthem flowing freely from his cracked lips. When they passed the cage where Paul and Wilson were being held, Pierce swiveled his head, his eyes fixed on his friend.

"Tell my parents that I loved them," he said in passing, his voice strong, without a quiver. "And that I die like a man…with honor. Good-bye my friend."

Paul Gallagher heard the words of his friend and his heart stopped beating, resuming a second later with such force that his whole body shook like a wheat stalk pushed by the wind. He held to the bamboo wall, shaking his head at the extraordinary events taking place right in front of him. Surely Hue was playing a game now, he thought grimly. He would not dare kill an American officer just like that, would he? But then his mind went back to the day that the young man had been shot by Hue in the jungle and with a cold shudder, he realized that Hue would not hesitate to kill them all if he didn't get what he wanted.

He shook his head in consternation, his mind refusing to believe what his eyes were telling him. Was Hue playing some kind of diabolical game with their heads or was the son of a bitch for real now?

"Damn you, Hue," he yelled at the top of his lungs, enraged now. "Wait a fucking minute, you murdering bastard. You can't do that."

Hue continued walking; not paying him any attention and Paul realized that he was powerless to stop whatever Hue had in mind.

"Hue…Hue…damn you, you son of a bitch," he yelled again, banging his head against the bamboo poles in desperation. It was futile, he knew, his heart racing now, beating painfully against his ribs, his mouth dry at the enormity of what he was witnessing. Hue was going to murder Alton, of that he was sure. He felt his throat constricting, the pain incredibly sharp, emotions running wild inside his head.

"Alton…Alton please, give him what he wants," he yelled again, as he watched the figures disappear into the jungle. "Alton!!!"

He sighed deeply, and slumped to the ground, his knees so weak that he couldn't stand any longer. "Jesus…oh Jesus, that bastard is going to kill my friend," he thought, feeling like he was going to drown in his despair, his brain screaming. He closed his eyes, praying to God Almighty to do something, to spare his friend from whatever Hue had planned.

And then a shot ran out. For a second that seemed an eternity to Paul Gallagher, he stood still, the awful import of that single shot searing his brain. And then he screamed, a primordial, inhuman scream full of pain and rage that chilled the blood of the VC guard outside his cage. For a long moment, the horrible sound of the scream lingered in the air and then it was gone, leaving Paul Gallagher shattered. He closed his eyes and the tears came, hot and burning, his body rocking slowly back and forth, his mind closing itself, relegating the incredible pain away from him.

* * * *

Alton Pierce walked past the cage holding his friend and felt his mouth go dry. This was the hour of reckoning and he was determined not to show any weakness in front of his enemy. He squared his shoulders, putting on a brave face for his friend, forcing his voice to remain strong.

"Tell my parents that I loved them," he said. "And that I die like a man, with honor. Good-bye my friend."

He saw Paul flinched at the words, the face loosing all color and then he heard the yells and the words of his friend directed at Hue. But this time Hue would not be denied and they continued the walk toward the jungle; Pierce still softly singing the lines of the national anthem. The lingering sound of Paul's voice followed him until finally Hue stopped, turning around to face him. The two VC guards pushed him roughly to his knees and Hue took a step toward him. He took a cigarette from his tunic pocket, lighting it and taking a drag, exhaling the smoke slowly. Alton Pierce looked at the man and then he glanced around him. Everything was crystal clear to him, the sounds of the jungle, the warm breeze ruffling his clothes, caressing his skin. He looked at Hue, fixing his eyes on him, waiting now.

"There is still time," Hue said softly, almost in a whisper and Alton had to strain his ear to catch what the man was saying. The hard, cruel eyes were fixed on him now, unwavering and Alton Pierce knew without a shadow of a doubt that if he didn't give Hue what he wanted, he would be dead within the next few seconds. He wasn't ready to die, hell he didn't want to die, but he was not about to give in to communist propaganda and he was not about to beg for his life. He just couldn't do that and be at peace with his soul.

"Forget it, Hue," he said, shaking his head at the same time.

Hue didn't say a word, just nodded his head. He threw his cigarette butt on the ground, stepping on it and grinding it down and then he walked behind Alton Pierce.

"Captain Pierce," he began, his hand reaching for the revolver at his side. "You are being executed by the orders of the National Liberation Front, due to your criminal actions against the people of Vietnam," Colonel Hue paused for a second, his hand coming up with the revolver, aiming at the base of Pierce's skull. "Do you have anything to say?"

Alton Pierce raised his head to the impenetrable jungle canopy above his head, wishing he could see the sky one more time before dying, but he was not given that wish and he just nodded his head.

"It's a good day to die," he said simply and bowed his head again.

The shot rang out and then, for a tenth of a second Pierce felt pain and a great blinding flash, and then nothing. His body slumped forward, the eyes staring upwards, bulging from the incredible pressure of the shot, his face almost unrecognizable, and blood and brain matter slowly seeping onto the ground. Captain Alton Pierce, 5th Special Forces was dead.

*   *   *   *

Paul Gallagher breathed deeply, trying his best to control the tide of emotions over-whelming him. He felt like a wild animal trapped in a cage with no way out. The fact that he didn't know what had transpired concerning Alton was eating him alive. The voice of Colonel Hue outside the cage brought him back to reality with a start and he whirled around to face the smiling, odious face.

"Your Captain is dead," Hue said, the words like punches, hitting Paul in the middle of his stomach. "And soon it will be your turn." Saying that, he signaled the guard and the cage was opened. The VC guard signaled Paul to come out and he did so reluctantly, wondering what the hell was going to happen now. The two guards pushed him roughly away, in the direction of the jungle and Paul started walking. In a few minutes they had reached the place where he had seen Hue and the guards go into the jungle and at a turn of the small trail, Paul saw the body of his friend. Alton Pierce was slumped on the ground, a puddle of blood disappearing fast beneath him. Flies and ants were already lapping at the blood and Paul rushed to his friend's side. The eyes that were always alive and full of mischief were wide open now, staring blankly at nothing. He tenderly cradled the form of his friend in his lap, unmindful of the blood and the brains staining his clothes, feeling the tears running down his face at sight of his friend.

"Oh Lord…oh Lord," he whispered gently, his hand closing the staring eyes, his heart braking. An incredible rage took hold of him at the inhumanity of the foul deed, his eyes clouded and he glanced up at his tormentor standing close to them, the smirk etched on his face.

And then Paul Gallagher exploded, his body uncoiling in a swift move, his face contorted with pent up rage. He wanted to get his hands on Hue, choke the life out of the bastard, and make him pay for the life of his friend. He had barely started his move when he heard his father's voice whispering to him, the words so clear that it was just like he was standing there next to him. *Don't do it son, please don't.* Through the mist of tears clouding his eyes, he saw Hue take a step back, his eyes registering surprise at the sudden move, the guards moving forward, their rifles leveling at him. With an incredible effort, he stopped himself, the hands balling into fists, his eyes showing all the hate and rage he was feeling at the moment.

"You...you miserable son of a bitch," he said, spittle flying from his lips, his face contorted by the inner rage and the emotions surging through him, the tears flowing freely down his cheeks. "Someday, somehow you will pay for this."

For long seconds the scene was frozen in time and then Hue shook his head and turned away, leaving Paul and the VC guards alone. A shovel was thrown at his feet and once again Paul Gallagher dug a grave for one of his friends. His mind was numb, unable to accept the fact that Pierce was gone. Slowly he dug until finally the VC stopped him and Paul lowered the body of Captain Pierce down. Just like he had done with Ashworth, he did with Pierce and finally he stood up, his lips moving silently in a prayer. When he was finished, he sighed deeply and turned around, walking away, his mind made up. There would be no giving up now and no matter what Hue dished out to him, the answer would be the same as Pierce's.

Chapter 27

U Minh Forest
VC Prison Camp
Republic of South Vietnam
July 1965

It wasn't long after Pierce's death that Colonel Hue decided to start on Lt. Gallagher. Pierce had been stubborn, but perhaps the Lieutenant would prove more malleable. The first time Hue approached Gallagher's cage it was just days after Pierce's murder and Paul was still numb from what had occurred. The death of his friend and superior officer had changed him, giving him a sense of inner peace and a different outlook on the pain and torture that would be forthcoming to him. Alton Pierce had gone to his grave believing that a man's honor and beliefs were something important and that no matter what, a man was nothing if he didn't have faith and courage to stand for his convictions. He had died because he refused to acknowledge the power of life and death that Hue held over him. He had laughed at Hue, taking every torture dished out to him and refused to break or even bend. And in doing that, he had become an inspiration to Paul who knew well that he couldn't do any less than Pierce and be at peace with himself. The road that stretched in front of him was going to be a long, hard one, but he was confident now that somehow he would make it.

He was alone now even with Wilson next to him. The man had malaria and was in bad shape and most of his days were spent in agonizing pain, thrashing wildly on the ground, whimpering like a baby at the onslaught of fever and pain. If something wasn't done soon, Wilson would be the next one buried in the jungle. He glanced at Hue and his eyes closed to slits, hard and uncompromising. Colonel Hue watched him closely and then came straight to the point.

"Are you going to cooperate with me?" he asked in his accented English. Paul looked at him for long seconds before answering him, his eyes speaking volumes. Hue saw a grim determination in the eyes and in dismay; he realized that the man in front of him was no different from Pierce and that he probably would end up killing him too.

"No," Gallagher said finally, his eyes never leaving Hue's face.

This time Hue didn't answer, just nodded his head. He turned around and signaled the VC guard who in turn opened the cage, pushing Paul out.

"Here we go," Paul told himself, knowing well that Hue would not give him any rest from the torture now. He shuddered briefly at what he knew was coming and then his mind thought about Pierce and his resolve turn to iron. Let the damn bastards torture him. He would show them.

The VC guards pushed him forward, stopping at a horizontal pole above his head. There were several tree stumps under the pole and the VC signaled with his head for Paul to climb one while they did the same on the others. With the help of the stumps they were able to reach the height of the pole, tying his arms by the wrist to the pole above. Once that was done, the VC guards dropped down and one of them immediately kicked the stump where Paul was standing. The whole weight of his body came down on his wrist, his feet several inches above the ground, his body swaying. Paul bit his lips, feeling his arms stretch to the limit, the weight of his body causing the ropes to dig into his flesh. He opened his fingers to grasp at the rope, but it was impossible to hold and he had to give up the attempt. Soon enough the circulation was cut off and his hands began to turn black. Hue stopped in front of him to observe the handy work and Paul fixed his eyes on him, a smile etched on his face. At a word from Colonel Hue the black pajamas were stripped from him, leaving him naked and then a VC guard made his appearance with a bamboo pole. Paul saw him approach and he bit his lips hard, drawing blood, knowing that a beating was coming. He clenched his teeth, willing his mind not to scream. At a nod from Hue the pole came crashing down on him, the impact leaving a red bruise on his chest. The pole came crashing down again and again and soon enough Paul Gallagher was screaming at the top of his lungs, cursing Hue, tears of pain and rage falling down his cheeks. How long the beating lasted he didn't knew, but finally a dark well came rushing at him and Paul lost consciousness. Hue glanced at the man swaying rhythmically on the ropes and he smiled sourly, walking away. For the whole day Paul was left to hang from the pole, the insects and the ants feasting on the sweat and blood of his body. During the day it had been hot, the humidity high, making him sweat his precious fluids while the mosquitoes feasted on his blood and then during the night it was so cold that his teeth chattered in one continuous motion.

When morning finally came, he had regained consciousness, feeling his body bruised and battered, covered by insect bites. His eyes were almost swollen shut from the mosquito bites and his body stunk from having defecated on himself. A VC guard approached him, climbing the tree stump to cut the ropes. Paul fell down on the ground and for a long moment, he remained there, absorbing the pain that permeated his whole being. A cup of water and the green looking soup was put next to him on the ground and his stomach revolted at the smell. Nausea welled up in his mouth and he vomited green slimy water, the heaves leaving him empty, his stomach cramping painfully. Several minutes later he took a sipped of the water and eventually was able to sip the nasty green soup. He knew that he needed to eat whatever he could get. He would need all his strength to withstand whatever Hue was going to dish out to him. As soon as he was finished with his meager meal, the VC guards lifted him up and pushing and shoving they threw him in the isolation cage, clamping irons on his legs, forcing him to lie on his back, unable to move or turn around in the cramped interior of the cage.

For ten days he laid there in his own filth and stench, using every available method he knew to escape reality, doing his best to overcome the pain and depression that were his constant companions. Most of the time he succeeded, his thoughts of Susan and his parents sustaining him in his darkest hours, the thoughts of the child he had never seen helped him to retain his sanity. When the pain got to be too much for his tortured body, his mind mercifully fell into unconsciousness, giving him a brief respite from the pain.

At the end of the ten days Hue let him out, returning him to the cage with Wilson who was still weak from the malaria in his body. Wilson took one look at the scarecrow coming into his cage and he was aghast at the apparition from hell. Every rib on Paul Gallagher's chest was visible and the man was covered from head to toe with bruises and welts. Insect bites also covered his body and the odor emanating from him was indescribable.

With a supreme effort, he crawled toward Paul, who was sitting on the ground, his back to the bamboo wall.

"Jesus Christ…Paul, what the hell have those bastards done to you?"

Paul Gallagher opened his eyes and glanced at Wilson, a tired grin playing on his face. Hue had dished out a lot to him in the last two weeks, but he had not broken down. Pierce would have been proud of him, Paul thought, sighing deeply. Even after all this time, it was hard for him to accept the fact that Pierce was gone; murdered by the sorry excuse for a human being that was Hue. He shook his head and glanced at Wilson again. Talking was an incredible effort, and the pain that coursed through his body was something alive, sapping his remaining strength. No matter what part of his body he moved, pain would shot from it. His nerves were raw and the thought of pain alone would send his body into spasms of shuddering.

Noise at the entrance to the cage caught their attention and their eyes grew with suspicion at the sight that greeted them. One of the VC guards opened the cage and another pushed a five-gallon can in, tossed a set of what passed for clean, black pajamas in, closed the door again and left. For a long second, Paul eyed the can with mistrust, wondering what the hell Hue was up to now, but finally curiosity got the best of him and he moved his body forward. Reaching the can, he looked inside and to his amazement he saw an almost full container of clean water. He put his hand in it gingerly, not really wanting to believe his eyes, expecting something to happened. The hand went in the liquid and it was cold, fresh. Without waiting any longer, Paul put his face inside the can and drank greedily, laughing and choking at the same time. Finally, realizing that Wilson was shouting at him, he sat back down on his haunches. Reaching for the can, he dragged it toward Wilson who attacked the water the same way that Gallagher had and soon both of them had their fill, their stomachs distended. After drinking the fresh water on and off through the day, Paul soaked a rag from his pajamas in it and cleaned himself fairly well and then he did the same for Wilson. For the next two days they were left alone and the food improved some. Paul knew this was just another way for Hue to mess with their minds, but he relished the water and the food, enjoying the psychological boost to his mind. If Hue was thinking that this would turn things around, then he had another think coming and soon he would find out and the torture would start again.

That night before Paul fell asleep he prayed for them all and for his friend Alton Pierce. Just when sleep was about to come, he thought he heard the drone of an airplane and he jumped straight up, wide-awake now, listening eagerly for the sound to repeat itself. But after much straining and listening, the sound was not repeated and Paul finally thought he had been dreaming. Reclining himself back on the hard ground, he closed his eyes, sleep finally overcame him.

Chapter 28

Somewhere Over The U Minh Forest
Republic of South Vietnam
July 1965
0237 hours

Lt. Colonel Matthew J. Murphy, United States Air Force, glanced at the altimeter to his left checking to see if he was high enough above the jungle canopy. The plane he was flying was the C-47, better known as "Puff the Magic Dragon." This was a vintage World War two plane, used extensively by the Air Force in Vietnam to support ground troops and Special Forces camps. He was returning to his base at Binh Thuy, down in the Mekong Delta after expending all his ordnance in the C-47 plane helping a Special Forces camp that was threatened to be overrun by Charlie. They had received the call for help early in the evening and had spent most of the night circling the camp, providing close air support with their side-fired General Electric SUU-11A/A 7.62mm Gatlin type mini gun. The mini guns were capable of dispensing thousands of rounds per minute, creating havoc with the enemy and keeping their heads down. Now he was low on fuel and completely out of ammo, heading for home in a sky that was getting cloudier by the minute.

Colonel Murphy glanced out the window, his experienced eyes checking on the weather conditions. The Air Force weathermen had said that it would rain, but he was sure that they would make base camp way before the rain started. His plane was assigned to the 4th Air Commando Squadron (4th ACS), flight E, stationed at Binh Thuy Air Base. Colonel Murphy had been in Vietnam all of two months and he could tell already that this war was different from any other he had seen. He had flown jets in the Korean War in support of ground troops when he was a young fighter pilot, but this was different.

Murphy wiggled his rump on the seat, trying his best to find a spot that wasn't sore from the long vigil at the Special Forces camp. He was satisfied with the mission, knowing well that their help had broken the heavy concentration of VC trying to overrun the camp. Another C-47 had taken his place and they would continue flying over the camp until daylight or until everything was over for good.

He looked at his instruments again, checking everything and then his eyes stray to the black monitor box that had been installed in his plane just before this mission. Some skinny little runt of a civilian had briefed him extensively about the box. The monitor was hooked to a ball-shaped pod below the fuselage of the plane and according to the civilian "puke", the pod was able to detect heat from any object below with the help of a night periscope and an infrared system in it. The heat source could be from humans or machines, walking or even hiding under the jungle canopy. The "black box" as it was called, was top secret and had arrived recently in Vietnam, with several of them being tested on other aircrafts and helicopters, especially the YO-3A Quiet Aircraft and the OV-1B Mohawk.

Murphy shook his head thinking about the box and his eyes glanced at it again. The greenish tint of the monitor was alive with pulsating red dots, hundreds of them and Colonel Murphy jumped in his seat, surprise etched deeply in his face.

"Well…I'll be damned," he said, getting his co-pilot's attention. "Eddie…look at this shit," he said, his eyes glued to the display on the monitor. Something big was down there, what he didn't know, but if it was men, there was a whole bunch of them in one place. He banked the plane sharply, making a wide circle, seeing the dots disappear on the screen. He checked his altitude and coordinates, making sure of his position and set himself to make a second pass. Within minutes the plane was back on course and both he and the co-pilot centered their eyes on the monitor. Once again the screen lit up like a Christmas tree when the pod reacquired the heat signature below. A small grin of satisfaction flickered across Murphy's face.

"Mark our position exactly, Eddie. We need to pass this on."

"Yes sir," Eddie said, busy already with the coordinates.

Murphy looked out the window at the impenetrable darkness of the jungle below. Nothing could be seen, not a light or a cooking fire, nothing. But the damn machine was telling him that a big contingent of men was down there. He shook his head, thinking that it was probably an enemy camp. He would write a report on the sighting tonight, giving the coordinates and then the report would be passed on down the line, all the way to MACV headquarters (Military Assistance Command, Vietnam). In a couple of days Army intelligence would be looking at it and if somebody thought that it required a second look, an Army unit would be sent to check it out or an Air Force wing would be detached to bomb the hell out of it.

With those thoughts in mind, Murphy banked the plane again, heading for home, while down below, under the jungle canopy, Lt. Paul W. Gallagher put his head down again, thinking that he had being dreaming about a plane overhead.

*   *   *   *

MACV Headquarters
Office of Military Intelligence
Saigon, Republic of South Vietnam
July1965

Colonel (full bird) Jason Albright, MI (Military Intelligence) read the report in his hand for the second time. Something in the back of his mind was telling him that he had seen something similar to this before, something about the area. He threw the paper back on his desk and stood up, searching for a cigarette, finding one and lighting up. He inhaled the smoke deeply, walking back to his desk, his eyes fixed on the damn report. What was it about the area that kept surfacing, he wondered. A C-47 driver had spotted a heavy concentration of men with the new "black box" and the report had being passed down to him for further action, if needed.

He sat down in his chair, his mind searching for whatever it was that kept coming back and finally he had it. He jumped from his chair, snatching the door open with a yank.

"Connelly…get in here," he said, loud enough for PFC (Private First Class) Connelly to hear him despite the noise of several typewriters going on at the same time. "Yes Sir," PFC Connelly answered, getting to his feet and approaching. Colonel Albright held the door open until PFC Connelly made his way into the office.

"Read this," Albright said, handing the report to PFC Connelly. While he read, Albright watched him, thinking that the young man would make a perfect spook. He was just a PFC right now, something that Albright was getting ready to change, but the young man was exceptionally bright, with a razor sharp, almost photographic mind.

He finished reading and raised his eyes to Albright. "Yes sir?" he said softly, his left eyebrow rose in question.

Albright ran his fingers through his short, brown hair, a characteristic gesture when he was exited.

"The area the pilot is talking about, Connelly," Albright started, pacing the floor of the small, cramped office. "What do we have on it?"

PFC Connelly grinned and immediately the answer came back. "Several weeks ago an Army unit, the 173rd Airborne Brigade (Separate), A Company, 1st Battalion of the 503rd Infantry, had a run in with a heavy force of regular NVA and VC in that area. We have reason to believe that the VC unit is the 371st Main Force Battalion." PFC Connelly paused for a second, his forehead creased in concentration and then he continued. "After a firefight, the VC retreated and the 173rd lost contact with then. A few days later we had to pull the 173rd out of the area, so we never had a chance to confirm the report on the VC Battalion."

Albright shook his head, his face etched with a smile. "I don't know how you do it son, but you are the greatest. Thank you."

"Thank you, sir," Connelly said, a grin flickering across his face. He whirled around and exited the office.

Colonel Albright picked up the report again, his face pensive mood showing on his face. Finally his mind set on the course to follow. He sat down to write his report and recommendations, requesting a combat patrol to check the area. If there was a VC battalion in that area they would find out soon and then the bombs would rain down, obliterating everything.

Chapter 29

U Minh Forest
VC Prison Camp
Republic of South Vietnam
July 1965

Soon enough it was back to reality for Paul Gallagher and Wilson, with Colonel Hue making his appearance the next day. All his attention was now on Lt. Gallagher, his mind set on controlling him, breaking him and if not, then he would kill him just like Pierce. He would stop at nothing to get what he wanted from them, even if he had to kill them all. He glanced at the prostrate form of Wilson on the ground, listened to his moaning and then he looked at Paul.

"Did you enjoy the food and water?" he asked softly, the eternal smirk on his face.

Gallagher didn't answered him, his eyes fixed on Hue. After a few seconds of waiting, Hue shook his head slowly.

"Very well…then we will see if you like more punishment." He turned swiftly to the VC guard next to him, talking fast and nodding his head.

Paul sighed deeply, getting his body ready for what was coming. His whole body was still in bad shape and the thought of more pain sent shivers through him, eating at his resolve to endure, but he was not going to be any less than Alton had been and he sure as hell was not going to be weak in front of Hue.

When the door was opened, he didn't wait for the guard to come in. Walking out on his own, he stopped close to his tormentor. Two guards got behind him and he was pushed roughly forward. He started walking when he was pushed again and he tripped, falling down. The moment his body hit the ground the guards were on him, the kicks searching for his stomach and head. Paul rolled the best way he could to avoid the kicks, doubling over to safeguard his groin. For what seemed to him like an eternity, the kicks rained on him, until at a nod from Hue, the VC guards stopped. Paul rolled over again, feeling the nausea filling his mouth, the pain coursing through his body, and stars in front of his eyes.

When the stars faded, he glanced at Hue who was standing next to him, his eyes laughing. "You wish to speak now?" he asked.

Paul laughed, a slow guttural laugh and then he said: "Go to hell, Hue."

Colonel Hue heard the words from Lt. Gallagher and his face became clouded with rage.

"How dare you…you," Hue spit out angrily, never finishing, his booted foot striking Paul in the face. In seconds the man went berserk, striking with the riding crop and kicking the prostrate figure on the ground, curses and yells coming from his mouth. When the rage had been vented enough, Hue stopped, his breathing was ragged, his eyes open wide, filled of fury. He signaled the guards who pick up Gallagher roughly, dragging him to an isolation cage, and throwing him in. For a long moment he was unconscious, blood seeping slowly from cuts on the face and back. He murmured softly to himself, pushing his battered body up, struggling to sit up. But he was too weak and in too much pain. His eyes opened briefly, closing again in blessed unconsciousness and he fell down on his face, remaining still.

How long he remained unconscious he didn't know, but eventually his eyes opened and he struggle to sit, desisting when he realized he was in the isolation cage. His entire body was covered with bruises and his chest was on fire every time he took a breath. He touched the sore spots on his chest gingerly and when the fingers found it, he moaned in pain. He had a cracked rib, possibly more, all courtesy of Hue's kicking him repeatedly. The isolation cage was small, dark, with barely enough room to move. It was also stifling hot and Paul felt the sweat rolling down his body. He touched his face, feeling the swelling under one eye and the soreness on his jaw. This bastard is going to kill me sooner or later, Paul told himself, moving his body to find a better position.

For five days he was left in the isolation cage, the only respite from the intense heat and the cold at night was the periodical trips to the waste hole and the brief time given for a meal. At the end of five days his brain was mush, the forced isolation playing games with his mind, forcing him to extend himself to the limits in the fight to keep his mind sharp, escaping reality by any means whatsoever. Finally, when he was on the edge of going insane, he was let out and thrown in with Wilson. For a change, Wilson was lucid, the fever giving him some momentary respite. He was aghast at the sight of Gallagher when he was thrown in his cage.

"Jesus, man…what have these bastards done to you now?" he asked, his eyes taking in the gaunt figure of Paul Gallagher.

Paul didn't answer, taking a short breath of air in order to minimize the pain from his ribs.

"I believe I have some broken ribs," he said, touching his side. Wilson dragged himself slowly toward Paul and with his help they set the cracked bones of two ribs and using the tops of their pajamas, they tightly bound the chest. After that they talked, Paul grateful for the chance to do so. He had found out that physical isolation was more painful for him than blows, the loneliness praying on his mind, making his tired brain susceptible to all kinds of weird thoughts, eroding his confidence and pushing him slowly into the abysm. And once you start thinking everything is lost, he told himself grimly, then you are dead.

He had to find a way to transcend the physical pain and the desolation imposed by the forced isolation or his life would not be worth much, he thought wearily. He sat still, his mind taking stock of his body and his mental condition, realizing that the constant pain and inhuman treatment were slowly eroding his will to live and more and more his mind was escaping reality, sending him into a world where nothing could touch him. There was a danger in that. If his mind pushed to hard, the trip into the subconscious level could leave him a doddering idiot, unable to face reality again. He had to walk a fine line between allowing his mind to drift away from reality in order to deal with the ever-present pain and keeping his thoughts clear and sharp, dealing with the pain as it came.

An incredible weariness took hold of him and he felt himself sliding into blackness. How he wanted this to be over, he thought, almost giving in to the allure of rest with no pain involved. It would be so easy just to let go completely, surrendering to the pain and despair. All he had to do was call Hue and tell him he would cooperate with him and give him what he wanted. Yeah…so easy, and then his soul would be damned forever and his honor would be just a thing of the past. And he would have betrayed the spirit of his friend, Alton.

He fought the feeling with every ounce of mental strength he could muster, his thoughts going to his wife, Susan, his brain bringing up the image of her. He held on to the image, his eyes closed, refusing to let himself surrender to the darkness, thankful for the strength garnered from Susan. He knew that he had to be strong for her and for the child he had never seen or he would have endured for nothing.

Slowly the feeling passed and when he opened his eyes, it was to find Hue standing by the cage, his eyes fastened on him. He recoiled from the presence of the man, his eyes haunted.

"Tomorrow, you will give me a confession," Hue said, his eyes fixed on Paul, his voice soft. "If you don't, I'll kill you."

Paul didn't answer, not wanting to betray himself. His throat was dry and he felt that if he opened his mouth to talk, nothing would come out. Hue had just given his ultimatum and in the morning, he would die. For a moment longer, Colonel Hue remained standing in front of the cage, the cold eyes of the man never leaving Paul's face. There was a puzzled expression in then, like a man wondering about something and then he whirled around, walking slowly away, leaving the condemned man alone with his thoughts of impending death.

Sleep for Paul was hard to come by that night and it wasn't until the early hours of the morning that Paul Gallagher, his mind and body almost shattered, fell into a troubled sleep.

Chapter 30

Somewhere in the U Minh Forest
Mekong Delta
Republic of South Vietnam
July 1965

1st Lt. Samuel Kennedy glanced at the impenetrable jungle surrounding his platoon and then he glanced at the watch on his wrist, noticing the time. Behind his platoon, elements of the 173rd, 1/503rd Battalion, Bravo Company, were waiting for him to move. His platoon was the point element on a search and destroy mission given to them by the spooks of MI (Military Intelligence) in Saigon, concerned about a possible Main Force VC battalion operating in the area. Kennedy recalled being in the same area several weeks before and engaging a VC and NVA contingent and now every nerve was tense and ready for more of the same. If Charlie was somewhere near, they would find out soon enough.

He glanced at his watch again, noticing the first sliver of daylight diffusing the shadows in the jungle. They would be moving in twenty minutes and he let his eyes drift slowly in front of him. Everything was quiet, the only noise the sound of metal hitting softly against metal when a man moved his rifle and the muffled cough of men waiting impatiently, nervously for the order to move into combat. They had approached the area the day before, slowly and carefully, unloading the choppers several clicks (miles) away from the coordinates given to the CO (Company Commander) in order to approach the site without being detected. They had walked into the area, going to ground late into the night, making a cold camp and holding noise to a minimum. The enemy they were hunting was nothing but smart and cunning and it was foolhardy to just walk in to the enemy's lair advertising your presence. Behind Bravo Company, several clicks away, the rest of the Battalion waited for word from the patrol elements. Even the Brigade Commander, Brigadier General Mobley was there, waiting impatiently to see what would develop. If a sizable VC force were found, then the rest of the battalion would move in, dropped from the sky by Hueys, encircling the enemy in a pincer movement. Once they had the enemy pinpointed, the helicopter gun ships would be called in and then the planes would make their appearance, bombing everything back to the Stone Age.

The shadows diminished slowly, and Kennedy could smell the fear and excitement in the air surrounding his men. He came to his feet swiftly and his hand signaled the rest of the men to get up. Slowly the platoon came to life, like a snake uncoiling and soon everybody was ready to go. Rucksacks were tightened and the olive drab towels wrapped around the necks to catch the sweat that soon would be rolling down their necks. Every one of the paratroopers re-checked their rifle, making sure they were loaded and soon the platoon was ready. Once again, Kenney nodded his head, signaling the point man to move and Corporal Bobby Smith took the point. The young man move slowly, watching his steps carefully, searching for booby traps or anything else unusual in his surroundings. Sweat trickled down his face and his throat felt parched already. His heart beat furiously at every step, adrenalin coursing swiftly through his blood, making him aware of every branch and tree around him. 'Charlie' was a wily enemy and he could be anywhere. He glanced at the tree tops, looking for any movement there that would tell him a sniper was above, his eyes constantly roving, searching, his ears attuned to his surroundings and any noise. The trigger finger was wrapped around the trigger of his M-14, the selector switch on automatic.

When the hair on his neck stood on end, Corporal Smith stopped cold, his right hand coming up, halting the platoon. Lt. Kennedy saw the hand and he did the same, the men coming to a complete halt, waiting. Eyes glanced at the jungle all around them, trying to find whatever had caught Smith's attention. For long moments that seemed like an eternity to men heading into combat, Smith remained still, his eyes glued to something to his immediate left. Even in full daylight, the jungle was dark and he couldn't make out exactly what he was seeing. Finally his eyes caught a slight movement and now he was sure. He snapped his head around, the expression on his face one of fear, his eyes bulging in their sockets, the rifle in his hand coming up at the same time he turned. His mouth opened up to scream a warning, but it was too late. The sound of a machine gun opening up filled the silence of the jungle and bullets like angry bees searched for them. They had found the VC.

Corporal Smith's scream died in his throat as bullets slammed into him, the sound of the bullets hitting him coming to Lt. Kennedy quite clearly. Smith dropped in place and Kennedy rushed to him, at the same time he was yelling orders to his men to return fire. In a short time, a furious firefight erupted all around Kennedy's platoon, men dying and killing in a wild frenzy. The sound of small arms weapons broke all over the jungle and the sound of a 60 mm mortar soon joined the battle.

Kennedy dragged Smith away from the murderous fire of the machinegun emplacement, feeling bullets creasing his clothes. He checked the young man quickly, but Smith was beyond help, his eyes staring into nothing. Kennedy settled the body down and then he looked around. In front of him and his men, he could see that more than one machine gun had them pinned down and he realized that the enemy was well emplaced. He glanced around quickly, finding his RTO (Radio Operator) and he yelled, signaling the young man to him.

The RTO crawled to him and Kennedy snatched the handset of the PRC-25, screaming into it, requesting artillery and gun ships.

"Bravo one, Bravo one…" he screamed, his eyes darting to the front, his face glued to the ground, feeling the clammy hand of fear turning his intestines to jelly.

"This is Bravo-one…go ahead, over."

"Bravo one, this is Ramrod zero-one-niner. We have contact, repeat we have contact, over," he yelled into the handset, making his body small.

The reply was fast, the radio crackling almost immediately in response. "Roger Ramrod zero, one, niner. We read you loud and clear. State your request, over."

"Roger Bravo one. Ramrod requesting support and artillery barrage, coordinates…Kennedy stopped for a second, his hand busy searching for the map, and then he swiftly read the coordinates, screaming to make himself heard, repeating himself above the din of battle rolling over him like thunder in the night. That done he threw the handset back to the RTO and glanced around, taking stock of his position. The sound of the firefight was getting stronger, the sound washing over the jungle, an incredible cacophony of noise that was like the sound of a hurricane, dulling the senses and filling the world with noise. He shook his head to dispel the buzzing in his ears and glanced around, checking on his men. The "Sky Soldiers" were doing a good job holding the enemy at bay and in minutes he knew that help would be there. A grin flickered on his face and he wiped sweat from his eyes, listening to the wild thuds of his heart beating against his chest, thinking that the VC were in for a surprise if they stayed put and fought. He raised his head to the sky above and listened closely. Yes, oh yes, he exulted, the Huey's were coming, the sound of rotors rending the air above the jungle canopy coming to his ears clearly.

CHAPTER 31

VC Prison Camp
U Minh Forest
Republic of South Vietnam
July 1965

Colonel Hue finished his breakfast and dabbed softly at his lips with his handkerchief. He lighted his first cigarette of the day and inhaled the smoke deeply. He was addicted to the American cigarettes, Marlboros, and he enjoyed their strong taste. He flicked ashes onto the ground and for a moment he thought about Lt. Gallagher. The man was just like Pierce and Hue wondered if all the American Special Forces were the same, stubborn and unwilling to sacrifice their so-called honor. He wanted Gallagher to give him a written confession of their war crimes, but he knew that wouldn't happen. He was going to have to kill the man and then, maybe, Wilson would see his way clear to give him what he wanted. He was sure Wilson was not of the same caliber as Gallagher and Pierce and probably could be broken more easily. The part of him that was a soldier, felt a grudging admiration for Captain Pierce and he had to admit to himself that Pierce had died with honor. The man had guts, no doubt about that, but in the end it had been Hue who had determined his fate. And it would be the same with this other one, he told himself.

He glanced at his watch, feeling the sweat running down his back, soaking his tunic. He cursed under his breath and stood up, pulling at his tunic, adjusting his belt. How he wished he were out of this stinking jungle, he thought, nodding his head at the VC guard next to him, making his way toward Gallagher's cage. It was early morning and already the heat and the humidity were almost overpowering. He continued on his way, his thoughts on Gallagher again. Soon he would have his answer and if the lieutenant wanted to be stubborn and refuse, he would kill him too.

Reaching Gallagher's cage, he stopped, seeing Gallagher standing close to the bamboo walls. Hue stared icily at the lieutenant and something in the man's stance and look told him that Gallagher was not going to cooperate with him, not this morning or ever. He sighed deeply and a smile came to his face. If the man wanted to die, well, that was fine, he would help him.

"Are you ready to cooperate?" he asked, expecting the answer that he got.

"No way, Hue," Gallagher said, tired of the game now. He walked to the gate, waited for the VC guard to open it and stepped out. His arms were tied behind his back and Hue started walking, the VC guard pushing Paul after him. They walked the same path that Alton Pierce had, finally stopping at a bend. Paul looked around, his eyes taking in the surroundings and then he fixed his eyes on Hue.

At a signal from Hue, the VC guard untied his hands and his feet and dropped a shovel in front of him.

Paul looked at the shovel and then he raised his eyes to Hue. The son of a bitch wanted him to dig his own grave, Paul thought, grinning at the irony of the moment. He bent down swiftly and picked up the shovel, finding a convenient place. He started digging, his mind running wild with thoughts of his family and his wife. He had come to terms with his death the night before. Or at least he thought he had, but he didn't want to die and his heart was breaking at the thought of dying alone in a stinking jungle, never to see his child or his parents and wife. He dug slowly, feeling himself losing control, the pain from his broken ribs making the job difficult. He could write the damn confession and live, he knew that, but living under those conditions was like not living at all and so he knew that he would die today. He struck the black dirt angrily, the sweat running down his back with the effort, soaking his clothes and getting in his eyes.

He stopped for a second to wipe his face and suddenly the jungle was rent with the sound of gunfire. He raised his head, watching Hue, the swarthy face registering surprise at the sound of the firefight reaching his ears. The sound of a 60 mm mortar and small arms fire was added to the machinegun fire, the sound washing over them like a giant wave. The firing increased and suddenly the sound of an artillery barrage started to rain down on the camp. The rounds were falling several hundred meters away and Hue started yelling and screaming orders. Soon several hundred VC soldiers were running in the direction of the fight, while Hue ordered Gallagher out of the hole, the VC guard pushing him roughly toward the camp. Paul glanced back once to see Hue running into the jungle, VC soldiers with him. The sound of the fight increased, the volume of fire reaching Paul's ears now a constant cacophony of noise. He was pushed roughly into his cage, the VC guard barely locking the gate completely with the rusted lock before dashing into the jungle. Soon enough, wounded VC soldiers could be seen running back into the camp, while overhead, the sound of helicopter rotors split the air, the sound of machine gun fire adding to the crescendo.

Paul's heart was in his throat as the firefight inched closer and closer to the VC prison camp. A shrill whistle above him made him flinch and an artillery round exploded close by, the fragments hitting the cage where he and Wilson were crouching. One round followed another, the sound straight from Dante's Inferno, the crying of men wounded and dying adding to the incredible confusion surrounding the camp. Above the jungle canopy, the sound of machine guns and helicopters could be heard, a constant sound now, coupled with the steady sound of mortar rounds falling everywhere. Men ran into the jungle, firing wildly at anything that moved in front of them and they in turn were cut down by a hail of bullets coming in from the force attacking the compound.

Paul went to Wilson, pushing the man up, realizing that he was too weak even to stand. Paul let him drop again. Going to the bamboo gate, his hands pushed, hoping like hell that a round didn't fall on top of the cage. Nobody was paying them any attention now and if he could kick the damn gate open, maybe, just maybe they could run into the jungle and escape in the confusion. He kicked and pushed, but the damn gate held and Paul's eyes filled with tears of frustration. So close, damn it, so close, he thought, realizing that he was just too weak to do much more. Regardless, he continued his pushing and shoving until he saw the disheveled figure of Colonel Hue coming toward the cage. The man was filthy and his tunic was in disarray, the eyes wild and haunted.

There were two VC guards with him and at his orders the cage was opened. "Get out…get out," he yelled, his face contorted in rage. His revolver was in his hand and he gesture wildly for Gallagher to step out.

"I'm not going anywhere unless Wilson is going too," he said, refusing to come out.

Hue ranted and raved, but it was to no avail. Paul was determined to take Wilson with him if Hue forced him out. If the son of a bitch was going to kill him, it would be better to get Wilson out. Whoever was attacking the camp might just be able to save one of them if they were together.

Hue finally relented and Paul bent down to Wilson's gaunt form and dragged the man to his feet. Hue started walking fast, in the direction of the jungle, the same spot where Paul had started to dig the grave. He was supporting Wilson, following Hue, while the two Viet Cong guards were behind them. Their eyes were wild and it was obvious that they would have rather been somewhere else than in the middle of a firefight. The artillery barrage continued to come down on the camp, hutches blowing up, men going down with terrible wounds. The small arms fire was also still intense and Hue crouched his body, making himself small. 88 mm mortar rounds started coming in, one falling so close to the fleeing group that all of them were sent sprawling on the ground. One of the VC guards didn't get up, his body ripped apart by the razor sharp fragments and Wilson had several pieces imbedded in his back, the pain of the wounds making the man scream like a banshee. The remaining VC soldier looked dazed and blood could be seen running from his nose, his eyes clouded. Paul picked Wilson up again, glancing at the small wounds that peppered his back, his mind centering on the fact that even a skinny man like Wilson was still too heavy for him. He felt his strength ebbing, his heart racing wildly, and his breath coming in gasps, the red-hot pain of his broken ribs searing his chest. Paul glanced behind him again, noticing that the other VC guard had somehow disappeared and his brain focused on the possibility that he could escape. But he could never do it with Wilson in the shape he was in and he sure as hell was not going to let him go. He continued to struggle after Hue, the pair bursting into a small clearing. The sound of the artillery barrage had ended, but the noise from mortars and machine gun fire could still be heard all over the jungle amid the roaring noise of rocket explosions and machinegun fire. Overhead, the infernal sound of rotors could be heard and from the edge of the clearing Paul could see "slicks" flying by low, the sides of the choppers spitting lead everywhere. Colonel Hue stopped momentarily, his eyes huge, confused, glancing back for any sign of pursuit, satisfied that for the moment there was none. He pushed into the clearing, oblivious to the fact that he was alone with the prisoners and that Paul Gallagher was behind him. They were half way to the end of the jungle clearing when Paul saw his chance and dropping Wilson swiftly on the ground, he rushed Hue from behind. Above him, the sound of rotors filled the air and Paul prayed that whomever was flaying the "slick" would hold fire or recognize him as an American. He and Wilson were dressed in the ubiquitous black pajamas and from above he doubted he looked any different than any other Viet Cong to the door gunners. Like an angel of death, he ran, his eyes centered on the figure of Colonel Hue, his brain closed to anything else around him.

The first inkling Hue had that something was not right was a noise from behind. He snapped his head around and his eyes opened wide in surprise at the sight that greeted him. The damn prisoner was attacking him!

He raised his revolver at the same time he tried to turn, but Paul, even as weak as he was, got to him first, his body crashing into Hue, who lost his footing and went down heavily. Paul came to his feet, gasping for air, the searing pain on his ribs making him nauseous. He fought the swirling darkness threatening to overwhelm him and he sucked air into his lungs. His heart raced wildly, adrenalin giving him the strength he needed. He came up swiftly and kicked at Hue's face, the foot connecting with the man's jaw, snapping the head back. Without preamble, Paul turned around, snatching Wilson from the ground, pulling at him with his remaining strength, lifting him and dragging him away from Hue as fast as he could. He glanced back, to see Hue pushing himself up, his face bleeding, his hair falling over his eyes, rage etched deeply on the swarthy face. An animal sound escaped from Paul's lips, a cry of desperation, realizing that there was no way for him to get away with Wilson before Hue put a bullet in his back. He glanced back again, this time to see Hue's hand raise, the revolver aiming at him. He pushed forward and staggered, becoming entangled in his own feet, waiting for the shot to ring out, his back cringing at the expectation of a bullet smacking into him. A shot rang out and he heard Wilson scream, his legs giving on him, the two of them crashing to the ground. In wild desperation, Paul glanced back at Hue, seeing the man start to run toward him, the pistol in his hand, a gloating smile of satisfaction on his face. He staggered to his feet, his hands bunched into fists, feeling the rage and fury overwhelming him. So close, so damn close, he thought, his eyes watching Hue swiftly cover the distance toward him, the hand with the pistol sneaking upwards.

CHAPTER 32

Above the Skies of the U Minh Forest
Close to the VC Prison Camp

CWO 2 (Chief Warrant Officer 2) David J. Wray, a member of the 119 AH Company (Attack Helicopter Co.), banked his chopper sharply over the jungle clearing, his eyes registering the movement of men clad in black pajamas down below. He flared over the trees and came back around one more time, trying to get a clear picture of what he had seen. He could swear that he had glimpsed several black clad men running after another man in Khaki uniform. This time he lowered the chopper almost at tree top level and then he hover in place. He looked out to his immediate front, his finger ready to touch the button that would send one or more 2.75-inch rocket toward the men below. He held the chopper steady and then his eyes took in the drama unfolding below.

"What the hell…," he mumble to himself, his eyes refusing to acknowledge what he was seeing.

"Hold your fire," he yelled to his door gunner on the right side, his eyes fixed on the three men below.

Down below, the man in Khaki uniform had been tackled by one man dressed in black, who had turned immediately, snatching a figure from the ground and limped away from the soldier in uniform. The Huey pilot saw the NVA soldier regain his feet, his right arm extend, a pistol in it, and then the man fired and one of the black clad men fell down, dragging the other with him. CWO Wray looked closely at the man struggling to get up, all the while wondering what the hell was going on below and something inside told him that the man was not a Viet Cong. He was too tall, almost Caucasian looking, a growth of beard on his face. The man helping the other one looked up at him and with his heart in his throat, Wray realized the man was an American. For a tenth of a second, he thought about releasing a rocket, but realized that if he did, he would kill all three men below. He saw the uniformed man running now to shorten the distance between them and he touched the chopper controls slightly, swinging the chopper to his left, giving the door gunner a clear field of fire and at the same time, he yelled into his mouth piece. "Tony, shoot the man in uniform…shoot him!"

The words were scarcely out of his mouth when the door gunner opened up with the M-60 machine gun and a hail of bullets stitched the ground in front of the soldier. A second later the bullets found its mark and the man toppled over, his body riddled with bullet holes. For a moment longer, Wray hovered in place, his heart beating wildly. He saw the man on the ground raise his hand, the expression on his face one of incredulity and Wray touched the controls one more time, the chopper finding its way into the clearing, touching down. The moment the chopper was down the door gunner opened up, stitching the edge of the jungle, making sure nobody there would interfere with the crew chief who had jumped out, running toward the men in the field, a rifle in his hand. The crew chief reached the men, slung his rifle on his back and reached down to pick up the wounded man. He lifted the man easily enough and turned around, heading for the chopper, the other man following closely.

CWO Wray saw the men approaching and his eyes centered on the last one. He was tall, emaciated looking, a filthy black rag strapped around his chest. His hair, what was left of it, was black, short and there was a growth of beard on his face several days old.

"Oh sweet Jesus," he said softly to himself, sure now of what he had thought, "they are Americans."

The crew chief reached the chopper and hastily pushed his burden onboard, while the other man leapt aboard clumsily.

"Lets go…go…go," the crew chief yelled into his mouthpiece, his eyes glued to the jungle surrounding them, expecting gunfire to come after them any minute now. In seconds Wray had increased power to the rotors and the chopper came up. The nose went down slightly and the slick sped away, swiftly clearing the treetops and gaining altitude.

CWO Wray glanced behind him and his eyes took in the face of the man immediately behind him. His eyes were huge and tears were running down his face. For a second, the man's eyes fixed on him; the blue eyes incredibly sad and the man nodded his head in recognition. CWO Wray felt a lump in his throat and he nodded back. The crew chief was bent over the wounded man; bright red blood soaked the floor of the chopper and the other man went to him, cradling his friend's head in his lap. CWO Wray turned his head around and got on the radio, breaking the engagement, giving the news that two American POW's had been rescued. In ten minutes, he had landed at an army base and in moments, the two men were transported to the field hospital.

* * * *

Lt. Paul Gallagher couldn't believe what had transpired in such a short time. He was sitting on a chopper, Americans all around him and Hue was dead. After all he had endured, after all the pain and suffering, he was free. His eyes became wet and he sighed deeply, unable to comprehend the magnitude of what had transpired. He felt eyes on him and he lifted his head up to find the pilot looking at him. He nodded his head and then he glanced at Wilson. He saw the crew chief leaning over him, the man's blood soaking the floor and he moved to help him. Wilson was alive, the bullet going all the way through his leg, but he was hurt bad and was losing a lot of blood. Gallagher held on to him, speaking softly and ten minutes later, the chopper banked sharply and landed. Immediately, several people approached and the two men were on their way to a field hospital.

Wilson was taken to some place away from him and a woman in uniform guided him to a bed. He glanced at her, realizing she was a nurse. She directed him to the bed and he sat down, glancing at the place. Several other GI's were there and the closest ones were looking in his direction.

The sound of the woman's voice brought him back and he glanced at her, his eyebrow raised in question. He had not heard a woman speaking to him for quite a while and the sound was soft and warm to him.

"I'm sorry, mam" he said softly, gently "I didn't catch the question."

She had a clipboard with her and her hand was poised to take notes. He noticed her eyes, a soft liquid brown taking him in and he smelled her perfume.

"I'm Lt. Donnelly and I need your name, please," she said, looking at him, her nose wrinkled in disgust at the smell coming from the man in front of her. The black pajamas were a mess, full of mud and Wilson's blood and his shoeless feet were bleeding.

I must smell real good, he told himself, his nose moving, probing the air, unable to get a whiff of himself. He felt an incredible weariness seeping slowly into his body and he closed his eyes, realizing how tired he was. He sighed deeply and opened his eyes, trying to concentrate on the nurse. He needed a change of clothes and a place to take a shower, he thought. His brain reeled with pleasure at the thought of clean, cool water falling from a showerhead and he sighed deeply again, finding that it was hard to concentrate on anything for long.

"I'm Lt. Paul W. Gallagher, United States Army, 5th Special Forces Group," he finally said.

The nurse looked at him again and wrote on the clipboard, her eyes coming back to him.

"And what seems to be the problem, Lieutenant? she asked. Paul looked at her closely, realizing that the woman didn't have an inkling of why he was there.

He smiled a tired smile and stood up. "Today I was rescued from a prisoner of war camp, mam," he said, his voice a mere murmur in the confines of the bay. "I was there for almost two years."

The nurse's mouth came open in surprise and her eyes widened at the unexpected words.

"And now if you don't mind, before we do anything else, I want to take a shower and get some clean clothes," Paul said.

"But...but you are wounded," she finally blurted out, her eyes fixed on the bloody clothes, her hands coming up to get the clothes off.

"No...I'm not," Paul said softly, his fingers going to the filthy cloth, wiping at the blood. "This...this is not my blood. It belongs to a friend."

The nurse didn't answered him, just nodded her head, her face etched in consternation.

She turned around and left swiftly and moments later a male orderly entered the bay, heading for Paul.

"Sir, if you will follow me, please," he said and Paul grunted his approval, following the man. He was taken to a shower room, the orderly indicating hot and cold to him. Soap and towels, shaving cream and a razor were left on a bench and the orderly left him alone, promising to return with clean clothes. Slowly, Paul stripped the rags from his body and turned the water on, stepping gingerly into it. For long moments he closed his eyes, the feeling of the water running down on his battered, used body was something of indescribable pleasure. How long he remained there he didn't know, but he washed and scrubbed his body, feeling the layers of dirt and pain and suffering washing from him, the scalding hot water like a balm to his soul. He touched the place where his ribs were broken and pushed gently, feeling the sharp pain. He needed to get that fix, he thought, lathering his chest carefully, smelling the scent of the soap.

When he finally exited the shower, he found clean clothes on the bench, way too big for him, but clean nevertheless and sandals. He put them on and then approached the mirror on the wall. For long seconds, he remained looking into his own eyes. The pain and sorrow that had been his constant companions for almost two years were clearly reflected there and he closed his eyes, feeling the wetness in them. After a while, he was able to open them again, proceeding to scrape the hair from his face. He found a toothbrush and paste and proceeded to clean his teeth and gum, seeing the blood coming from his mouth at the touch of the brush. His teeth were all loose and the pain inside his mouth was all too real. After that he made his way out, returning to the bay.

This time there were several people there, waiting on him and his eyes took in the gathering. He noticed a tall, skinny man, the rank of major on his collar and the medical caduceus on his shoulder. His eyes went to the nameplate on his left side, Walker, MD. The nurse was back and there was also a man with a Green Beret on his head, the eagle of a full bird Colonel on it. Their eyes watched him walking toward them and he stopped, waiting. The Green Beret Colonel was the first one to speak, coming toward Paul, his hand extended.

"I'm Colonel Travis, son and it sure is great to see you," he said, his voice strong, just like his handshake. "I'm the Commanding Officer of Special Forces and we have been waiting a long time to know what happened to you, Captain Pierce and Sgt. Ashworth."

"Captain Pierce and Sgt. First Class Lee Ashworth are dead," Paul said, and then he added, "sir," his eyes infinitely sad, his voice almost a whisper. Then he said almost to himself, "That bastard of a Colonel Hue killed them."

Colonel Travis flinched at the news and he ran his fingers through his short, blond hair, his face clouded. He gave the Lieutenant a blue-eyed stare, taking in the scarecrow countenance of the man, the hooded eyes and he continued.

"When you guys were ambushed, we lost track of all three of you. We never found the bodies, so we suspected that you guys were prisoners of war," he said, pausing, his mind recalling the facts of almost two years gone by. "We never obtained confirmation that you guys were prisoners, so you and the other men were listed as missing in action."

Paul sat on the edge of the bed, his mind trying to cope with everything that had happened in such a short time. Just a few hours before he was at the point of getting killed and now things were moving so fast that his head was spinning. That he was a free man was hard to believe and his brain was not functioning right just yet. He was glad he was free and at the same time mourning again the loss of his friends, Ashworth and Pierce, wondering why he had survived and not them. Emotions surged and ebbed inside him and his eyes had trouble focusing properly.

He blinked hard to cope with the wetness in his eyes and took a deep breath, wincing at the pain that assaulted him. He had forgotten about the ribs again. The doctor saw the expression on his face and was instantly alerted to him.

"Are you okay, Lieutenant? he asked with concern in his voice.

"I believe I have a couple of busted ribs, Sir."

The nurse moved to him immediately, helping him to the bed, solicitous now of his well being.

Colonel Travis turned to the doctor and talked to him softly. That done he whirled around and spoke to Paul.

"These people will take care of you now, Lieutenant and I'll be back in the morning," he said. "I'm sure MI (Military Intelligence) would like to debrief you about your ordeal and I'll also make arrangements for your family to be notified of your rescue."

Paul came to his feet, came to attention and saluted Colonel Travis. "Thank you, Sir," he said.

Colonel Travis came to attention himself and returned the salute to the young man in front of him.

"Welcome home, son," he said. He nodded his head, whirled around and was gone.

As soon as the Colonel had departed, the doctor and the nurse started on him and for the next thirty minutes his body was probed and pinch and his blood was drawn. When his shirt came off, he heard a sharp intake of breath from the nurse. He glanced at her to see her eyes fixed on his chest. From bullets scars to recent bruises, cuts and abrasions, his chest and back were full. Some of the scars were old and some still healing, a testament to what the man had suffered at the hands of the VC. In due time, his ribs were taped in place and he was pumped full of antibiotics. After that, the nurse excused herself and Paul was left alone with the doctor who continued to ask questions. Paul was tired, wanting to be left alone with his thoughts, but he knew he needed to answer the questions and he kept at it. Once Dr. Walker was finished, he closed the chart and faced Paul.

"You are way below your weight, Lieutenant," he started, "which is to be expected on the starvation diet you were forced to endure, also you are suffering from vitamin deficiency and probably have parasites in your system." He stopped talking, consulted the chart again and then continued. "Your stomach has probably shrunk to the size of a child's, so you are going to have to be careful with what you eat for a while." He closed the chart again, moving back and forth on the ball of his feet while he talked. "You will be leaving here shortly, on your way to Walter Reed. They will do a more comprehensive exam on you. Any questions?"

"No sir, nothing right now," he said softly, wishing the questions would end.

Dr. Walker nodded his head and then he said, "I'm sure that you have experienced something that most human beings never encountered in their lives and its beyond me to even begin to guess half of what you have endured son, so in the morning I'll send Dr. Weaver to see you. He is a psychologist and I'm sure he will be of help to you."

Paul's eyes remained fixed on the doctor and slowly he nodded his head, wishing the man was gone.

Walker glanced at him one last time, his eyes hooded and a speculative look on his face and then he whirled around, leaving Paul to himself.

CHAPTER 33

Phuoc Vinh Aid Station
Republic of South Vietnam
1965

Paul Gallagher sighed deeply after the doctor was gone and reclined on the bed, his eyes surveying the place. A couple of GI's in the medical bay were not paying him any attention any more and he closed his eyes, trying to find a comfortable place on the soft bed for his body.

His mind was a whirlwind of thoughts and he tried hard to put everything that had happened into perspective. He was free, he told himself over and over, willing his mind to accept the fact. And in a short, few days he would be able to see his wife and child and his parents. So why I'm not happy? he asked himself, knowing well what the answered was; he was alive, his friends were dead, their bodies rotting away somewhere in the jungle. An overwhelming sense of loss swept over him and he closed his eyes, breathing deeply and slowly.

"Lt. Gallagher, sir," a voice next to him made him jump and he opened his eyes. The same orderly who had helped him with the shower was there, a cup of water and some pills in his hands.

"Yes?" he asked.

"I'm Specialist Five (E-5) Keller, sir, and this is your medicine, sir."

Paul took the offered pills and the water, downing them and giving the cup back.

Paul glanced at the orderly, a black man in his mid twenties by his looks. "Let me…let me ask you something," Paul, said and the orderly came to stand by the bed, waiting.

"Yes sir?" he said, his left eyebrow rose in question.

"My friend…Wilson…the man who was brought in with me…is he okay?"

"Yes sir," the young man answered promptly. "The doctor patched him up and he's probably on his way to a hospital on Cam Ram Bay by now."

"Thanks…thanks," Paul said reclining on the bed.

Sp. 5 Keller looked at the man on the bed, wondering about him. He was curious about it, but he sure as hell was not going to ask any questions. He had overheard the doctor and the nurse talking about him, about being a prisoner of war for almost two years and he felt sorry for the man.

"If you want something to eat, sir, I can get you just about anything you want," he said.

Paul thought about that for a moment, his mind conjuring up all kinds of food that he would like to have and then he remembered the doctor's advice.

"Just bring me whatever you want to," he said and the orderly nodded his head, whirled around and walked away.

Thirty minutes later he was back with an overflowing tray. There was chicken smothered with gravy, mashed potatoes, green beans, apple pie, juice and milk and Paul's eyes opened wide, his mouth salivating ferociously.

The orderly set the tray down, handing Paul a set of silverware and stepping aside to let him eat. Paul looked at the food on the tray and took a bite of the chicken, then the mashed potatoes. Everything was hot and well seasoned, the smell tantalizing. He ate slowly, pacing himself, enjoying the taste and the smell of food that he had forgotten existed. And then, just when he was about finished, his stomach turned and the nausea overwhelmed him. He felt his stomach churning and the bile rose in his throat and before he could stop it, the hot vomit came gushing out of his mouth. The orderly jumped away, avoiding most of it and Paul pushed the tray away, falling on the floor, the contents spilling.

"Shit," he heard the orderly say and Paul's face blushed a deep, crimson red, embarrassed at the turn of events.

"Sorry...about that," he said, wiping his lips, the bile taste in his mouth.

"Nothing to worry about, sir", he said.

The orderly left and moments later was back with a broom and a mop, cleaning up the mess, Paul helping as best he could. When everything was back to normal, he glanced at the orderly saying, "Bring me a piece of bread and some cooked rice, please."

Sp. 5 Keller glanced at him, his head nodding. Once again he left and returned shortly afterwards with the rice and bread and a clean set of clothes. Paul ate that and drank some water afterwards. When he was finished with his meager meal, he stood up, walked to the shower room again, cleaned himself up and put on the clean clothes. He glanced at himself on the shiny surface of the mirror and the face that glanced back at him was something from the past. This time he didn't closed his eyes, but inspected himself closely. The eyes were sunk and every bone on his face was prominent, the flesh wasted away. He had aged an eternity and he almost didn't recognized himself. He walked back to his room slowly and again he settled on the bed. The damn thing was soft, much too soft after sleeping on the ground for almost two years and after awhile, Paul stood up and walked outside. It was dark outside and he glanced at the sky above, a million stars shining like sparkling diamonds. He heard laughter and the voices of people talking close by and a strange melancholy took hold of him. He remained still for a long moment, his senses absorbing the noise of the place and his surroundings. A Huey flared up just above the building, coming to land close by and he saw women and men running toward it with a stretcher. Several minutes later, the slick was airborne again, the sound of the rotors diminishing in the distance until it was gone.

Paul sighed deeply, making his way back into the bay, finding his bunk and laying on it again. He closed his eyes, feeling incredibly tired and lonely. For a moment he thought about the incredible gift he had being given, his life, and he said a prayer to his God Almighty. His thoughts then turned to Alton Pierce and Lee Ashworth and he felt the wetness in his eyes. He wiped at then angrily, thinking that it was unfair for him to be here now, while his two friends were dead, their bodies in a shallow grave that he had dug for them. He sat on the bed, the emotions surging inside of him until finally exhaustion took over and he lay back down. Within minutes he was asleep, his tortured body finally relaxing.

He woke up in the middle of the night for a brief moment; his befuddled brain wondering where he was. When it finally came back to him, he stood up and stretched out on the hard floor, falling asleep again in seconds.

*   *   *   *

The next time he woke up was to a world of pain. Screams reverberated in his ears and he shot straight up on the floor. Someone was next to him and in the dim light his befuddle brain thought it was a VC guard. He jumped away, lashing out in rage his body rebelling at the touch of hands searching for him.

"Get away…get away from me," he yelled. In the semidarkness, his body made contact with a table and he went down, crashing to the ground.

Strong arms wrapped themselves around him and he struggle, listening to the animal sounds escaping from his lips. Suddenly a light came on overhead, bathing the interior of the bay. He blinked his eyes repeatedly and finally the scene came into focus. A nurse, a different one now, and the orderly Keller, were there. Keller was holding him, while the other patients in the bay were sitting up, their eyes glued to the crazy man who was screaming.

"Jesus…I'm sorry…I'm sorry," Paul said, over and over, realizing that he had had a nightmare.

Keller finally let go and Paul stood up. Sweat was running down his face despite the air conditioning in the bay and his clothes were wet. He had a terrible headache and his eyes were sore.

"It's okay, Lieutenant," the nurse said, her voice soft, gentle, reaching out to him, pushing him gently to the bed. He reclined again and she produced a wet cloth from somewhere and wiped his face slowly, tenderly. Paul closed his eyes, feeling the wild staccato of his heart, until it finally slowed to its normal beat. The nurse stood up, left the room and was back shortly afterward with a pill in her hand.

"Take this," she said, "it will help you sleep."

He did as he was told and took the pill, doubting very much that he would be able to sleep, pill or no pill, without the nightmares.

*   *   *   *

The next time he woke up, it was to the sound of soft, muted voices. He opened his eyes, amaze that he had been able to sleep at all, realizing that it was daylight. A new orderly came with breakfast and this time Paul was able to eat a few bites before the nausea assaulted him. He stopped eating and sipped the strong hot tea instead. Eventually the churning in his stomach ceased. He glanced around, noticing the time, seeing the doctor and the same nurse from the day before approaching. Colonel Travis was there also, a smile on his weathered face and he approached the bed rapidly. Just behind him, Paul could see two other men in civilian clothes and he wondered about them. Probably MI, he thought, his eyes fixed on them.

Colonel Travis looked at him, his blue, intelligent eyes taking him in. "Well Captain, how are you," he said, the blue eyes full of laughter now. Paul was standing by the bed and he came to attention when Colonel Travis arrived

"I'm…fine, sir," he said, his forehead creasing in question at Travis' words. A grin flickered on Travis face and his right arm came up, holding a new Green Beret with the silver tracks of a Captain on it.

"It appears that you have been promoted son," Travis said. "Congratulations." He gave the Beret to Paul, who stood there in complete silence, his mouth hanging open.

"Well…sir…thank you," he finally stammered, his face breaking into a happy smile for the first time.

Travis nodded his head and then he was all business again. With a nod of his head, he pointed at the men in civilian clothes, saying; "These gentlemen would like to get your report and debrief you, if that is okay with your doctor," Travis said, looking at Dr. Walker.

Dr. Walker shrugged his shoulders in a non-committal way, deferring to Paul. "If the Captain feels up to it."

He shook his head in the affirmative and moments later the two men, Colonel Travis and Paul were led to a private office and the debriefing began. For most of the morning, Paul talked, relating his experience at the hands of the VC and Colonel Huc. Once the story was told, the two men started asking questions, making Paul go over the story over and over again, getting every piece of information and detail of the death of his friends, and the eventual escape with Wilson, until all was said and a silence descended on the room. Colonel Travis finally stood up, his eyes fixed on the man who had endure so much and his heart went out to him. He had a son, just about Paul Gallagher's age, serving in Germany and he prayed to God everyday for his safety. He could not begin to understand what the young man in front of him had gone through, but it sure looked like it had been some kind of hell. He approached him, his hand going to his shoulder, squeezing it affectionately.

"Well done Captain, well done," he said, his voice choked with sentiment. Paul shook his head, trying his best to control the tide of emotions surging through him. He sighed deeply, controlling himself and finally the idea that had been in his mind all night, came to his lips. He raised his head to the Colonel, saying; "Colonel, I believe that I…I can find the grave of Captain Pierce. If we…we can return to the place I can find it. We can get his body back home, give him a proper burial."

Travis heard the words and his eyes flared. He paced the room, his arms across his chest, his forehead creased in thought. After a few minutes, he glanced at Paul, saw the determination in his face and nodded his head.

"If it can be done, we will do it," he said, his voice flat. His eyes were fixed on Paul, his forehead creased in deep thought. For long seconds, he didn't say anything, obviously mulling something important over in his mind. And then he said, "What about Sgt. Ashworth?"

Paul thought about Ashworth, wondering if he would be able to retrace his steps and find the first camp, but after careful consideration of the events that had taken place and given the fact that they had been blindfolded when transported to the second prisoner's camp, he doubted that he would be able to retrace the steps back to Ashworth's grave. Paul thought about it, closing his eyes and attempted to recreate the whereabouts of the place, but too much time had passed and the images kept flashing out, never allowing him to pinpoint the exact location. His friend would remain buried in this strange and unforgiving country, unless by some miracle or by the grace of God, his body was found.

He glanced at Travis who was waiting for an answer from him, saying, "I don't believe I could find his grave, sir."

"I understand, Captain," Travis said, his voice reflecting the sadness in him. Lee Ashworth was one of them and it galled him just as much as it did Gallagher that he would never be able to return the body of one of his men home.

The two men in civilian clothes left the room and shortly afterward Paul and Colonel Travis made their exit. After conferring with Dr. Walker, the two of them exited the medical bay and shortly Colonel Travis' helicopter was on the way to pick them up. While they waited, he got on the radio and by the time his chopper had arrived, another Huey had made its appearance, a detachment of Special Forces in it. Seven Green Berets exited the slick, making their way to Colonel Travis. The men came to attention, snapping a salute to their superior officer, their eyes taking in the man standing next to their commanding officer. By now all of them had heard about Paul Gallagher and they clustered around him, offering congratulations, slapping him on the back and exulting about his good luck. It was a happy moment for Paul, and once again, he felt like he belonged there with those men, fighting for freedom. Once the men quieted down, Colonel Travis came straight to the point. The Green Berets toned down when they realized the kind of mission they had volunteered for.

Without another word, the men leaped into the waiting Hueys and in moments the two birds were speeding away. Twenty minutes later, the choppers banked sharply and Paul's stomach lurched. They were approaching the area of the VC prison camp. The damage from the artillery barrage and the firefight were clearly visible from the air. Trees were still smoldering from the Napalm bombs and here and there a crater where a bomb had fallen could be seen. The choppers slowly circled the immediate area twice, finally landing in the clearing where Paul and Wilson had been rescued. Travis exited the chopper, glancing at Paul. The young man was pale and his eyes were hooded, but he was game. He glanced around and swallowed hard and at a nod from Colonel Travis he walked a few paces away from the Huey, his eyes scanning the area slowly, orienting himself. When he was completely certain of his whereabouts, he started walking, the rest of the Green Berets closely followed, their eyes searching the jungle, their fingers close to the triggers on their rifles. The area was a mess, with hundreds of trees down from the artillery barrage, the smell of rotten corpses heavy in the hot, humid air, the hungry flies thick and loud. Paul stopped and his eyes rested on the human form lying on the grass, the face bloated, the flies and ants still feasting on him. The man was naked, except for his underwear, the belly swollen with gases.

"This was Colonel Hue," he said, his voice cracking, the eyes open wide, an unholy light in them. His face was twisted in a snarl of pure hate, the corners of his mouth tight at the sight of the man that was responsible for so much pain and suffering.

Travis took a look at the fast decomposing body and he wrinkled his nose in disgust at the stench emanating from it. For a moment everybody was still and then Travis put his hand on Paul's shoulder, saying, "Lets go."

Paul whirled around and walked away. Hue was dead, that was all that mattered, he thought. He retraced his steps from the day of the battle, stopping often to make sure he had it right and eventually, he stopped again. He glanced up at Colonel Travis who was closely following.

"This is the place," he said, emotions about to take control of him. His friend was buried in the ground in front of him and like a bad dream, all the days of torture, pain and suffering came to him. He closed his eyes, swaying gently and the face of Alton Pierce came to him, the ever-present grin on his face, the eyes laughing. Paul opened his eyes and wiped angrily at the wetness pooling there. As he stepped aside, two of the Green Berets started shoveling dirt away from the place Paul indicated while the rest of them walked a few paces into the jungle, their ears and eyes searching for movement or noise. The place appeared deserted after the battle that had taken place there, but this was Vietnam and the war was still going on.

After several minutes of digging, the shovels hit something and the digging progress at a slower pace, until the body in the shallow grave was completely free. A black body bag was brought up and the remains of the body of Alton Pierce was put inside. Carefully, the bag was picked up and once again the Green Berets made their way to the waiting choppers. The body was put in one of the Hueys and shortly the birds lifted up, speeding away. Paul looked down at the body bag and the tears welled up in his eyes. This time he let them come, flowing freely down his cheeks, feeling the burning in his eyes. His friend was going home. And so was he.

CHAPTER 34

Headquarters
U.S. Army Special Warfare School
Office of the Commanding General
Ft. Bragg, NC
August 1965

Brigadier General Raymond A. Brown put the phone down slowly, a smile of pure happiness spreading on his rugged face. He pushed fingers through his thinning hair and stood up from his chair.

He walked a few paces to the window in his office, glancing out. The setting sun was almost gone, the last rays of daylight creating an incredible panorama of color in the sky. A few GI's could be seen walking by, heading for God knew where after a day of hard training. He stood by the window for several seconds, his eyes really not seeing anything outside. He was enjoying the moment of knowing that one of his men had managed to escape from the hands of the VC after years of confinement and that the young man would be going home soon.

General Brown walked to the front door and opened it, saying, "Sgt. Major, please come in."

Sgt. Major Wilhelm walked in the office of his commanding officer, his eyes taking in the General's demeanor. Some good news had just come in, he could tell. Probably that phone call from the Pentagon, he thought as he came in and closed the door after him.

General Brown had been the commanding officer of the Special Warfare School almost a year now; since General Woods was promoted to Major General and Wilhelm liked him. The General was a no nonsense man, a good leader and he really cared about his men and their welfare.

Brown smiled again and fixed his eyes on Wilhelm. "You remember Lt. Gallagher, Vietnam, 1963?" he asked softly.

Sgt. Major Wilhelm looked at General Brown, his eyes searching for any indication on the old man's face that would tell him more.

He nodded his head in the affirmative. "Yes sir, I do. He was either killed or captured, together with Captain Pierce and Sgt. Ashworth."

"Well, Gallagher is alive and he has escaped from the VC. Probably by now he is on his way to Walter Reed Hospital."

A smile of pleasure spread over Wilhelm's face, glad at the tidings. "By God, that is good news, sir."

"Yes it is," Brown said, laughing softly.

"What about Pierce and Ashworth?" Wilhelm asked.

"Don't know the whole details, but according to the phone call I just received, Pierce is dead. His body has been recovered and is on its way to Hawaii for proper identification and eventual return to the U.S." He paused for a second, sighing deeply, his weathered face serious now and then continuing. "Ashworth is also dead, but so far there is no way to find out where he is buried."

"I see," Wilhelm said. He had known Lee Ashworth for years, had served together with him in far off places, sharing the dangers and the hard life which is the lot of soldiers everywhere and now he would grieve for his soul.

"He was a good soldier," Wilhelm said softly and General Brown nodded his head in assent. He knew that coming from Wilhelm that was a compliment to a fallen comrade.

For a moment, there was silence in the office, finally interrupted by General Brown. "See if you can find the telephone number for Captain Gallagher's family. I'd like to give them the good news."

Sgt. Major Wilhelm nodded his head in assent, whirled around and left the office.

* * * *

Mason City, Iowa
August 1965

Bill Gallagher closed the barn doors and headed for the house, walking slowly after a long day of farming. His back hurt and his shoulders were a mass of tight muscles and he grumbled to himself as he started to walk in through the back door. He was getting old, no doubt about it, he thought, a grin playing on his rugged face at the thoughts in his mind. He stopped at the entrance, bending down to unlace the work boots. They were full of mud and Carol would give him a hard time if he went in the kitchen with them on. He finished the unlacing and pulled them off, throwing them to the side. Later on after dinner was finished, he would come back out and clean them, ready for another day of work in the fields. He glanced at the sky, already full of glimmering stars and realized he was late for dinner. He could hear his sons and the women talking in the dining room and he hurried to get washed, knowing well that they would be waiting for him. As he stepped in, the telephone on the side of the kitchen wall started ringing. For a second he thought about letting it ring, but them his hand reach for it, his stomach fluttering.

"Hello...hello," he said, listening to the static on the line. "Hello," he said again and this time there was a voice on the line. Susan and Carol walked in the kitchen, still talking and then they stopped, watching him.

He listened to the voice at the other end and his face turned deadly pale, his knees buckled, having to reach to a chair for support. Tears started running down his face, intermingled with laughter. For a second Carol thought her husband had lost it, taking a step toward him.

"What is going..." she started, never finishing, Bill hung up the phone and looked at them with tears streaking his face.

"Oh merciful God…he…he is alive," he said, his voice rough, his weathered face breaking into a huge grin, his eyes bright and wet, the tears flowing freely down the weathered cheeks.

"What are you saying, Bill?" Carol asked, rushing to him. She had heard the words and her heart was pounding painfully in her chest, her legs about to fold on her.

"Our boy, Carol…he…he is alive, on his way home."

Susan came to their side and all three of them hugged each other, the unexpected news thrilling them to no end. After all this time, Paul was alive and coming home. Bill Gallagher held on to his women, his heart about to burst. He raised his head to the ceiling and whispered softly, "Thank you Lord…thank you." His prayers had been answered and his God had seen that their son returned to them.

Chapter 35

Key West, Florida
August 1965

Major General Pierce sat still on the chair of his study, the telegram hanging loosely from his fingers. His face was etched with anguish and his old heart was braking, silent tears streamed down his wrinkled face. The news that he so desperately never wanted to hear had finally come. His son, Alton, was dead—killed in Vietnam. His body had being recovered with the help of Lt. Gallagher and in a few weeks the remains would be in transit to the United States for proper burial. He stood up, wiping the tears with the back of his hand, missing his son as much now as he did when his fate was unknown.

He walked to the corner bar, filled a glass with the amber liquid and took a long swallow of it, the liquor burning his throat, doing nothing to dissipate the lump in there. He felt the tears in his eyes again, and this time he let them come, heart-rending sobs shook his whole body, until his knees folded on him and he went down on the floor. "My son...my son," he murmured softly, all the pain and loneliness of a lifetime surfacing now.

How long he remained like that he didn't know, but eventually the sobs subsided and Robert Pierce stood up, making his way back to the chair. He rummaged in one of the desk drawers and his hand came out with a piece of paper, a number scribbled on it. He would call his friend, Lt. General Donovan. He wanted to know all the details of

Alton's demise. Then there was the burial. He wanted his son to be buried with full military honors, in Arlington Cemetery, close to the thousands of other young Americans who had given the ultimate price for freedom.

With a heavy heart, Major General Robert W. Pierce picked up the phone and dialed the number.

Chapter 36

Walter Reed Hospital
Washington, DC
August 1965

Captain Paul W. Gallagher fidgeted impatiently in his seat, waiting for the doctor to come in. He had been in the hospital for three days—since arriving from Vietnam—and he was eager to be on his way. They had pinched and poked at him again for what he thought was an eternity and finally the doctors had agreed to let him go. He was waiting now for final confirmation and if everything turned out all right, he would be on his way home soon. He was looking forward to that, to the pleasure of seeing his son, his wife and his parents again. The Army had given him sixty days of leave and he was prepared to use them all.

The door to the small office where he was waiting opened and a small, bespectacled man in uniform came in.

"I'm Captain Moore from Personnel and Finance," the man said, dropping a briefcase on the desk, rummaging through it and getting a number of papers from it. He put papers in front of Paul while he continued to talk as fast as he could. "These are your leave papers, Captain, and your new orders after the leave is complete." He handed the papers to Paul who took them without saying anything. The Captain rummaged some more and put another paper in front of Paul, saying, "Sign here."

Paul did as he was asked and then the Captain continued. "Here is a check for all the pay and allowances you are entitled for the time you have been gone and here is a number for you to call if there are any problems while you are on leave."

The man finally quit talking, gathered all the forms and closed his briefcase. He extended his hand to Paul, saying, "Welcome home, Captain," and without further ado, he was gone.

Paul shook his head and stood up. There was a mirror on one side of the small office and he saw his reflection in it. For a moment he had the awful impression that he was looking at a ghost and then he shook his head, willing the bad memories away. His face was beginning to fill up, but the blue eyes were still haunted, incredibly sad, accentuating the pallor of his face. His hair was also finally starting to come out and he was grateful for that. Much of his strength was back, his body filling out again, but he knew it would be a hard road ahead before he was himself again.

He returned to the chair, forcing himself to be patient, waiting. A small grin flickered across his face, thinking about being patient. He was an expert at that, after all the time spent in cages during the last two years, waiting for Hue to make his appearance and the torture to begin.

He was dressed in class A Greens, the Green Beret that Colonel Travis had given him on his head. The Colonel had seen him out of Vietnam and before leaving he had pinned a Silver Star on his chest, together with a Purple Heart and a CIB (Combat Infantry Badge). A noise at the door brought him out of his reverie and he turned around to face the man coming in.

Colonel Julius R. Lowell came in, a file in his hands. Taking a seat behind the desk, he opened the file, read something in it, closed it again and looked at Paul.

"Captain Gallagher, we have reviewed your medical condition and we are happy to tell you that besides some minor problems, everything else is fine. You have a mild form of protein-calorie malnutrition due to the starvation diet that was forced on you, but it is nothing that cannot be cured. You will probably have stomach problems, off and on for the rest of your life, your weight is off by quite a few pounds and your ribs are healing nicely." He stopped for a second and then continued.

"Watch what you eat for a few days and see what happens, continue with the vitamin supplements and have a good vacation." The Colonel stopped then, his eyes fixed on him and something told Paul there was more to come.

"It has been our experience with prisoners of war who have survived, that there is a period in which the mind refuses to settle down, to allow a person to be at peace with themselves. Especially if friends have died and they are the ones to survive." He paused, breathing deeply, continuing then. "They tend to blame themselves for being alive, for having survived while their friends died. Nightmares and bad dreams are usually present immediately or soon after being released and the experiences can be rough. These things might happen to you, might not, but if they do, please feel free to call me anytime. We can help."

With that, the man stood up and extended his hand. "Good luck, son," he said, smiling.

Paul stood up too, shaking the Colonel's hand. He was ready to go.

CHAPTER 37

Mason City, Iowa
August 1965

Paul W. Gallagher arrived home late in the evening the next day, his body tired from the trip, but eager to be there. He had come without calling his family, wanting to surprise them. He exited the taxi that had brought him home, stopping it at the entrance to the driveway. It was a beautiful summer day, with not a hint of rain, the sun shining in a blue sky, a gentle breeze rustling the leaves on the tall trees that lined the long driveway. He stood still for a minute, his eyes taking in the land and the familiar sights he knew so well, the wheat fields extending in long lines of shimmering gold into the distance. Hefting his duffel bag, he started walking toward the distant house, his footsteps stirring the dust on the road. He walked on, coming closer and closer to the house, his eyes detecting movement suddenly at the front. Somebody had come out of the house, probably wondering who could be walking on the path toward the house and he extended his steps. Soon enough, another figure joined the first one, a taller person and Paul new without a shadow of a doubt that it was his father. The figure on the porch took several steps forward and then the man was running. Paul dropped the bag on the ground and felt himself running too, burning tears running freely down his face. The tall man's figure soon evolved into his father and a moment later they both reached out for each other, the strength of their embrace threatening to crush them both.

Over the roaring sound of his heart, Paul heard his father voice saying, "Thank you Lord, thank you."

With tears and laughter, the two men looked at each other and Bill Gallagher thought his heart would explode in his chest, his emotions getting the best of him. Soon thereafter, his mother joined them, her face radiant with happiness. Her son was home. A sound on the porch and the voice of a toddler made Paul raise his eyes. He saw the door open and a small child came out, about fourteen months old, his long, blondish hair fluttering in the wind, his blue eyes looking at the stranger. He took a tentative step toward his grandpa and then stopped, not knowing what to make of the other man. He heard the sound of his mother's voice behind him and he turned around, jumping in her arms when the porch door came open again. Susan came out, busy with the child, talking at the same time.

"What is all the com..." she said, never finishing. For a long moment she stood transfixed, her eyes unable to believe what she was seeing. Her whole body stiffened, muffled sounds escaped from her mouth and then she was running, the baby in her arms crying, the words rushing out of her mouth in a torrent.

"Paul...oh Paul, my God, oh my God." Tears of happiness came tumbling out and she reached him, crushing the baby to his chest in her attempt to get to him. He reached for them, his tears mixing with hers, incoherent sounds escaping his lips as he held onto the people who meant the most to him. He held her tight, thinking about all the long months he had spent wishing she was next to him. When he finally let her go, she looked into the saddest blue eyes she had ever seen and she stifled a sob.

"God in heaven, what have they done to you?" she whispered, taking in the gaunt figure, the sad, haunted eyes and her heart went out to him. The once beautiful, powerful body was now nothing but skin and bones and his face was carved in stone, the cheekbones pronounced, all the flesh gone.

He shook his head, unable to speak then and just reached for her and the child again.

Charles and Ralph finally made their appearance and soon the whole family was there, sharing the life that had come back to them.

When emotions had finally abated some, they made their way into the house; everybody talking at the same time while Paul Jr. watched the stranger, fascinated by all the shiny things in his uniform. Bill Gallagher lingered outside for a moment, watching his son walk in. He raised his face to heaven, his lips moved in a whisper, his face breaking into a grin. He felt as if the gates of hell had been opened and his soul had been given a reprieve. All the pain and suffering that had been his constant companion were now gone and in its place an incredible sense of happiness overflowed his heart.

"Thank you, Father, for giving my son back," he said humbly, the tears flowing freely again. He stood still for a second longer and then he made his way inside. Everything was going to be fine.

CHAPTER 38

Arlington Cemetery
September 1965

Captain Paul W. Gallagher and his family looked in awe at the field of crosses extending in front of them. In the hallowed ground of Arlington National Cemetery rested the remains of thousands of men and women who had given their lives for the sacred principles of duty, honor and country. Paul glanced around at the people who had gathered there today, his mind going back to the letter he had received from Major General Pierce a week ago. Alton's body would be interred in Arlington Cemetery, with full military honors and he wanted Paul and his family to be there. Paul had accepted the invitation, thankful to General Pierce for allowing him to pay his final respects to his friend. He glanced around again, recognizing some of the men gathered around. Colonel Travis was there and also Brigadier General Raymond Ashley Brown. Major General Winfield Woods was also present, his old commander, who was now the Commanding General of the 82nd Airborne Division at Ft. Bragg, NC.

Paul's thoughts went to his friends, Ashworth and Pierce and the incredible ordeal that had taken place in the VC camp. The VC had been extremely cruel, inhuman really and the death of both of his friends still weighed heavily on him. Just like the doctors had said back at Walter Reed, the nightmares had started almost immediately after he got home, torturing his sleep, waking up screaming, haunted by the ghosts of Vietnam. Susan did her best to understand his suffering, drawing him out slowly, allowing him to vent his pain and frustration, talking about it, until he was finally able to go back to sleep, his head cradled on her bosom. It got so bad that he was almost afraid of going to sleep, the thoughts running through his head a torture in itself. And then finally, his father had intervened.

Bill Gallagher had watched his son, had heard the muffled cries and the terror in his son's dreams and he knew without a shadow of a doubt that his son was blaming himself for being alive while his friends had die.

He had being sitting atop the small hill overlooking the farm one evening when his father walked up next to him and quietly sat down. For long moments, they were silent and then Bill Gallagher glanced at his son's face. In a soft voice, almost a whisper, he started talking.

"Son…I know what you are going through…what your mind is telling you. You feel sorry for yourself and for your friends. And you also blame yourself for being alive, wondering why it was you and not them." He stopped then, breathing deeply, not at all sure what it was that he wanted to say, knowing that he needed to do something to stop the pain eating at his son. "I know what it is to lose friends in combat, the pain that eats at you when you think, why me? Why was I allowed to live when my friends are dead? He stopped again, his eyes glancing at the fast approaching darkness, the last rays of the evening sun almost gone over the horizon, the sky turning blood red. "All I can tell you is that the ways of the Lord are unfathomable to us and that if He gave you your life back, it is for a reason. You are alive and I believe that your friends, wherever they are now, would not have wanted it any other way." He stopped then and stood up stiffly, wiping the seat of his pants. He touched his son's shoulder, squeezing it gently. "I love you son," he said softly, walking away.

After that Paul had thought a lot about his father's words, realizing that the old man was right. He was alive and the good Lord was responsible for that and he should be thankful for the gift.

His body had slowly healed, the only thing remaining was the incredible sadness deep in his eyes, eyes that had the look of a man who had seen death and incredible pain staring him in the face and had been tempered by it.

He glanced around the National Cemetery again, wishing that the same thing that was being done for Alton could be done for Ashworth, but without a body, that was impossible. His thoughts went back to a week prior and the ceremony conducted at Ft. Bragg for Lee Ashworth. Brigadier General Brown had requested the memorial service and the ceremony had taken place at the Special Forces chapel on Smoke Bomb Hill. He and Susan had been able to attend and in some small way, it had been a redeeming experience for him.

He shook his head slowly, feeling the gentle pressure of Susan's fingers in his hand and he willed the memories away.

The day was windy, almost cold, with a watery sun showing its face every once in a while among dark clouds, and he thought that it would rain soon.

There was movement to the side of him and he glanced around, seeing the hearse carrying Alton's body approaching. Everybody stood up, their eyes glued to the hearse making its way. The Special Forces Honor Guard opened the door of the hearse and the casket came out slowly, the men holding it tightly. They made their way to the grave, the flag wrapped coffin holding everyone's attention. The Honor Guard stopped and the Army chaplain gave the oration and after that the flag was folded. The Captain in charge of the Honor Guard walked toward Major General Pierce, handing him the flag, he came to attention and saluted. He made his way back and the casket began its journey down into the grave. Paul felt the tears coming and he swallowed hard, the lump in his throat extremely painful. As the casket reached the bottom of the grave, the rain started coming down, a gentle shower that soon had everybody wet. The crack of the rifles firing in the air shook Paul to the core, his body reeling with the sound of the shots. A lone soldier stood still close to the grave, a bugle in his hand. Then the mournful sound of "Taps" rent the air and Paul's body trembled like a man shaking with a fever, his chest feeling like it was going to explode. Susan looked at him, taking in the face contorted in agony, the eyes bulging in his grief and the tears came freely into her eyes. Paul tried in vain to control the tide of emotions surging through him and suddenly his father was there, an arm pressing on his shoulder. Like in a dream he heard the words; "Steady son, steady," and once again, he was himself.

As the dirt was pushed into the grave, the people started dispersing, until there were just a handful of them left, among them Paul and his family.

"I'll be right back," he said, his hand wiping at the tears mixing with the rain on his face.

He made his way to the grave, stopping next to General Pierce, he looked down at the casket that held the remains of his friend.

General Pierce sensed his presence and he turned his head to him, the grief that he was experiencing clearly visible in the tired, red-rimmed eyes.

"General, sir," Paul said softly and the General's eyes focused on him. "I'm Paul Gallagher, sir."

"I know who you are, son," the old General said softly, his voice tired, sad. "My son talked a lot about you and Sgt. Ashworth in his letters."

"That's true, sir," Paul said, remembering Pierce's habit of writing to his father every day.

Paul fidgeted for a few seconds, not at all sure what he wanted to say to the old General, knowing that he needed to say something that would make sense to him, give him some comfort in his hour of need.

"General," he started, the words tumbling out. "I don't know if what I'm going to tell you will make things easier for you, but I believe it will." He paused for a second and then he continued, saying; "Alton was my friend, and I regret his passing. He died for what he believed, holding out until the end, his conscience clean with the knowledge that he had not betrayed his country or helped the enemy in any way. He die for his ideas…for the belief that it was his duty to his fellow men and to his country to resist."

Paul paused again, clearing his throat. He shrugged his shoulders, soaking wet now, his hair plastered on his forehead, the Green Beret in his hand. "General…your son died like a man, and he died with honor." He stopped then, the tears falling down his face intermingled with the rain. "I'll miss him, just like I know you will and by remembering him, I'll honor his passing. I'm…I'm sorry for his death and…and," he stopped, his mouth unable to continued, the pain in his heart so very real that he felt he was choking, unable to get enough air into his lungs. He was alive and his friends were dead, and by what whim of fate he had made it, it was unfathomable to him. But he knew that in some way, he owed his life to Alton Pierce. He had endured when there was nothing left in him, buoyed by the example of his friend, taking everything that was dished out to him by Hue, always remembering Pierce and what he stood for.

The eyes staring at him filled with unshed tears and the General nodded his head at the words. His hand went out to Paul and he embraced him, pulling him tight against his chest.

"Thank you son…thank you," he said and let go. "I know that wherever Alton is, he would be glad to know that you are alive, back with your family and wife. That's the way he would have wanted it."

For a few minutes longer, Paul Gallagher stood still, his eyes on the grave, then he put his Green Beret on, came to attention and rendered a perfect salute to the soldier buried there. He turned around slowly and made its way to his family, the rain falling gently down. His blue eyes took in the tall figure of his father, the dear one of his mother and then he glanced at the woman holding the child, a look of undying love on her beautiful face and a promise of a new life to come and he thanked God for all of them and for the prize that he had been given; a second chance at life. He came to them; his eyes moist and then he whirled around, listening to the gentle breeze whispering among the headstones.

And the ghosts of war whispered softly; "Well done soldier, well done."

* * * *

0-595-24173-5